Mist in the Pines

Mel G Smith

MIST IN THE PINES

ISBN 978-0-615-67907-5

Self-published by Frances C Smith Ltd
Printed in USA by 48 Hour Books

Cover by Frances C. Smith
Commercial Artist/Publisher
Morehead City, NC

Dedication

I dedicate this book to my patient
and cherished wife, Frances Ann, for her
loving and quick-witted companionship; and,
kindly understanding the Lawman's Call of Duty with
its many interruptions;
for her solid trust in my skills, and, most importantly,
knowing without a doubt,
The Lord was with me at every turn.
Her faithful encouragement is never-ending.
I'm a lucky man.

Note from the Author

As a native of Carteret County, I have a deep love for the area. My writings are much like having a conversation with everyday folks who live along the coast. It will include some not so proper grammar and a little slang.

People move here from all over the world after falling in love with our colorful dialect and friendly laid back lifestyle.

Simple living close to nature, salt spray in the air, the constant roar of the ocean, a bowl of conch chowder, and a good book; I ask, what could be better?

Enjoy your read.

Come...Sit with me by the Sea.

Mel

INTRODUCTION

This is a story about
a young man who wanted 'to belong' who took the wrong
turn with the wrong boys.
Author, Mel Smith, former 30 year veteran lawman,
will take you on a journey as seen through
the eyes of the young man, as well as law enforcement.
Like many fine officers,
Smith tried to keep young people from getting criminal
records; a few did not.
You'll get into the heart and soul of this young man,
learn of his survival skills taught to him
by his best friend, Snake Woman,
who lived in the woods
along the water of Black Water River.
You'll see why the hunters referred to him as
'mist in the pines'.
You think you see him, but when you
get there, you can only feel his presence.
You can't see nor hear him.
You'll travel down the road of mischief turned criminal, as
he repeatedly loses his way in life.
It's all there;
arson, imprisonment,
bank robbery, escape, chase,
survival, betrayal, and
ultimately murder.

MIST IN THE PINES

ONE

With only a few hours left on my shift, I went to the Sheriff's Department to turn in my papers. While sorting through thcm, I heard voices speaking in low tones coming from the office of the High Sheriff. As I eased closer to the door, I could hear the voices of Deputies Antonio Denardo and Francis Gaza of the Investigative Division. They were informing the sheriff about the department's involvement in a bank robbery and shootout that occurred the day before in Cape Shore, a small town located at the far west end of Seaside County. I recognized the name of the boy they were discussing and it piqued my interest. When I learned it was young Michael Schomeck, it really took me back because I knew the boy.

I remember Michael Schomeck being different than the other nine-year olds in his class. Michael's hair was a little shorter than most, but that was expected, after all, his father was a marine. He was a good-looking kid with brownish-blonde hair and clear blue eyes. Michael was a little taller and slightly thinner than most of his classmates, yet something about his look made him stand out in a crowd. There was also something about Michael that made you think this kid had something to prove.

Before moving to Seaside County, Michael never lived anywhere long enough for him to call it home. Michael was born on United States Marine Air Station, Iwakuni, Japan. His father, a career marine, was assigned to two other military bases before Michael's tenth birthday. At that time, Michael was a fun-loving kid with a quick smile and laugh-craving social contact, but a little shy and reserved. Michael's personality wanted to develop and come out but every time it started to, his father would beat it down which was a tough row to hoe for a fun-loving kid like Michael. To say Michael was a victim of an iron fist puts it lightly.

Michael had one older brother, Joseph or Joe Jr. as he liked to be called, who graduated from high school in May. Joe Jr. had been preparing his whole life to go into the "family business". Joe Jr. was scheduled to report to the US Marine Corp. Induction Center on July 25, eleven days after he turned eighteen years old. Joe Jr. was definitely his father's son, a chip off the old block, strong, straight, ruggedly handsome, yet dumb as a stump. Lettering in four sports, everyone knew there were very few men better than he was on the athletic field; unfortunately, this was the only area in school where Joe Jr. excelled.

Michael's father, Joseph Sr. thought Joe Jr. had what it would take to become a Marine officer, but ROTC was out of the question for Joe Jr. It had been everything he could do to keep his grades high enough to graduate. Joe Jr. was physically strong but just didn't pack the necessary gear it took for him to become a Marine officer. But this was okay with Joe Jr. because becoming an officer was his father's dream. It had always been Joe Jr.'s intention to follow in his father's footsteps and become a recon marine, and he was about to have his dream come true.

Michael's mother June was your typical southern mother, born and raised only a few miles outside of Atlanta, Georgia. June, the baby of the family, had been raised in the same house where her mother was born. Living on the farm and never really having much contact with the outside world, her mother shielded the children from big city life. They were taught what they needed to know to succeed in life only by their parents and church family. Around the age of fourteen, June's mother began to instill in her the duties necessary to be a good wife when her time came. She was taught to submit, support, love and obey her husband. "Once you get married you're in it for life," her mother told her. "There will be times when you'll have to ignore your own feelings and take care of your husband, no matter how you feel about it," June's mother would say in a deep southern drawl. "Till death do you part, no matter how hard it may be." June was a good student of her mother's teachings and was determined to live up to her wedding vows no matter what.

June doted on the boys and made them her life. June showered them with all her love knowing it was likely the only parental love they would get. June had known for years that Joseph Sr. had no love to give. Joseph Sr. thought it a sign of weakness to show his love for June and the children. Using his Marine Corps background and training, he had hidden his emotions so deeply that he was no longer able to make contact with them. M/Sgt Schomeck was a Marine and knew two things for certain, he knew right and wrong. ***He knew he was right and everyone else was wrong.***

When June met Joseph, he was twenty-one and she had just turned eighteen. June had never had a boyfriend before and quickly became infatuated with the good-looking young Marine. June's mother volunteered June to serve coffee at a USO dance. Joseph and a couple of his buddies had seventy two-hour passes and were looking for a good time and some female companionship. Joseph met June, asked her for a dance and the rest was history. Eleven weeks later Joseph and June were married. From the beginning, Joseph made it clear to June that he was Marine Corps ***green*** right down to his green eyes and would remain a marine for the rest of his life. June knew that she, the children and nothing else would ever come between Joe Sr. and the Marine Corps.

Joseph's first posting in the Marine Corps was Germany. There he began to refine his skills and set out on the career trail of becoming one of the Marine's elite: a Recon Marine. It was no surprise for Joe to be very good at learning the specialized skills needed to become Recon.

November 1963, Lance/Corporal Joseph Schomeck requested and was approved for duty in Southeast Asia. Six weeks later, he found himself on a transport plane with one stop in Japan for fuel and the next stop Cambodia and then Vietnam.

The more time Joseph spent in Vietnam, the less time he thought about home. When Joseph did write, his letters were distant and rambling, and as time went by, they became so disturbing to June that she no longer looked forward to hearing from him. He told graphic stories of violence and gore that he had witnessed and participated in while serving in "The Nam." Vietnam took its toll on Joseph, a toll that seemed to eat a hole right into his soul. Already introverted, Joseph seemed to turn even more inside himself as he shut out his family and friends.

February 12, 1966, Sgt. Schomeck was wounded when he stepped on a booby trap during his second tour of duty. He was awarded the Purple Heart and a one way ticket back to the 'world'. With his second Purple Heart, a Metal of Valor and more medals than he would talk about, and enough experience to last a lifetime; it was time for Joseph to go back home. On the long flight home, Joseph remembered thinking he never would leave Vietnam, now he thought Vietnam would never leave him.

After release from the naval hospital, Joseph requested to be assigned to the United States Marine Corps training depot in California. Marine unit commanders needed instructors with experience, and who could better instruct raw marines than someone who had served in and survived Vietnam. Sgt. Schomeck was exactly what the Marine Corps was looking for, experienced, motivated, dedicated and committed to excellence in every aspect of his life, except home life. Sgt. Schomeck spent the next five years as a Marine Corps drill instructor turning inexperienced boys into the killing machines the Marine Corps needed.

During his years on the field at San Diego, Sgt. Schomeck's graduates had the unique distinction of having the highest percentage of marine trainees to survive their first tour of duty in Vietnam. This was more than any other drill instructor in the US Marine Corps. This accomplishment didn't go unnoticed by Sgt. Schomeck's command staff and he was rewarded accordingly and promoted up through the ranks at a record pace.

Shortly after being promoted to Master/Gunnery Sergeant, Vietnam assaulted Joseph's conscious and threw him into a serious tailspin. Haunted by nightmares and trying to fight off the nightly fears, Joseph began drinking heavily. The drinking led to staying out late at night, sometimes only to get home in time to shower, put on his uniform and report to the base for duty. The bazaar behavior happened more and more frequently until it began to affect his training methods and his fitness reports, inevitably spilling over into his family life.

All of Joseph's troubles came to a head one night when he got into a bar fight. No one was injured, no charges were filed and the police weren't even called. Everyone went on their merry way and it was all over until Joseph got home and decided to finish the fight by taking the issue up with June. Joseph pushed June around, voices got loud, June was heard crying, and dishes were thrown. Joseph got pushy and louder, so loud that a neighbor hearing the ruckus, called the military police. When the M.P.'s arrived, the fight was over and Joseph was passed out drunk in a chair, but Joseph's liberty was secured anyway. Joseph was taken into custody and transported to the Provo Marshall's Office where he was charged with conduct unbecoming, drunk and disruptive behavior and spousal assault. He was thrown in the brig and confined until his commanding officer came to get him out. These were the first disciplinary actions ever entered on Sgt. Schomeck's records.

Sgt. Schomeck had an outstanding military record until now so concessions had to be made. After receiving a written reprimand and first class dressing down by his commanding officer, June was taken into the CO's office and convinced not to pursue a criminal complaint and after that everything was white-washed over. Sgt. Schomeck was fined with a loss of one month's wages and ordered to transfer out of San Diego.

On 02 June 1980, M/Sgt. Joseph Schomeck requested transfer to the First Marine Division, Force Recon Battalion, First Marines, Camp Ironside. Because of his outstanding record, experience, and a very high recommendation from his commanding officer, M/Sgt. Schomeck's transfer request was processed and approved and the Schomeck family was on their way to eastern North Carolina.

M/Sgt. Schomeck reported for duty at Camp Ironside on 03 August 1980. For the first time in years, Joseph was excited about a new assignment. Life around the Schomeck household was bearable for a little while. Joseph and June found a nice house with a big yard and a water view just outside of Cape Shore, NC.

Cape Shore is a small bedroom community located ten miles from Camp Ironside. It would be a good place for June and the kids to live while M/Sgt. Joseph trained men to defend the country against enemies foreign and domestic; the rent was reasonable, the owner of the house, a retired marine himself, was happy to have a decorated marine living in his house; and, finally things were looking up, they thought.

Since moving to the coast of North Carolina, Michael had made a magical discovery that there was something he never knew about himself. He discovered that he had the ability to become invisible. Whenever his father was ranting and raving with his mother, Joe Jr. or him, Michael would simply become invisible. When Michael saw his mother being abused, pushed around or hit by his father, he would very easily become invisible. With no friends to speak of and going nowhere fast, it wasn't long before Michael wanted to become invisible and stay that way.

Living in a small town, Michael was free to come and go without much supervision. His house was only a short walk down a dirt path to the ICW- Intracoastal Waterway. Michael usually started each morning the same way. His father would leave a list of chores, saying, "Your chores are to be completed before you do anything else, that's an order!" Today was no different, #1. Take out the trash, check. #2. Rake the yard around the front door, check. #3. Set the sprinkler up to water that spot in the yard we seeded two days ago, check. #4. Clean the glass on the front storm window, check. "Have your mother check your work and then and only then if all items have been completed satisfactorily, you are dismissed." Michael's mother had to check each item after Michael completed it. June knew she would have to account for them later so she could never cut Michael any slack on his chores. Checking off the last item on his list, she would turn to Michael with a big smile, salute and say…"dismissed," laughing as the words escaped her lips. FREEDOM! The rest of the day was Michael's and out the door he ran. A short run down the path and onto the pier and finally Michael could escape from all the pressures and burdens that had been heaped upon his narrow sun-tanned shoulders.

On a typical day you could catch Michael swimming, picking up a few clams, maybe doing a little fishing, skipping shells on the water and tanning in the hot North Carolina sun. However, today was going to be anything but typical. "Nary a whiff of breeze was blowing, which was unusual living this close to the sound," Michael said to himself as he wiped the heavy beads of sweat from his forehead. The stillness made the salt from the water hang heavily in the air. Michael didn't realize how hot it was until his bare foot stepped on the first pier board. The heat from the boards was nearly unbearable. For a second, Michael thought his feet might just catch on fire! "I can't take another step," still he did. The first few steps Michael walked on his tiptoes. Taking a few more steps, he switched onto his heels. A few more steps, he switched to the sides of his feet; making it past the HUGE "No Trespassing Sign" mumbling, "I'm more than halfway there, I can make it… just a few more steps. The end of the pier is right there…I made it. I did it and I did it without stopping to soak my burning feet in the cool waters of Bogue Sound." As Michael got closer to the end of the pier, he started peeling off his tee shirt and picking up the pace. His slow deliberate walk had now become a trot…throwing his shirt and towel down close to the edge of the pier … SPLASH! AHH…brought immediate welcome relief from the sweltering heat. The cool salty water surrounded Michael like the love of his mother's arms. His imagination soared…a swim out to the sand bar… it's only a football field's length away. The swim would give a frogman plenty of time to attach some magnetic mines to the steel hulls of an imaginary enemy's ship. Plenty of time to look for the sea monsters he had sent to the bottom of the ocean yesterday. Lots of time to dive for buried treasures and, of course, time to save a lady from drowning. Michael's fears were gone. He had no worries for these brief minutes. "Because of my heroics, the world is a safe place to live a little while longer," Michael said as he climbed up the ladder and back onto the pier. Just as his feet touched the pier, a feeling of despair rushed into his gut. It was a feeling Michael knew all too well...a feeling of impending disaster. Out the corner of his eye, Michael could see them coming down the beach.

TWO

Robert Thompson was the ring leader of five or six of the meanest kids in school. Buddy, he liked to be called, was fifteen going on thirty-five. He came from a broken, dysfunctional home. His father never married his mother, then left home before Buddy's seventh birthday, "It‘s all your fault, if you weren't here, he would've stayed home and I'd be happy," Buddy‘s drunken mother would often tell him. She never missed the chance to tell him how his dad left because of him, and each time Buddy heard the story, he became more resentful. Buddy's broken home was all the excuse he needed to carry a chip on his shoulder two feet wide and he took out his anger on everyone who got in his way.

Michael remembered hearing a rumor that Buddy had been sent to juvenile detention once. The story was told that Buddy and two other kids broke into the local high school one night after a football game. They spray painted graffiti on the walls, dumped trash cans in the hallways and broke the toilets in the teacher's lounge. A kid that Buddy had a beef with earlier, heard that Buddy had done the damage and turned him in to the cops. The story goes that Buddy caught ninety days in juvenile and the kid who turned him in caught six months in the hospital.

Buddy's red hair glowed like a match burning on top of his head in the bright North Carolina sun as he walked down the beach towards Michael‘s father's pier. "Michael! Hey, Michael!"

Buddy yelled. Michael tried to ignore the hailing as he leaned over spreading his towel on the pier. Michael whispered to himself, "I'll lie down right here, I'll become invisible, they'll go on down the beach. They won't come down the pier...they'll see the giant, (No Trespassing - This Means You) sign his father put at the end of the pier. I'm safe, I'll just lay right here," Michael continued softly. In a loud voice Buddy yelled again, "Michael don't act like you don't hear me you wus, get down here. Get down here right now...don't make me come out there and get you!" Michael thinking, "I'm trapped, what can I do? I guess I could jump in the sound and swim away, but if I did that, I would never be able to live it down; or, I could go meet my fear face to face. I may get beat up, but at least I'll be able to hold my head up at school," Michael whispered quietly.

Giving in, Michael started down the pier to meet Buddy. With each step he took, the sick feeling in his gut intensified. A voice in the back of his head kept telling him this probably wasn't going to turn out good. Michael fought back the fear with each step down the pier, making his long trek to meet Buddy. As Michael walked down the pier, he thought it was funny how the pier boards that were so hot only a few minutes ago, now had no effect on his feet, as his mind thought about the encounter he was about to face with Buddy Thompson.

Funny how a reputation gets built by pushing little kids around, just kids trying to prove to everybody that they're big men by showing everyone how much of a bad guy they are. When in fact, you ain't no bad guy; and, you sure ain't no man. Buddy's strength was intimidation. Catch him by himself he was a puppy, but catch him with his gang behind him and he's a pit bull, today he was a pit bull.

"What's up bro, what's the deal?" Buddy asked as Michael stepped off the end of the pier. "You better be glad I didn't have to go out there and get you! So tell me, why can't we use your old man's pier? Don't give me that mess about your daddy saying that he didn't want them punks on my pier either," Buddy scoffed. Buddy struck a sour cord with that statement. Michael's memory immediately went back to one evening about a year ago when he made the mistake of calling his father 'daddy' and was smacked sharply across the mouth for his disrespect. "You will address me as ***Father*** or as ***Sir***," kept echoing from the thundering voice of his father in Michael's head. Buddy continued, "You could put in a good word for us, if you weren't such a wimp." "My father says no and there's nothing I can do about it," snapped Michael. Buddy snapped back, "Bro, don't be such a chicken. Your father ain't even home, come on man, let us use the pier. We'll be gone before he gets home and besides, who's going to tell anyway, you . . . not us, who else has the guts to tell? Nobody who cares about staying healthy, I'll tell you that much," Buddy concluded.

Michael thought for a minute; Buddy was right, who's gonna know and who's gonna tell. Buddy now speaking in a soft friendly voice, "Come on bro, let's be friends. You do this one thing for us and we'll let you join our club." Michael thought for a quick moment, "this just might be my chance to fit in; it's my chance to be a part of something…even if it's something bad, and at least I'll belong to something. Maybe these guys aren't as bad as they've been made out to be ...maybe they're just like me, you know, they're trying to fit in too. Suddenly turning toward the pier, Michael motioned with a swinging arm...come on boys follow me. "I'll race you!" At that second, all the kids turned and ran behind Michael down the length of the pier. Running like they were taking a hill in a battle, running at full speed the boys raced to the end of the pier and jumped into the cool soothing salty water.

Michael and the boys played, swam and had the greatest time the rest of the afternoon. Michael thought, "What have I been thinking all this time, these guys are all right. I never saw them in this light before. Look what I've been missing; I had these guys all wrong. They're just like me, they are just kids, fun loving kids, no better, no worse...wow I've got friends, and I made some friends today." The day was spent swimming and playing and forming memories that would last the rest of their lives.

As the brilliant red sun sank slowly into the Atlantic Ocean, Michael thought to himself, "I've seen the sun set a million times before, but I don't remember it looking like this before. Funny how having friends make things look different." Walking toward the end of the pier, the boys cut up re-living the fun of the day. As they stepped off the foot of the pier, Buddy said, "We'll meet at the big water oak tree behind the hardware store at 11 o'clock tonight." "We'll see you then," the boys replied collectively as they broke up and began to walk away." "Yeah, man we'll see you then," Michael said hesitantly. Buddy's voice, "We'll meet at the big water oak tree at 11 o'clock," kept ringing in Michael's head. "I can't meet nobody at no big live oak tree," Michael kept telling himself. "I hadn't been out of the house without my parents after ten o'clock in my life. Michael kept going over this in his mind, "Twenty-one hundred hours, nine o'clock p.m. lights out in the Schomeck house…"Father makes a bed check and head count at twenty-one-thirty. Twenty-two hundred, Father and Mother go to bed…they've never checked on me after lights out before," Michael kept telling himself, "I could get out then," Michael said trying to convince himself to go! "As long as I'm back home by zero-six-hundred hours I'll be okay…they won't even know I'm gone," Michael whispered to himself over and over. Tic, tic, tic of the clock echoed throughout the room.

The minutes clicked by like seconds. Time was fleeing and Michael still hadn't convinced himself to go. "What do I do? What do I do?" Michael kept asking himself expecting some type of spiritual answer. "These are my friends, if I wimp out now they'll treat me worse than ever, I've gotta go. I've used that old oak tree a million times to crawl in and out the house." "I've just never used it at night," Michael said quietly trying to convince himself.

The hot summer breeze blowing through the branches of the oak tree outside Michael's window seemed to beckon him--come on Michael get moving it's time to fish or cut bait. "That's it, I'm going…my mind's made up," Michael said out loud. Slapping his hand over his mouth, Michael threw back the covers pulling on his clothes in record time. Michael shimmied out the window like a cat, slid down the curved limbs of that live oak tree and landed on the ground as light as fog. Stopping only long enough to gather his senses, Michael took a quick look around and down the road he ran. It was about two miles to the hardware store and Michael made the run in just over ten minutes. Michael approached the gathering spot slowly and quietly like his father had taught him. Michael stopped a few yards from the old oak tree in the darkness and waited quietly.

From his location, Michael could see he wasn't the last one to get there, which gave him a feeling of relief. As Michael stood in the darkness observing before he moved in, he smelled a whiff of smoke lingering close to the ground near the base of the tree. Buddy and two other boys were squatted down smoking cigarettes. "Hey guys it's me," Michael whispered. "Come on in," Buddy replied in a low voice. "Well, well, well I guess I owe you some cigs," Buddy said talking to the boys squatted by the tree. "I thought you'd wimp out or maybe I had you figured wrong all along! What do you think, Michael did I have you wrong?" Buddy asked. "Well, I'm here, ain't I?" Michael replied sharply. As Michael approached the tree, Buddy reached out and handed Michael a lit cigarette. Michael took the cigarette with trembling hands as he was afraid of what would happen if he didn't. Michael slightly parted his lips and stuck the burning cigarette between his lips and held it there. Cigarettes were a big no-no around Michael's house, "Affects your cardio health you know! No smoking, it's a filthy habit and you are not allowed to have any bad habits," rang in his head as he had heard his father barking orders to him and Joe Jr. as they performed military P.T. "Yeah, it's okay for you to drink yourself blind every other night and beat the hell out of your wife but we ain't supposed to have any bad habits," Michael thought as the smoke from the cigarette rolled up and into his eyes. "What we gonna do Buddy, we gonna wait all night for those wimps," asked Billy. "I didn't come here to sit under no stinking tree, I want to get drunk and tear something up," Billy said loudly. Michael had known Billy for more than two years and these were the first words he could remember having heard Billy speak. Billy usually just stood around looking dumb and let Buddy do the talking for him. 'Billy the Bully' was how he was known around school. Billy Fulford was fourteen years old, had long dirty blonde hair usually worn in a surfer type style, but he wasn't laid back and cool like a surfer, Billy was just mean, you know the kind, mean right down to the bone. Known for being mean, sneaky and destructive, Billy was the kind of kid who would laugh at you while he was stomping the guts out of your cat just to see you cry. Michael had made it a point to stay as far away from Billy as he could and now he was thinking, "This guy's my new friend, wow! We'll give them five more minutes then we're out of here," barked Buddy. "We're not gonna wait around all night for those wimps, but I'll tell you one thing, they'll have hell to pay tomorrow if they don't show up." Without a word, Buddy stood up and peeled away from the tree. While disappearing into the darkness, he paused for only a second and called out, "Well…you guy's coming or you going to stay here and play horseshoes?" Billy, John and Michael rose to their feet and followed like robot soldiers. There was no talking or noise as the boys followed the path through the woods that led down to the shoreline. None of them had the guts to ask Buddy where they were going or what they were going to do, their destiny was in Buddy's cigarette stained hands. Reaching the shore in less than ten minutes, Michael and his new friends headed west down the shoreline for another fifteen minutes.

THREE

It was here they came upon a one story cottage, "Gather up right here," Buddy whispered as he pointed in a circular motion. The boys gathered like chicks around their mother hen. "I came down here and checked this place out the last three nights in a row," Buddy whispered. "Ain't nobody been here since last Sunday afternoon. The house belongs to some rich guy who only comes down here on weekends. He comes down to drink, eat and party and he won't be back until at least Friday night, so...you know what that means...this is all ours for the next two days," Buddy said with excitement in his voice.

Buddy rose slowly and said, "Follow me and keep quiet." Buddy walked slowly along the shore line using the tall break water to hide his movement. Moving to a position just behind the backdoor steps of the cottage, Buddy held up his fist signaling to the others to stop. Popping his head above the break water looking around, Buddy whispered, "Let's go." The boys jumped across the break water and moved quickly up the steps to the back door.

Pausing on the stoop Buddy told Michael, "You go around front and check things out, take a good look around and make sure the coast is clear." Without hesitating, Michael followed Buddy's orders as if they had been issued from M/Sgt. Schomeck himself. He sprang over the porch rail and moved quietly to the front of the house for a recon patrol. Making sure to stay in the shadows, he made his way to the front corner of the cottage. Stopping briefly for a quick look around, he climbed up the porch rail and took up a location where he could see the entire area. Michael squatted there in the shadows looking for any sign of movement. From his location, he could see all the way down the lane to Hwy 18 nearly a half a mile away. He paused silently in the dark while listening to the sounds of the night. He listened carefully for several minutes and didn't hear anything unusual…no cars, no music playing, no unusual voices in the night, no nothing. He didn't even hear a dog barking . . . the coast is clear, Michael thought. He hopped over the porch rail and quickly moved to the rear of the cottage. As he rounded the corner, he looked directly into Buddy's eyes and motioned all clear.

At almost the same instant, Buddy used his elbow, "CRASH," he broke out the bottom glass pane in the door. He quickly shoved his hand through the broken window and directly onto the lock. With the flick of his wrist the door lock popped open, in another second the boys were inside the cottage.

The interior of the cottage was well lit by the near full moon glistening off of Bogue Sound. "They make it so easy," Buddy said as he walked over to the fully stocked bar. He then started taking liquor bottles from behind the bar and handed each of his crew a bottle. John and Billy grabbed two bottles each and took a seat on a blue and white flowered sofa overlooking a huge picture window that opened to a beautiful view of Bogue Sound. Kicking his feet up on the white washed coffee table Billy said, "This really is the life ain't it John?"

John following Billy's lead, kicked his feet up on the table too. "Sure is," John replied as he unscrewed the bottle top and lifted the bottle to his lips taking a long drink. The boys took several pulls from their bottles as they sat drinking, staring out the window enjoying the view and slowly becoming dazed.

"Here you go Michael, I got one for you too," Buddy said as he reached out and handed him a bottle. Michael reluctantly took the bottle. "Go over and stand by the front door and keep a good eye out," Buddy said. "If you see anything unusual, holler out!" Michael assumed his position next to the door peering out between the curtain and the window. While keeping a vigilant lookout, every once in a while Michael would hold the bottle up to his lips and pretend to drink from the liquor bottle. "Who am I kidding, I don't belong here but how do I get out," Michael thought as he pulled back the curtain and looked out.

It didn't take very long before the boys started feeling a buzz with jokes and fun flowing like the free liquor. Laughing and making fun of each other suddenly switched to kids they had screwed with over the years. Everyone was telling stories and feeling great when suddenly Buddy jumped up and said, "Well now . . . let's see what else Mr. Richie Rich has to offer us this evening. If this guy makes the kind of money it takes to own a place like this, then maybe he's got a safe or a stash of cash hidden around here somewhere, you know for an emergency or something. Get off your butts and get to looking," Buddy yelled in his bossiest voice. Billy and John slowly got up from the sofa and began looking for anything they could steal, sell, trade or destroy. Billy pulled drawers from the dressers dumping what was inside onto the floor. He'd then kick his feet through it looking for loot. Billy would then throw the drawer across the room up against the wall. Every time a drawer hit the wall it would leave a large gaping hole in the sheetrock. Each time a drawer bounced off the wall Billy let out a loud, Yahoo!

With drawers flying past his head and Billy screaming in his ear, John was afraid he was going to be hit by a flying drawer so he went into another room to continue his search. John had been in the bedroom for only a couple of minutes when he let out a yell. "Get in here, get in here right now!" Everyone stopped what they were doing and ran to John's voice. "Michael, you stay at the door and keep a sharp eye out," Buddy yelled as he ran to the bedroom where John awaited.

Coming through the bedroom door Buddy spotted John standing several feet away from an open dresser drawer. By the way John was staring, Buddy thought it must be full of snakes. Buddy yelled, "What is it? Jack Pot? Buddy yelled as he neared the dresser, what the heck is it?" Stopping dead in his tracks, Buddy was able to see what had taken the wind out of John.

Buddy and John stood there unable to speak, mouths gaped open, looking at a black wallet with a small gold badge pinned on the front. Buddy reached in the dresser and picked up the wallet. As Buddy was reaching for the wallet he felt the urge to turn and run but he knew he couldn't. There was no way he could let his crew see the panic that he felt racing from his head to his feet as his fingers touched the black leather of the wallet.

Buddy gently clinched the wallet between his thumb and index finger as he began to lift it from its nest in the back of the drawer. Buddy raised the wallet like he was picking up a ticking time bomb. Little did he know at the time, it was. With the utmost care, Buddy reached over with his hand and opened the wallet. As Buddy opened it he could feel the blood leaving his face and fear replacing it.

Quietly, Buddy began to read, "John L. Perkins, Sr., Special Agent, State of North Carolina." Their hearts were beating so hard they nearly jumped out of their chests. "What now?" yelled John. "We're in some real trouble here... the owner of this house is a SBI Agent. They don't play with you; they won't stop until someone's butt goes to jail. Our fingerprints are all over this place. What in God's good name are we going to do?" "Shut up, let me think," snapped Buddy. "Just shut up, who's the one with the brains around here . . . shut up and let me think for a minute," Buddy said trying to calm the boys down.

After several minutes of silence Buddy said, "I saw a movie the other night and the bad guys burned down the house to hide their identity." "Movie, we're going to jail and you're telling us about a movie, this ain't no movie Buddy, once the SBI gets involved...we're all going to jail," John yelled in a panic. "Shut up and let me talk," Buddy yelled. "How'd they do it?" asked Billy. "They made a delay timer from a book of matches and left the house to establish their alibis. When the timer started the fire, the bad guys were all sitting around a bar having drinks and nobody could pin the fire on them because they weren't anywhere near the house when the fire started," Buddy continued. "They burned down the house and destroyed all the evidence...no evidence, no charges...they got away with everything!" "That's what we'll do, we'll burn this place to the ground," Buddy spouted.

The boys gathered around Buddy in the living room as Buddy motioned toward the sofa. "Pour the rest of that liquor on the sofa and on anything else you find that will burn. Pour it on the furniture and in all the other rooms too. We've gotta make sure there's nothing left that they can get evidence from. Y'all get started while I find something to make a timer out of," Buddy ordered.

John and Billy toted as many bottles as they could carry while walking around the cottage pouring liquor out in every room. Michael stood at his post terrified and afraid, Terrified to stay and afraid to run. It was everything he could do to not fling the front door open and run like a scared rabbit. This failed decision would haunt him for the rest of his life.

Foraging through drawers, Buddy found a book of paper matches. He took out a cigarette, lit it and fumbled with the match pack. Opening the book of matches, Buddy wedged the butt end of the smoldering cigarette between the double rows of paper matches. Buddy then took a long deep breath and blew gently on the tip of the cigarette making the tip glow like a fire-brand. Slowly walking to the sofa, Buddy bent over and laid the matchbook on the liquor soaked sofa, "Let's get out of here--we'll meet back at the old live oak tree."

The boys ran out of the cottage and down the beach as fast as they could never looking back. When the boys got to the oak tree they were gasping for breath as if Satan himself had been chasing them. Panting for breath John was the first to speak, "Now what we gonna do? I didn't count on this crap... I never meant to get mixed up in anything that I could go to jail for."

"Shut up," Buddy yelled! "I've had about enough of your chicken attitude. I'll tell you what we're gonna do! We're gonna keep our mouths shut! That's what we're gonna do! Look, the fire hasn't even started yet! Everybody, go home and make sure when you get there you let your parents know you're home! By the time the cops figure out what time the fire started, we'll all have our alibis set!" Buddy said with a smirk, "Who's gonna give you a better alibi than your parents?"

Speaking in a voice none of the boys had ever heard before, Buddy said, "I'm warning all of you, if you talk to anyone about what happened tonight, I'll kill you, I mean it, I'll kill you. I ain't going back to jail for none of you punks! Now, get out of here-- get home right now and you better keep your mouths shut!"

Without saying a word, Michael turned and ran home as fast as he could. Michael went up the old tree faster than he had come down it. He was undressed and in bed before he stopped long enough to take a deep breath. Letting out a sigh, Michael whispered, "What have I gotten myself into?" Michael waited until his heart rate got back to normal before getting up and going to his Mother's door and knocking gently. "Mother, may I see you for a minute?" Michael pled.

Michael's mother's answered back gently, "Yes, honey I'll be right there." A minute later Michael's mother appeared at the door. "Michael what's the matter," she asked. "Mom I have a sore throat can I have something for it?" Michael asked pitifully. "Yes dear, get back in bed and I'll bring you something," June replied. June walked back into Michael's room, "Here honey, take this and you'll feel better shortly...now get back in bed and try to get some sleep." Michael took the pill, yet he thought there would be no sleeping tonight. Climbing back into bed, Michael looked at the clock; it was 2:07 a.m. Normally, not much of a guy to pray, Michael quietly slipped from between his sheets and landed on his knees next to the bed. Bowing his head Michael began to pray. At that exact second he heard the wail of a siren in the distance. The moaning cry of the siren paralyzed him with terror; Michael knew it was on the way to the fire. Michael hopped up and went to the window, leaning out as far as he could; he looked toward the western town limits. "If I lean out far enough, maybe I can catch a glimpse of the fire," Michael whispered.

What Michael saw next sent terror deep into his soul. Michael could see the flames from the fire rising seventy-five to a hundred feet above the tops of the pine trees that grew along the Intracoastal Waterway. Michael jumped back into bed, pulled the covers up over his head and prayed with all his heart.

Zero-six hundred hours on the tick, Michael's father banged on the door yelling, "Rise and shine, get dressed, chow in five clicks. If you're late you won't get any grub. Now move it, move it, move it!" Michael didn't need five minutes; he had been awake and dressed for hours. Knowing what they had done at the cottage was uncontrollably compelling Michael to return to the scene of the crime. Breakfast was over at 06:30, Joseph Sr. out the door and headed to work. As soon as his father was out of sight, Michael ran out the door with no thought of his chore list. "I'll take the whipping," Michael said as he ran down the path. Michael figured that the best place to get a good look down the shore was from the end of the pier. While running down the path, Michael saw two men standing near the pier on the shoreline. Michael couldn't make out who they were but as he got closer, he could see one of them was a Deputy Sheriff.

FOUR

Quarter past two a.m. Deputy Sheriff Daniel Fairlane, who was assigned to the western area, received a call from county communications. "313, we are dispatching Live Oak Point Fire Department to a house fire at 407 Seashell Road, Live Oak Point." Daniel picked up the microphone and replied "10-4 Seaside County, 313 will be en route, leaving the Decker Field area at this time ETA ten minutes."

Daniel Fairlane joined the sheriff's department in 1974 just a few months after he retired from the Marine Corps. After twenty years in the Marine Corps, Daniel and his family were happy to settle down in a small town close to the ocean. His statue wasn't imposing as he didn't cut a very wide path. Daniel sported a very well-groomed and very short mustache. He was neat in appearance and had an excess of attitude. With steel gray eyes that seemed to look through you, Daniel was soft spoken with the hint of a northwestern accent that let you know in a moment he wasn't a laid-back Seaside County native. The guys working a shift with Daniel knew he was a bulldog with a ''stick to it" attitude and get the job done with whatever it takes state of mind. Responding to the fire call, Daniel sped west down NC Hwy 18 with his blue lights flashing and siren wailing.

Rounding a curve just outside of Cape Shore, Daniel was able to see a large reddish-orange glow in the western sky indicating the fire's proximity. Daniel thought, "That is one heck of a big fire for me to see it from this far away." Three a.m. Daniel advised the communications center that he was 10-23 at the fire scene. Approaching a fireman, Daniel asked, "Where is the Chief?" "This is what we firefighters call a hot fire," the fireman replied. "No, no I said, where's the Chief?" The sound of the diesel running full speed coupled with the constant throb of the water pump made it impossible to communicate with the fire fighter. "This fire was started with some highly flammable accelerant," the fire fighter shouted. "You can smell it in the air-- take a deep breath-- you can smell it." Daniel took a deep breath, "All I smell is smoke," Daniel said. "Well you don't have a fire fighters nose. If you did you'd be able to smell it," the fireman said laughing. Daniel walked closer to the fire scanning the working fire fighters looking for the Chief. Not wanting to get in the way of the firemen, Daniel stood on the outskirts with a drove of people who had gotten out of bed during the middle of the night to come see the fire.

The intensity of the fire was amazing. "I can literally feel the heat on my face and body." Daniel thought standing more than a hundred yards away. Daniel moved a few yards closer until the heat from the fire started feeling uncomfortably warm. Daniel watched the fire fighters dressed in heavy fire protection suits working only yards away from the roaring fire and wondered what makes a normal man want to be a fire fighter. He headed back to the air-conditioned comfort in his patrol car.

The house was too far gone, there was no saving it. The only thing for the fire department to do was contain the flames so it couldn't jump to another house and burn it down too. It was a heck of a fight and the fire was winning.

Six-thirty a.m. The fire fighters had done their job and kept the fire from spreading to any other structures and they were letting it burn out. Seven forty-five a.m., the Fire Chief ordered one truck and its crew to remain at the scene to make sure the fire didn't flare up. All other trucks were ordered back to the fire department. Eight a.m. Daniel opened his trunk and took out a roll of crime scene tape and walked to the scene of the fire. Once there, he started taping off an area twenty-five feet outside the fire zone. As he walked from point to point tying off the tape, Daniel got a good smell of the heavy smoke clinging close to the ground. The smell nauseated him. The smoke from the burned cottage mixed with the fumes from the diesel trucks nearly made him throw up. Daniel's mind compared the smell to that of napalm from his days in Vietnam... an odor he hoped he would never smell again. Daniel tied off the tape as he surveyed the damage and thought the carnage and amount of damage was unbelievable. "How does a fire get to this type of intensity without help?" Daniel asked himself as he started a new string of tape. "Yesterday this pile of smoldering rubble was someone's beach house and today it's all gone," Daniel muttered. "Where do I get started?" Daniel thought as he looked over the fire scene. Other than a basic fire investigation school, Daniel attended during law-enforcement basic training five years ago; he had never received any training to prepare himself to investigate this type of crime scene.

"Daniel, Hey, Daniel!" Joe Miller, the Live Oak Point Fire Chief hollered, "Can you come over here for a minute?" summoning Daniel to his vehicle. Daniel laid down the roll of crime scene tape and walked over to Chief Miller's truck. Arriving at the Chief's truck, Daniel stood patiently waiting for Chief Miller to finish a conversation on the cell phone. Hanging up the phone, Chief Miller said, "Daniel, I thought before you get too deep into that mess, I'll let you know, in my opinion, this is definitely arson." "My problem is this; I don't have the resources necessary to investigate it properly. I'm going to call in the Fire Marshall to help us with this investigation. That is, if it's all right with you?" Chief Miller asked.

James Edward Harris, Seaside County Fire Marshall had worked for the county for about nine years. Prior to that, J.E. led the arson investigations for the largest fire department in the state. J.E. had a hee-haw charm, but don't let that fool you when it comes to arson investigations. He had few equals! His instincts were pure reasoning, very clear and knowledgeable to an extreme. In other words, he was a first-class arson investigator. J.E., as he was called by friends, was 64 years old, a little more than six feet tall, around 240 pounds. He had a face that wasn't at home without a smile on it. He was quick with a joke, easily approachable and first in line to offer help anytime it was needed. When J.E. wasn't actively conducting or assisting in a fire investigation, he was performing duties as the liaison between the volunteer fire departments in the county and the Board of Commissioners who is charged with the funding of all the volunteer fire departments within the county. Needless to say, J.E. was a very busy man.

J.E. was well liked by the majority of the fire fighters he worked with, envied by a few, and despised by others. Most of the people who didn't like J.E. were jealous of him because the county commissioners had gone outside of the good-old boy network to hire a Fire Marshall. Some of the volunteers felt that qualified applicants already existed among local fire fighters and didn't see any sense for the job to be given to an outsider. This attitude caused dissention among some fire fighters and J.E.

Daniel and Chief Miller walked around the fire scene looking for evidence while waiting to hear from J.E. Taking a break from the heat, they walked over to the breakwater to enjoy the cool breeze blowing across the sound. "Daniel, look at those foot prints down there; what do you make of them?" Miller said. "I wouldn't give too much stock to them if I were you Chief, they're probably just footprints from kids playing on the beach yesterday," Daniel answered. "There are kids up and down this beach all day long. They could have been made at any time, there's no way to know when they were made." Daniel continued. Suddenly a wad of tobacco spit hit right between Daniel's feet from behind him. "You two just don't know nothing about nothing do you?" Without looking around to see who it was, Daniel snapped, "Fred McDaniels if you don't stop sneaking up on me, I'm gonna shoot your butt."

Fred McDaniels was a well-known hunter and tracker who lived in a little community called Madison about five miles from Live Oak Point. The biggest attraction about Madison is Decker Field, Marine Corps Auxiliary Landing Field. Decker Field is an open field where the Marine Corps decided to build a full-scale aircraft carrier landing deck on the sandy coastal soil. This landing deck is used to train marine aviators. This isolated field is in the middle of nowhere. Marine aviators learn how to take off and land on an aircraft carrier deck without the danger of an actual at-sea landing. The four hundred and eighty-two occupants of Madison had grown used to the daily sounds of the Marine Corps jets landing exercises; therefore, they blocked out the roar of the engines and didn't even hear them anymore.

Fred was a young man when the worst of the great depression hit Seaside County. Everything the family needed to survive was dirt-cheap. The only problem was his father didn't have any money to buy what the family needed. So at the wise old age of sixteen, Fred realized his inability to bring money home to help his family. It was causing an undue burden on them so he decided it was time to join the Marine Corps.

May 12, 1930, Frederick Augustus McDaniels put his hand on a Bible and swore that he was eighteen years old just like the recruiter told him to do. An oath was given and ten minutes later, "Congratulations you're in the Marine Corps," snapped the recruiter with a quick hand shake and pat on the back. Fred was lead to the bus, bound for Jarvis Island, South Carolina for basic training. Fred told me that this was the first and only time he ever swore to tell the truth and not do it and he vowed to never do it again. Fred, normally quiet, reserved and hardly ever outspoken, told me once that from the day he received his first military pay check till the day his mother and father passed away, he sent money home to help them. That was the kind of fellow Fred McDaniels was. After serving honorably for eight years, Fred was discharged from the Marine Corps. Within a few weeks, Fred joined an outfit that was hiring men to guard the United States / Mexico border. The outfit became known as The United States Border Patrol.

Graduating at the top of his class, Fred's instructors discovered that Fred had more tracking experience than all the other men in his unit put together, and on more than one occasion, Fred taught his instructors a thing or two about tracking and woodsmanship. "Whoever ends up with McDaniels on their squad is in for a pleasant surprise," John Sneed, Head Training Officer for the US Border Patrol said to James Garth, Commanding Officer US Border Patrol. "James, if I had a hundred more just like McDaniels, I'd put a real dent in the problems we're having between Sonora and Arizona."

Fred received his first assignment on July 12, 1938. He was assigned to the desert between Baja, Mexico and California. Fred used the open country along the border to refine and even further his tracking skills. It didn't take long before Fred had honed his skills to a level that was legendary. Fred was known far and wide as the 'go to guy' when it came to tracking man or beast. Fred would say neither man nor beast can avoid me for long. Just put me within five miles of where the prey was last seen. With my ability and knowledge of tracking and my natural sense nature, I can find 'em." He would then follow up by saying, "It ain't bragging if you can do it."

Fred knew he had about half way irritated Daniel, so he slapped him on the back, chuckled that old Fred McDaniels chuckle, to smooth things over. Reaching out to shake Chief Millers hand, Fred said, "How's it going Chief? Looks like you boys need a little help here. You know you're looking at the fellas who did this, don't you?" Fred asked. "What the heck are you talking about, I don't see nobody," said Daniel. "Well you're looking right at them but you just don't know it yet," Fred said with a squeak in his voice. Fred hopped up on the top of the break water, pausing for only a second, he pointed with his long thin finger. "See that line right there Daniel, that's the high water mark. I checked the tide chart and high tide was at eleven o'clock last night. All the footprints that were laid down here yesterday during the daytime would have been wiped out last night when the tide came in. See these prints right there?" Fred asked. "All of these prints were laid down after the tide ebbed which was between eleven o'clock and about six o'clock this morning before you two geniuses rolled up to this fire call," Fred paused and spit. "Do you notice anything about these prints right here?" Fred asked. Daniel answered, "Yea they're small, looks like they might be girl's feet." "Or small boys," Fred replied. "Now look at these footprints. See how you can see just about the entire footprint? Whoever made these prints were in no hurry. They were taking their time moving real slow. They were trying not to be noticed I suspect. Several people walking real slow one behind the other, you know, single file. There were three maybe four people total, all heading west towards the house. Now look right here, see these prints? If you didn't know what you were looking at, which apparently you don't," Fred chuckling again, "you could hardly tell these are footprints at all 'cause they're way too distorted. But if you know what you're looking for, you can tell these are footprints right here too. The way these prints are distorted tells me that whoever made them was in a real hurry 'cause they were running hard. Yep, they were running hard and running fast," Fred concluded. "Daniel, I believe these footprints right here are the footprints of your suspects running away from that fire scene running real fast." A little frustrated Daniel said, "Fred, I just don't know how much stock I can put in all that footprint mess. All I see is a bunch of footprints that we don't know who they belong to, so what are you gonna do, find who made 'em?" asked Daniel. "We don't know for sure if they even belong to our suspects. Do we really want to base this whole investigation on a bunch of footprints in the sand? I'm not convinced that you can tell much from footprints anyway," Daniel said skeptically. Fred replied, "Let me tell you something Daniel Fairlane, I'll bet you a cold cola that these footprints don't belong here and if they don't belong here then why are they here?" asked Fred again. "I'll bet my bottom dollar if we find out who these footprints belong to, we'll be one step closer to finding out who burned that house down, and you can take that to the bank," said Fred in a cocky tone. "No faith in footprints...huh," Fred said as he squatted down real low! You see this one right here. This is the footprint of a thirteen to fifteen year old boy. He weighs between a hundred and a hundred twenty five pounds." Fred reached into his pocket and pulling a tape measure and measured the length of the stride. "He's somewhere between five foot two and five feet and five inches tall. He has a three inch scar on the bottom left of his right foot. It's close to being fully healed 'cause there's no scab on the wound. He cut it about four weeks ago and it didn't need stitches," Fred concluded with a spit.

Mumbling sarcastically under his breath, Fred stepped back away from the footprint, "Now if I'm finished giving the two of you a tracking lesson, and if you two will stay off the beach and out of my way, I'll follow these footprints that can't tell us anything about the suspects and see if I can gather some information about the boys that didn't burned down that house." "You need my help?" Daniel asked. "No thank you, you've done enough. I'll let you know what I find out." Without saying another word, Fred turned slowly and walked eastwardly down the water edge of the beach analyzing footprints and looking for signs.

J.E. Harris' radio call sign is 700. "700 Seaside County, I'll be 10-23 at 407 Seashell Point Road." "10-4, 700 I'll notify Chief Miller you are on scene," came the reply from the county communication center, "Zero-eight-twenty-four hours. Proper protocol dictates that upon arriving at the fire scene all officers assisting in the investigation are to check in with the Chief of the Fire Department or the Officer in charge of the fire scene. That way, additional help can be directed to join the ongoing investigation or be assigned to another task that needs to be performed. As required, J.E. met with the Fire Chief Miller to see how he could aid in the investigation.

"J.E., you can see I don't think we have much left to work with here. Yea it burned pretty good didn't it?" J.E. responded. "It's definitely arson, so I've called you in to give us a hand with this one," said Chief Miller. "Oh yeah, definitely arson. I can smell the accelerant in the air," J.E. concurred. "The scene is still too hot for us to start combing through right now. I think the best thing we can do for now is leave a firefighter here to keep an eye on the scene until it cools down some and we'll get started first thing tomorrow morning." Chief Miller agreed. "We'll meet back here in the morning zero-nine-hundred if that's okay with you, J.E." "Yeah that's fine, I'll see you in the morning," J.E. replied.

Chief Miller was briefing Fairlane on their plans when Daniel's radio squawked; it was Fred. "Daniel, can you meet me down at the beach for a minute?" Fred asked. Daniel answered, "Yeah 10-4, I'll be there in a few minutes."

When Daniel got down to the breakwater, he noticed Fred sitting on the edge of the pier swinging his feet like a five year old, watching the water and enjoying the cool breeze. "Daniel, come down here with me," Fred said as he slipped off the pier landing on the sand below. "Follow my footsteps and I'll show you what happened here last night." Fred said as he led off. Walking along, Fred began to point out pairs of footprints in the sand headed west. "These are our suspects' footprints headed towards the house," Fred said surely. "The way I see it, there are at least four distinctive sets of footprints here. I drew them down on paper and did some measurements. I think I can do a little figuring and I'll be able to tell you the approximate ages, heights and weights of the four kids that made these prints," Fred said as he continued to walk down the beach. "Look right here, this is where they stopped and had a pow-wow. I don't know why, maybe they were having a meeting or giving out assignments, but they stopped right here for about five minutes." "How can you tell how long they were here?" asked Daniel. Fred replied, "See this match here. I figure it was used to light this cigarette," pointing to a cigarette stuck in the sand, "And by the amount of tobacco that's burned away, I figure it took about five minutes for that amount to burn. See this print right here," pointing at a particular set of footprints. "This is the leader. See how the others gathered around this one . . . he's the boss," Fred said. Picking up and continuing to walk down the beach, "I followed these prints until I come to this path right here," Fred pointing to a slightly used path under the canopy of the maritime forest.

"Daniel, I followed it about three quarters of a mile and it comes out right behind Mitchell's Hardware Store. There's a big water oak tree back there and it looks as if it was the fellas' rally point. There's a bunch of fresh cigarette butts and other trash up there and the best I can tell you Daniel, is that they are no more than six or eight hours old. There's some candy wrappers, soft drink bottles and that kind of stuff so nothing indicates adult traffic to me. Around the tree, I found at least six other paths that have been used recently probably to get to or away from the tree I'd guess," said Fred while wiping his brow. "I haven't followed the exit paths to see where they end up yet but I will. Daniel, you know something, I believe we're following a bunch of kids here. Everything I see just reads kids to me," Fred said sadly. Daniel snapped, "Fred, it just might be kids but I ain't going to let them get away with this just because they're kids. Somebody's got to go to jail over this; somebody's got to pay for this one!" Daniel said angrily.

"Follow me, let's go back down to the beach," Fred said as he led off. When Daniel and Fred got to the beach Fred said, "Look right here, all these footprints go into the woods and back …then back to the oak tree except this one. This one heads directly east in the sand. I followed these as far as that pier down there and that's when I stopped and called you. I picked up more signs that led directly up that path to a house," Fred continued. "I thought before I went any further, I should get you involved in case one of the young'uns live in that house," Fred paused. "You did just right, Fred you did just right," Daniel responded.

Daniel and Fred were standing on the beach looking toward the house down the path when they spotted a young boy running toward their location. "Maybe we won't have to go up to the house after all," Fred said cleverly.

Michael could see the two figures standing to the side of the pier as he ran toward the beach, but didn't know whether to keep running or turn and run away as fast and as far as he could. He knew either way he was done for. Michael slowed his frantic pace but continued jogging toward the pier. As he made the approach, Michael could see clearly that one of the men was wearing a uniform and the other man was dressed in green, they both looked like trouble to Michael. Michael's heart fell into the pit of his stomach as he heard, "Good morning young man," Fred speaking first said. "How are you on this fine morning?" "I . . . I'm fine," Michael replied. "Where you headed?" Daniel asked. "I was going down the beach to see the house that burned last night," Michael said as he slowed to a walk approaching Daniel and Fred's location. "You ain't been down to the fire yet?" Fred asked. "No sir, not yet," Michael answered. "Let me ask you something then, that is, if you don't mind?" asked Fred. "You say you haven't been down to the fire yet, is that true?" asked Fred again. "Yes sir, that's right, I haven't been down there yet," Michael responded. "Then tell me boy, how do you explain your footprint, this footprint right here," pointing at the footprint Michael just made. "How is it that this footprint, your footprints, are over here on the beach headed towards the fire and here they are again right here," pointing at the footprints returning from the direction of the fire. That is if you haven't been to the fire yet?" Fred asked. Daniel jumped in excitedly, "How can your footprints be on the beach going to the fire and coming back from the fire? Do you have some kind of special abilities? Can you do magic or something that lets you be able to do that?" Daniel asked. "Well, have you got something to tell me?" Daniel asked pressing for an answer. Michael froze speechless, "I was home all night, I never left the house, you can ask my Mom," Michael plead with the two men! "I think that's a good idea," Fairlane said, "I think we need to go up to the house and talk with your mom before we talk to you anymore."

As Michael and the two men walked up the path, the knot in his stomach grew to a new level of discomfort. Michael knew if the knot didn't kill him, certainly his Father would.

It was exactly eleven-hundred-hours when Capt. Forrest rolled up to S/Sgt. Schomeck's exercise location and advised him that he was needed at home for some very important business. Driving home a million disaster scenarios ran through Joseph's head but not one of them would come close to the disaster he was about to realize when he got home.

Turning down his driveway, Joseph could see two strange vehicles sitting at the front of his house. As he got closer he could see one was a Sheriff's patrol car and the other a beat up Chevy truck. Running into the house, Joseph's first concern was, "Is everyone all right?" "Yes," June told him. "Then what's so darn important that it couldn't wait until I got off duty!" Joseph yelled. Daniel stepped in, "S/Sgt. Schomeck, we think your son Michael was involved in the burning of a house on Sea Shell Point Road last night." "No way, no freaking way," S/Sgt. Schomeck responded angrily! "Michael was home all night. He was in bed at twenty-one-thirty hours. I bed checked him personally and I woke him this morning at zero-six hundred. There is no way he went anywhere last night," said Joseph. Joseph shouted, "Get Michael in here night now he'll tell you," "Michael get in here right now!" Joseph shouted again. "Now

Hear This! You tell this Deputy where you were last night when that house caught on fire and every word that comes out of your mouth had better be the truth! Now Spill it," ordered S/Sgt. Schomeck.

Michael had only seen this level of anger from his father one other time. He knew the kind of beating he had received when his father found out that Michael had not told him the whole truth. The command was tell me the truth and as afraid as Michael was to tell the truth he was twice as afraid not to. "I was there, I was there, I was there when the house was set on fire," Michael admitted. Joseph dropped to his knees and began to shake in anger.

FIVE

October five was four days before Michael's fourteenth birthday. Michael was arraigned before Judge Sedrick Cobles in Seaside County Juvenile Court. Michael had been charged with felony arson with a loss of property exceeding three hundred thousand dollars. Despite the threats, beatings and general harassment from Deputy Fairlane and his father, Michael still would not relent and tell who the other boys were involved in the arson.

Deputy Sheriff Daniel Fairlane was the first person to testify to the information uncovered during the fire investigation. Deputy Fairlane told the story of his part of the investigation leaving out nothing. Deputy Fairlane testified to how Michael was implicated in the crime by his footprints going to and from the crime scene leading directly back to his front door steps. Fairlane testified to how Michael was confronted by his father and thereafter confessed to his involvement in the arson. Deputy Fairlane made it crystal clear how Michael had described his involvement leading up the actual lighting of the fire. "When we questioned Michael about his accomplices, Michael told us that the kids that burned the house down were unknown to him." Michael told me that he met them the night of the fire and weren't together long enough for him to remember their names," Fairlane continued. "I tried to get him to tell me who they were but he refused to cooperate. Your honor, I believe that Michael knows the names of the other boys that burned down the house, and I do not believe that he will tell us the boys' names under any circumstances," Fairlane concluded. "Is that true?" asked Judge Cobles. "Judge, I don't know who they were, if I knew them I would have told Mr. Fairlane," Michael replied. "I am not about to give up my friends," Michael thought to himself. "If the shoe was on the other foot they wouldn't give me up," he felt in his heart.

The next witness to testify was Chief Miller. Chief Miller testified about the amount of damage and how in his expert opinion the fire had been intentionally set. "With the amount of accelerant used, there was no way to control that fire, Judge. There was enough fuel used to burn that house it could have been burned down three times over," testified Chief Miller. "All we could do was watch it burn," Chief Miller said as he put another nail in Michael's coffin. J.E. backed up the testimony of the other witnesses agreeing that the investigation had been conducted competently and professionally and in his professional opinion, the arsonist responsible for the fire had been taken into custody and was standing trial today. Within fifteen minutes of the District Attorney's closing remarks, Michael was pronounced guilty of all charges and sentenced without offering any defense.

During sentencing Judge Cobles announced, "Michael Schomeck having been found guilty of all charges, I hereby sentence that you will be taken into the custody of the North Carolina Department of Corrections, Juvenile Division at Sandy Dunes. There you will serve in maximum custody until your eighteenth birthday," Judge Cobles announced. "Michael, your failure to assume responsibility for your actions and your total lack of cooperation was the largest determining factor in making this sentence an active one. I pray you will use your time in custody to reflect on the mistakes you've made and make a decision not to repeat them when you are released from custody." With that statement Judge Cobles' gavel slammed down and Michael was carted away. With the slam of a gavel, Michael's whole world turned upside down.

Michael couldn't remember much about the ride to Sandy Dunes, about the only thing he could remember was it didn't take very long. Michael's mind was reeling not knowing what was going to happen to him next. His imagination ran wild as the Sheriff's patrol car sped toward Sandy Dunes. Every decision and every mistake Michael had made during his short life flashed before him as the patrol car neared ever close to its destination.

Standing at a locked chain link fence twenty feet high, Michael looked up at the sun glistening off points of the razor wire and thought, what in the heck have I gotten myself into, I don't belong here. Sgt. Otis Jones met the transportation Deputy at the main gate and assumed custody of the juvenile and escorted him into the facility and to the in-take area. Michael was officially taken into custody of the NC, Juvenile Justice System at zero-eight-hundred-hours. Michael was led to a room where a full strip-search, a full body cavity search was conducted, fingerprints and photographs were taken. Michael was issued two green jumpsuits, three pairs of skivvies, a pair of shower shoes, a pair of generic tennis shoes, two pairs of socks, a bar of soap, a roll on deodorant, a toothbrush, tube of toothpaste and two towels and a rulebook and issued an inmate identification number.

In a very loud and clear voice Sgt. Jones barked, "Listen up and listen good, you have been sent to me because you would not obey the rules and laws of society. My job is to teach you the rules you will now live by and to punish you if you do not. If you live by my rules, you may survive my camp and one day be returned to your home. If you do not obey my rules, you are in for a very long miserable stay in my facility. Learn the rules and make your time here productive. I am fair but I am firm, I will give you respect only if you earn it, you will give me respect because I own you."

Michael's in-take process took a little more than an hour. Ruled, schooled and totally humiliated, Michael was ready to enter general population of Sandy Dunes. The housing wing where Michael was assigned housed fifty juvenile offenders between the ages of ten to seventeen years old. The profiles of the offenders on Michael's wing were kids that parents couldn't handle anymore. Some of them couldn't afford expensive lawyers and a few had committed serious crimes. Some were throw away kids; some got mixed up with bad influences or drugs and some were just plain mean and dangerous. Because of Michael's offence he was considered a serious criminal. Michael thought because his crime was serious he would get some respect; unfortunately, among the other offenders, his was a victimless crime that meant he never faced anybody when he committed his crime, he was due no respect.

Sgt. Jones walked Michael to his room and was assigned the top bunk bed. "Sit down at that desk and do not leave this room until you have read your rule book from cover to cover," Sgt. Jones said sternly. "Make your bed and stow your gear according to the regulations; only after you have completed these tasks, you may join the other boys in the gym. Do you have any questions Mr. Schomeck?" asked Sgt. Jones. "No Sir," Michael shouted in his most obedient military voice. "Then carry on," Sgt. Jones said as he snapped, turned and exited the room stopping only long enough to slide a name card into a slot on the wall next to the door.

Two offenders are assigned to each room, the rooms are very small only five feet wide and nine feet long. The furniture consists of a set of bunk beds bolted to the wall with a mattress made from an orange plastic type material that was about two inches thick, and a pillow that looked like it had been run over by a large truck. A sink-toilet combination was at the end of the room and a writing desk with a steel chair both bolted to the floor.

Michael whispered as he sat to begin reading the rule book, "This place ain't that much different from home. I had rules I had to abide by there; I have rules I have to abide by here. All I have to do is learn and obey the rules and I'll be okay and the good thing about this place is I won't have my father here to scream at me every five minutes. Yeah maybe this place won't be that bad after all," Michael said trying to convince himself.

It took Michael an hour and forty five minutes to stow his gear, make his bunk and read the rule book. Michael exited his room, made a right turn and a few minutes later was standing outside the doors of the Sandy Dunes gym pausing outside for a moment, he thought. . . please don't let them see how scared I am. Michael walked into the gym eyes scanning from side to side without moving his head looking for a friendly face. This ain't so bad… looks like every other gym I've ever been in before… same smells, the same echoing of voices and the same kids horsing around playing ball… yeah, this ain't gonna be that bad. Michael told himself over and over again. If I keep telling myself this, everything will be okay.

Precisely at seventeen-hundred-hours, a loud horn began to blow, three one-second blasts over the PA system. Everyone stopped what they were doing immediately and began to file out of the gym. "Where's everybody going?" Michael asked a kid heading toward the door. "Whenever you hear that horn, go to your room, don't stop unless a guard tells you to," the kid replied. "Don't talk to anyone unless a guard asks you a question. Just get to your room as fast as you can without running. It's in the rulebook; everything you need to know is in the book," the kid concluded. Michael quickly walked down the narrow hallway making his way to his room. Stepping through the door, Michael was surprised to see another kid standing at the foot of the bunk facing toward the wall at attention. "Stand right here," pointing at a spot on the floor said the kid. Without saying a word, Michael snapped to attention as he and the boy stood perfectly still waiting.

One minute later, Sgt. Jones appeared at the door, looked inside and shouted, "Two men, unit one-fifty-seven." Without hesitating, Sgt. Jones slammed the door shut and locked it in the same motion. Michael's roommate sat down on the edge of the bottom bunk sticking out his hand and said, "I'm Tim Blackhardt." "Michael, Michael Schomeck," Michael replied. This was the beginning of a relationship neither boy would forget for the rest of their lives.

Michael and Tim spent fifteen hours a day locked in a room with no one to talk to but one another. Time dragged by slowly. Michael and Tim had nothing but time to get to know each other and tell each other all about themselves. At first, custody was like summer camp but once the new wore off, the time locked behind a steel door became more and more unbearable for both boys.

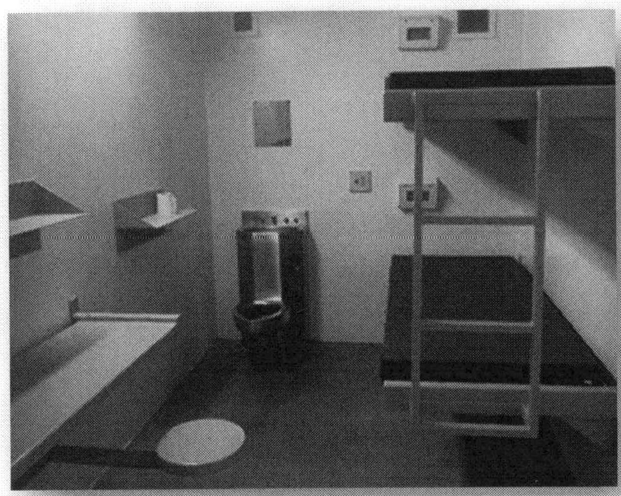

SIX

Timothy Blackhardt was a few months younger than Michael. Tim had lived in the mountains of North Carolina just outside the town of Greenbriar for most of his life, and life was good. Then the hosiery mills started closing down and moving to Mexico and work was hard to find. Tim's father lost his job and couldn't find work, so he did odd jobs until he was no longer able to put food on the table. He was three months behind on the rent, the electricity had been cut off, the water bill was past due and scheduled to be cut off; and, prospects for employment were dire.

Tim's Dad, desperate for work, spoke with his sister who worked at Memorial Hospital in Grantsville. She told him that there was work available, so Tim's dad packed up the family and moved to Grantsville leaving the mountains and all of their friends behind. Once in Grantsville, Tim's family of five, moved into a three bedroom doublewide mobile home with Tim‘s aunt until they could do better.

Tim was still in the fifth grade as he never was much of a student. The only reason he even went to school was because the law made him. Newly enrolled in the county school system, Tim became even less interested in school. The county was a much larger school system than Tim was used to, and he found it easy to be missing without anybody even noticing. Having a lot of time on his hands and little to no supervision, it was inevitable that Tim would get into trouble.

Tim's first run-in with the law was with the Grantsville Police Department one summer evening when he was trying to get home after crashing a frat party. Tim had partaken of a lot of free beer and drugs and was attempting to stagger home. The cops noticed this young boy intoxicated, stopped him, and because of his bad attitude, he was arrested.

Tim was charged with consuming and possessing alcohol while under the age of twenty-one, *Strike One*. Tim answered these charges in juvenile court where he was pled guilty and was placed on unsupervised probation. Less than a month later, Tim was arrested again. A college kid caught Tim breaking into his car in the Shop Mart parking lot, *Strike Two*. Tim was awaiting his court date on that charge when he was arrested for attempting to buy alcohol while under age and trespassing.

Tim's probation officer petitioned the presiding Judge to revoke his probation and he was immediately sent to confinement at Sandy Dunes. Tim had been at Sandy Dunes for nearly six months and would remain there until his court date for his new charges and probations violations. Tim told Michael, "I don't believe I will get out of Sandy Dunes until I either turn eighteen or until I can make an escape from this place.

Neither Michael nor Tim made much of an attempt to make friends during their time at Sandy Dunes. The boys hung out together and watched each other's backs and stayed to themselves. Some of the other offenders didn't think much of their arrangement. They thought they were putting on an air that said they were too good to associate with the other trash we're imprisoned with. "They thinks they's too good to associate wid us criminals I guess," Joe Green, the leader of a gang of red kerchief thugs said. "Well, we'll just have to see about that... we'll have to see about that real soon."

Seventeen-thirty-hours, Sgt. Jones came to Tim's room and advised that he was scheduled to appear in Juvenile Court in Grantsville at zero-nine-hundred-hours tomorrow. "We'll wake you at zero-six-hundred-hours, you will shower and get dressed, and then someone will pick you up at zero-seven-hundred-hours and transport you to your court appearance. Is that clear Mr. Blackhardt?" Sgt. Jones asked. "Clear Sgt. Jones. I'll be ready and waiting," Tim responded. Tim was removed from the room the next morning at exactly zero-seven-hundred-hours.

Everything appeared normal just like yesterday, the day before that, and the day before that. The only difference was that Tim was gone and hadn't returned from court yet. It's fourteen-hundred-hours one long horn blast means everyone to the gym for exercise. This was the one hour of the day when the offenders got to do anything they wanted to do.

This free time is used to associate with other kids, toss a ball, play basketball, work out with weights or just gather around and talk with the other kids. For some unknown reason, Michael felt a little uncomfortable today. Maybe it's because Tim isn't here... he couldn't quite put his finger on it. Michael had an eerie feeling that wasn't natural, "No problem, everything's all right," Michael kept telling himself. "I've been around these kids for more than a year now; I've never had a beef with anyone before...nothing about today would be different. What could happen today...it's just another day," Michael whispered as he walked in the gym. "Yo Michael," one of the kids hollered and motioned for him to come over. Michael walked slowly around the basketball court when suddenly the knot he used to feel in his stomach when his father was giving him the devil made its presence. For some unknown reason, that knot was beginning to form in the base of his stomach. Suddenly with no warning, four members of the red kerchief gang rushed out of the shower room and grabbed Michael by the arms while one put his hands over his mouth the others pulled Michael back into the shower.

Seventeen-hundred-hours; three one-second blasts came across the PA system, everyone starts heading toward their rooms. A few minutes later Sgt. Jones and his crew begin head count to make sure each offender was accounted for. Quickly walking down the hall, Sgt. Jones poked his head in each room and shouted out a head count of inmates in the room, "Two offenders room one-five-one." Moving to the next room, "two offenders room one-five-five." Then loudly Sgt. Jones called out zero offenders, room "one-fifty-seven. I repeat unit one-fifty-seven one man unaccounted for." Only a second passed before the horn began to blast with a one-half second blast repeatedly. Sgt. Jones continued his head count while other guards began searching for the missing boy.

Michael Schomeck was the juvenile offender that was unaccounted for. It was seventeen-hundred-ten-hours when Sgt. Rose located Michael. He was in the shower room where he had been laid out on the floor with his hands tied behind his back with a rope made from a shredded towel and a gag placed in his mouth. From all appearances Sgt. Rose felt that Michael had been sexually assaulted. The charge was never substantiated and no one was ever charged.

Michael was taken to the infirmary where he was examined and treated for minor cuts, scratches and bruises. After being discharged from the infirmary, Michael was then sent to a staff psychologist where he was asked about the assault. Asked if Michael could identify who assaulted him, Michael simply said, "Save your breath. I wasn't assaulted; and, if I was, I'd take care of it myself and no matter what happened or didn't happen, I'll never rat on anybody. That's all I have to say about the matter," Michael said as he crossed his arms and refused to answer any more questions. Refusing to talk about what happened, Michael was sent back to his room and never spoke about the incident again and was never the same after that day.

After the shower room incident, Michael and Tim drew even closer together spending all of their waking hours working out-- the order of the day. Sit ups, two thousand a day, pushups, two thousand a day, running in place, eight hours a day. Anything Michael and Tim could do to get a workout they did. . . filling a trash bag with water using it for weights, one boy sitting on the other boys back to add weight for pushups, doing back pull ups between the bed frames, whatever one thought of the other was willing to try. "One day we'll get out of this place and when we do, we have to be strong enough to take care of ourselves," Michael said, "Ain't nobody ever going to screw with me again, nobody," as he wiped the sweat from his face!

Over the next year Michael and Tim's bodies and minds changed radically. Michael read everything he could get his hands on about becoming a survivalist, hunting, guns, military and police tactics, equipment and all the bells and whistles that went along with it. Over the years, Michael became quite an authority.

Tall, straight and strong, the boys grew into men to be reckoned with. When either boy walked into a room or down a hall, other offenders would move to the side. One boy alone was extremely dangerous, but both boys side by side were unbeatable. No one at Sandy Dunes ever mustered the guts to challenge this dynamic duo again.

"In eight days and I'll be eighteen; they've got to let me out That's what that judge said . . . they have to let me out when I turn eighteen," Michael said repeatedly. "Don't let it get into your head man. . . you can't afford to lose it with only eight days left to go, stay cool," Tim said calmly. "Don't let anybody rile you, don't give nobody any reason to keep you here one second longer than you have to be, stay cool man," Tim whispered.

One week and one day, zero-six-hundred-hours, "Rise and shine," the familiar voice of Sgt. Jones rang in the window. "Mr. Schomeck, we are in the process of confirming your release date for today. We are currently waiting for Superior Court Judge Filmore to return our call. As soon as we receive his fax authorizing your release, you will be processed out and released back into the real world. Is that clear Mr. Schomeck?" asked Sgt. Jones. "Loud and clear Sgt. Jones," Michael replied.

Jumping to his feet, Michael started shoving his personal property into a cardboard box that Sgt. Jones had left outside of the door for him. Placing the last of his property in the box, Michael slid the box top onto the box and slowly sank down on the edge of Tim's bunk. "Man you know I couldn't have made it in here without you, don't you bro?" asked Michael. "No matter where I am, no matter what I'm doing, if you call me, I'll be there for you no questions asked," Michael said as he hugged Tim around the neck, "You're the best friend I've ever had and I promise I won't forget you. You've got the phone number for my mother and she'll know where I am and how to reach me, so when you get out and if you need me, promise to call me.

Zero-nine-hundred-hours, Sgt. Jones walked Michael to the front gate, "Michael you've done your time and your record is clean. You can start over from this day forward. You're free to take the best life has to offer you from this very minute forward." Stopping just outside the gate, Michael took a deep breath of free air and slowly turned around facing Sgt. Jones and said "Sgt. Jones, you treated me fair. Thank you for that and because of that, I thought I'd tell you I intend on taking your advice. I'm going to take the best of what life has to offer me from this day on." With that, Michael turned and jumped aboard the waiting bus bound for Seaside County. It was 1:25 p.m. when Michael arrived at the bus station. As he waited for his father, he nervously checked with the station attendant several times making sure the bus had been on time. The bus had been on time, yet his father had left no messages and the attendant was getting annoyed with Michael's constant questioning. "I guess I'll just sit outside and wait," Michael said to the attendant nervously. If Michael had learned anything while he was away, he learned patience and how to occupy his thoughts; so, he sat thinking of the grand reunion he was in store for when he got home.

Now 2:45 p.m., Michael was stretched out on the bench outside the front door of the bus station. There was a nice breeze blowing and the sun shining on his face made him think about his days on the pier. Kicked back enjoying his new found freedom, when suddenly Michael felt a tap on his shoulder. Michael leaped from his seat with a big smile on his face expecting to see his parents. He was disappointed when he looked into the eyes of the haunting Deputy Daniel Fairlane. The joy he felt only a moment before vanished completely, "What are you doing here?" Michael asked. Fairlane replied, "I thought it would be best if I came to meet you and we can have a little chat while I give you a ride home." "No thanks," Michael responded, "I'm waiting for my father." "I spoke with your dad a few days ago when we found out you were getting out and we felt you could benefit from me and you having a little chat. Come on Michael we can talk while I give you a ride home," Deputy Fairlane said as he motioned Michael toward the waiting patrol car. Michael grabbed his property box and walked slowly to the car with Deputy Fairlane. Michael carefully put his stuff in the back seat and climbed in the front with Deputy Fairlane.

As soon as Michael's seat belt snapped, Deputy Fairlane started laying down the law. "You've been gone a long time Michael and a lot of things have changed while you've been away," Fairlane said. "Usually the first thing a parolee wants to do is to get high or see some girl he left behind or get some payback to the guy that put him away." Fairlane continued. "I ain't no parolee," Michael interrupted in a strong voice. "I'm clean, I was sentenced as a juvenile offender and you know what that means, don't you?" Michael asked. "It means my records have been sealed and I'm as clean as if I had never been convicted of anything at all." Fairlane interrupted, "Yeah, keep telling yourself that mess boy! You're a convict no matter what anybody told you. Look boy, no matter how much jailhouse law you think you know, you're a convict and the best thing for you to do is remember that. One more thing you need to know is, I own you boy. If you screw up one time, I'm going to be on your butt before you have time to think about it twice. So before you go out and try to get some payback, you better think about that. I ain't kidding around with you Michael, if you screw up one time, you're going to jail. I ain't gonna give you no second chances or feel sorry for you or any of that mess. You're going to jail, and if I have anything to say about it, you'll stay there a long time," Fairlane said in an angry harsh voice. Without even realizing it, Fairlane had just let the cat out of the bag. Somebody ratted me out, Michael thought. He's trying too hard to make his point clear without just telling me to stay away from the rat. Fairlane continued with his rant, "The best thing you can do is get a job and spend your time working, going to church and staying out of trouble. Make no mistake about it, I'm going to be keeping my eye on you boy. If crime picks up anywhere near where you are, I'm coming straight to you. Keep your nose clean, stay out of trouble and don't cause me any grief and I'll be your friend. But if you get in any trouble, I'll be your worst enemy, it's your decision to make," Fairlane threatened. "Michael you're not a kid anymore. If you get in trouble again, you won't go to kiddie jail this time; you'll be going to prison." Fairlane sneered. Michael snapped "I ain't never going back to prison; you, and nobody else will ever put me back in prison."

Michael had enough, "Pull over and let me out," he demanded. "I did my time, I'm free and I don't have to sit here and listen to your threats. I haven't done anything to deserve your threats, pull over right now!" Michael shouted. Fairlane pulled over to the side of the road and Michael jumped out. As Michael reached for the back door handle, Fairlane said, "You go ahead and do whatever you want to do but just remember one thing, I'll be watching you." Michael opened the back car door and leaned in to pick up his box of property. Hesitating for a second, Michael looked Fairlane in the eyes and said coldly, "I ain't a little kid anymore Deputy! If you come after me, make sure you come prepared 'cause you know like you said, I ain't a kid anymore." Fairlane sat quietly shocked with nothing to say as Michael slammed the door on the patrol car and walked away.

Michael began to walk westward down the side of Hwy 18. Looking up he saw a highway sign that read seven miles to Cape Shore. Michael had only been walking a few minutes when an old man in a beat up farm truck pulled over and asked if he needed a ride. "Sure do, if it ain't too much trouble, "Michael replied kindly. "Jump in the back," motioned the old man. Michael jumped in the back and said, "Drop me at the Filmore 66 if you're going that far." "Okay," the farmer signaled with thumbs up as he pulled back onto the highway headed toward Cape Shore.

A short fifteen-minute ride and Michael was standing in the parking lot of the Filmore 66 station in Copper Cove. "YaHOO, I'm home!" Michael shouted to the top of his lungs, "After four long years, I'm back home!" Thanking the old man for the ride, Michael turned and walked up to the front door of the station.

The 66 station at Copper Cove had been a hangout for the kids of Copper Cove from the first day the place opened its doors. The station was originally built as a nightclub back in the sixties, but that didn't fly. So, over the years, it changed from a convenience store to a church, then a flea mall and now it was an arcade with a grill. The owner added some pool tables, a few arcade games and a jukebox. The kids flocked there. The owner thought it was great he was able to keep the place open for the kids to have a safe place to hang out. The place finally started making some money.

Michael felt the door close behind him. He shyly turned and nodded at the clerk behind the cash register. While at the same time, he glanced over to the game room to see if he recognized anyone. Not a lot of people there yet, just a couple of kids playing pool and one guy on the phone. Taking a cola from a wash tub filled with ice in front of the register, Michael pulled out a dollar and paid for the cola, then dropped the change in the tip jar before strolling over to the game room to have a look-see. Pausing in the archway entering the game room, Michael leaned up against the door and took a slow look around. The guy on the phone looked kinda familiar, "Oh my GOSH," he whispered, that's Billy, Billy the Bully." Michael walked over to where Billy was standing. Billy was leaning up against the wall holding himself up. He had one arm on his head while looking down at the floor. A cigarette hung from the corner of his mouth as he listened attentively to the voice on the other end of the line.

Michael stood only a few feet behind him taking a close look at the guy. There he was, Billy the Bully, older, fatter, and dirtier-looking like a shower was the farthest thing from his mind, but yeah, and it was definitely Billy. As Michael stood behind him, Billy shifted his stare from the floor to Michael's face looking Michael directly in the eyes, "Yeah man, what do you need?" Billy said. "What do you mean?" asked Michael puzzled. Billy asked again only this time real slow and sarcastic, "What…do… you…need?" Michael answered, "You don't know who I am, do you?" "No man, I don't know who you are and I don't much care. Look man, if you ain't buying, I don't want to know who you are, so get outta my face and leave me alone, or I'll be forced to deal with you!" Billy said combatively. Michael stepped back a couple of steps, squared his shoulder to throw a punch or defend himself if he needed to and said, "I'm Michael Schomeck." Billy's jaw dropped open, "Oh my Gosh man, when did you get out?" "I just got back man. This is the first place I stopped," said Michael happily. "Man, I never would have known you if you hadn't told me. Man, look at you, you're a monster. How did you get in this kind of shape?" asked Billy. Michael replied, "Picture this. . . you're locked in a six foot by nine foot room eighteen hours a day, day after day. You find ways to occupy your time so me and my cellmate worked out." Michael said. "Well, you look great man! Do any of the guys know you're out?" Billy asked. "Man, we really missed you. I can't tell you what you've missed while you've been away," Billy continued. Michael thought, "Yeah you guys missed me so much that none of you ever bothered to write or call or send me a magazine or anything else, yeah, you missed me all right.

Billy, although older, really hadn't changed much. "Hey man," Billy yelled, "Can you hang around for a while…the guys would really like to see you." "I'm not sure, I haven't been home yet, I'll have to play it by ear," Michael replied. "Well there's a phone right over there. Give your folks a call and tell them you're here and you're okay and you'll be home when you get there." Michael, still a little peeved that his father would have a Deputy pick him up instead of coming to get him himself, blurted out, "Hey you know what, forget about it, you're right, I'll get home when I get home! Heck yeah, I can hang out, HECK YEAH!" Michael said loudly. Shuffling his feet, Billy strolled slowly toward the cashier, pulled out a wad of wrinkled bills and boastfully said, "You see my friend over there? Whatever he wants comes out of this, as he placed the bills on the counter. If that runs out let me know, 'cause there's plenty more where that came from. He's an old friend of mine and his money ain't no good tonight. Anything he wants he gets." Then Billy let out a big laugh.

Billy walked over to the beer cooler while tugging up on his pants. He slammed back the cooler door and reached inside and took out two cold beers, held them up for the cashier to see and walked back into the game room. "Here you go bro," as he twisted off the top and handed it to Michael. "Down the hatch man, let's get this party started!" Michael took the beer, clanked his bottle against Billy's bottle and then down the hatch. Michael watched as the bubbles rose to the bottom of the bottle and thought, to heck with M/Sgt Joseph Schomeck. I'll get there when I get there. He didn't care enough to come pick me up himself so to heck with him.

Michael and Billy spent the rest of the afternoon laughing, joking, shooting pool, drinking beer and talking about the good ole days. Michael's order of the day was to talk about and think about anything except Joseph Schomeck or Sandy Dunes.

SEVEN

Michael glanced up at the clock; seven-fifteen p.m. there were only a few people in the arcade. It seemed like only a second later when Michael started noticing more and more people wandering in. By eight thirty there were at least fifty folks drinking, smoking, playing the juke box, playing games, dancing and having fun. "This place has really turned into the "SPOT" hasn't it Billy," Michael quipped as he took a long drink from a newly opened ice cold beer. "Yeah man, looks like there's gonna be a good crowd in here tonight.

If you're up for it, it's about time for us to make some bread," Billy said as he motioned for Michael to step out-side with him. "What do you mean?" "Look bro, me and Buddy's got us a little business going on in here. You know people want a little something, so I supply them with a little something, and they pay me a little money. I get what I want, they get what they want, and everybody's happy, you dig? And the good news is… you get to make a few bucks and you ain't even got to do nothing for it, 'cause you're one of us, you know, one of the gang." Michael responded sheepishly, "I don't know Billy, I just got out of jail, and I don't want to get into any trouble man. You know that Deputy Fairlane, don't you?" asked Michael. "Yeah I know him," Billy replied. "My *Father* sent that jerk to pick me up at the bus station today. He told me that he was going to be keeping his eye on me." "Hey man, forget Fairlane! He ain't got nothing on us." Billy said. "He ain't gonna come in here and mess with us; and, even if he tried to, we'd know he was here before he could get the door open on that fancy police car of his. Trust me man, you're as safe in here as you would be in your mother's arms. Buddy's got everything worked out and everything's under control, especially when it comes to the cops," Billy bragged.

Suddenly from behind Michael came a loud voice, "Well who in the heck do we have here?" He snapped around and saw an old face coming towards him that he hadn't seen since the night of the fire. "Well if it ain't Buddy Thompson, how the world are you?" Michael asked. "I'm doing good and now that you're home, you will be too," Buddy answered. "Billy told me you were here." Throwing his arms open, Buddy hugged Michael like they were the best friends in the world. "Come on over and have a sit down so we can catch up," Buddy said as he led Michael to a corner table. Buddy and Michael waded through the crowd to a table in the corner that had mysteriously been empty all evening. Michael had taken note that it was the only empty table despite all the other tables being taken up. "You must rate," Michael said as he slid into the booth. "You don't know the half of it," Buddy replied. Sitting down at the table, Buddy said to Billy, "Go get us a cold one." Billy obeyed just as Michael remembered… same old Billy nothing more than Buddy's flunky.

"Michael tell me all about it, you know, tell me all about your time in custody," Buddy said. "No man, I don't want to think about that right now, maybe some other time." Michael replied. "No, not some other time, tell me about it now," Buddy ordered sharply. "No I said, I don't want to talk about it," Michael snapped back assertively. Michael stood up and began to turn away, and as he did, Buddy forcefully grabbed his arm and said, "Look man, sit down, we've got lots to talk about. "I didn't want to talk about my mess either when I first got out." Michael eased back into the seat. Buddy continued, "We've got a pretty good deal going here. I guess you can say a few of us are in the supply and demand business. We supply our customers with whatever they want, and we demand top price for our goods. We make a pretty tidy profit from it too," Buddy bragged. "Last month alone, just me and Billy made more than five thousand dollars in pure profit," Buddy said with his normal sly grin. "Michael, I know you've been away a long time, and you don't know how things work around here anymore; but, because you're one of my boys, you're in for a full share from this day on. You see, 'cause you did the time and kept your mouth shut, that entitles you to a piece of the action," said Buddy. Michael responded, "I don't know if I want in or not. I ain't going back to lock up for you or nobody else. Buddy, I just got through doing four long years. That's four years out of my life that I'll never get back, and it's too early for me to think about this kind of stuff right now," Michael said. "Michael, you don't have to make up your mind right now; take a few days then we'll get back together and talk about it some more. Tell me, do you have any walking around money?" Buddy asked. "Looking away shyly, Michael said in a low voice, "No, not really." Buddy reached into his pocket and took out a roll of bills wrapped with a red rubber band. Holding the money below the edge of the table, Buddy peeled off several bills, then reached across the table and pushed the bills into Michael's shirt pocket. Buddy said, "Here's a couple of bucks to get you through the next few days. Remember, if you need anything, I mean anything at all, don't hesitate to call me. Contact me through Billy, he'll know how to get up with me," Buddy said. "Thanks man, give me a couple of days and I'll be back in touch,"

Michael replied. Walking toward the front door, Michael noticed the clock on the wall; it said eleven fifty five p.m.

Michael enjoyed the feel of the cold winter air blowing on his face as he walked down Hwy 58 toward his mother and father's house, not feeling at all that he was going "home". The weight of the box under his arm seemed as light as a feather. Rounding the curve three miles from home, Michael stuck his nose into the air and took a deep breath. "Aha yeah," Michael said out loud, "Just smell that salt air… oh how I missed that smell." Crickets were chirping, frogs croaking and an old owl hooting along with the other sounds of the woods, made Michael remember how much he had missed them while he was away. "Two more miles and I'll be at the road leading to the front of my house," Michael whispered. "I wonder how they'll greet me. How will my father act…? I wonder if they planned a welcome home party." Michael's every thought was on the upcoming reunion. Then without warning, deep in the pit of his stomach, the knot started to make its presence known. Oh no, Michael thought… there's no reason for that…I'm home . . . I'm home.

Michael paused at the end of the road looking towards his house and couldn't believe what he saw. No lights burning, no sounds and nobody moving. Must be a surprise party Michael thought. Quietly Michael walked down the lane and up to the front door listening carefully for any sound of movement inside the house. Peering through the front door, Michael's eyes fell upon a note taped to the storm door window. Michael's name was written on the front of the note. He reached out and pulled the note down and began to read.

"Michael, if you're reading this, it's obvious you decided to come home after lights out. Your mother and I have turned in for the night. Don't bother knocking; no one will open the door for you; you are not welcome here after lights out.

Since you decided not to come home at a reasonable hour, you can find somewhere else to stay for the night. If you want to try to explain your actions to me, come back tomorrow. I get home from the base at seventeen-thirty hours. You need to think about what you have done to your mother and me. If I decide to let you live in my house, you will obey my rules. You may see me tomorrow, and at that time, I will explain the house rules; and I will decide if you will be allowed to stay here or not. ***Welcome home convict****, maybe I'll see you tomorrow."*

Signed,

S/Sgt. Schomeck

Michael crumpled up the note and dropped it on the front stoop next to his foot. As he walked away, "I'll never live under his roof again."

Michael heaved his property box on his shoulder and walked down to the pier. Taking a seat, he closed his eyes and sat quietly in the darkness listening to the sounds on the water. He could hear the water gently splashing against the pilings, the drone of the shrimp boat motor and the voices of fishermen talking to each other while they hauled in their net, the faint squawk of a seagull, and of course that unforgettable smell of the salt air. Thoughts of the fire came fresh in his mind as he looked down the beach to where the house once stood. "I guess things really weren't all that bad after all, Michael thought as he wished he could take everything back to the fateful day when Buddy invited him to join the gang. Oh if I could only make that decision again, he regretfully thought. But it's too late to worry about all that now. I have to find somewhere with a roof over it so I can get some sleep and think about what I'm gonna do tomorrow," Michael said to himself as he shuffled down the pier. Wondering what his options were, Michael reached into his pocket and pulled out the money Buddy had shoved into it . . .

five one-hundred dollar bills. Now if there was only a motel on this end of the county I'd be set," Michael said aloud, as he tucked the money back deep into his pocket and walked down Hwy. 58.

Michael had been walking for what seemed all night when he came upon the dirt road that lead down to the Black Water River camp ground. "I'll go down there and sleep in one of the cabins. There're empty this time of year, and at least, I'll be out of the weather with a roof over my head," Michael said to himself as he walked. He was familiar with the camp because he, Joe Jr. and Father had stayed there a few times hunting and fishing as kids. Walking down the road it was just as he had remembered it. The camp ground was closed and the cabins were open, so he picked one out and settled in for the night. Sleeping soundly, Michael's dreams went back to the little pier over the sound. It had been his special place where he could escape for the past four years and couldn't help but to dream about it tonight.

Then suddenly all of Michael's thought left the sights and sounds of the river and zeroed in on the smell of bacon. Michael rose from his cot sniffing the air and thought… I must still be dreaming; nope it's bacon all right, there's nothing else in the world that smells like bacon, except bacon.

Michael reached under the cot, slid his box out and laid it across his lap. Lifting the lid, Michael peeked inside at the stuff he had been carrying around for the past two days.

Looking over his only personal belongings, Michael reached in and took out a bunch of letters his mother had written him bound together with a red ribbon. Thinking about her loving words for a minute, Michael laid them beside him on the cot. Admiring some drawings he had made, Michael then shuffled through the box and took out a couple of books. These books had been the center of his universe for the last four years, each having different meanings. Just holding the "Rules" book brought back a flood of bad memories. Michael threw it back into the box vowing to use it as kindling at his first opportunity. He then reached for the Sandy Dunes issued hard back Bible and held it close to his chest. The worn crumpled pages and circled passages reminded him of how much comfort it gave him to get him through each day with hope for a brighter day. Talking aloud to himself, Michael said, "Four years of my life are gone and what did I come home to… a bunch of so-called friends that want me to deal drugs with them, a father who can't stand the sight of me, and a deputy whose sole purpose in life is to put my butt back in jail . . . where do I go from here?" Michael snapped the lid back on the box quickly hoping it would seal all the bad memories and fears inside.

Suddenly a loud growl came from deep within his stomach. He pushed the box back under the cot, stood up, swung open the cabin door and stepped outside. "Now let's see if we can find out where that bacon smell is coming from," Michael said. Michael stuck his nose in the air and literally began to follow it toward the delicious smell of bacon. As Michael walked through the woods, he saw wildlife and nature like he'd never seen it before. Walking for a while, stopping to watch squirrels frolicking, he thought, "If I could get my hands on one of them, I wouldn't want that bacon so much." Another hundred yards, Michael saw a flock of wild turkeys but there was no sneaking up on them as they were quick to run away. I think the smell of that bacon is getting stronger.

EIGHT

Michael walked for more than an hour when he spied something up ahead looming in the morning mist. Maybe I'm just seeing things; no it's a cabin, a small rundown log cabin. Michael had walked within one hundred yards, squatted down in the tall grass and watched a plume of smoke rising straight up into the air. Michael wondered should he dare to go up to the house and ask for food. Looking around the outside of the cabin, He thought it looked like something out of a fairy tale. Spanish moss was hanging from trees, chickens pecking for feed around the yard and a large black caldron sitting partially over an open fire in the front yard. "Where in the heck am I," Michael murmured, "have I walked onto a movie set or stepped into the pages of a book?"

Suddenly, from out of nowhere, this rough voice echoed, "What you doing, boy?" Michael almost jumped out of his skin in fright. She was standing right beside him, "I… I… I smelled bacon," Michael muttered. "You smelled bacon?" the old woman asked in a deep stern voice. "Yes ma'am, I smelled bacon and I was hungry so I followed the smell, I followed it here." Michael said. "You smelled bacon huh?" she asked. "Yes ma'am," Michael said again. "Where'd you come from boy?" You ain't got no business being here on my property. I just soon shoot if'n you come any closer. Now, what you doing here?" barked the old woman. "I just come upon this place following that smell of bacon. I'll leave if you'll let me. I promise, I ain't doing nothing," Michael said nervously. I'm asking you one more time, boy, where'd you come from?" asked Snake Woman. "Over that way," pointing in the direction, where he had walked through the woods. "No, that ain't what I'ma ask'n you, boy!" snapped the old woman. Any dern fool wid two eye in their head can see you come from over dat away. What I mean, is where'd you come from?" asked the dirty, haggard-looking old woman again. Michael responded, "I thought you meant..." The old woman interrupted, "How far away did ya smell bacon?" "I don't know for sure; I walked a little more than an hour, I reckon," Michael said questioning his time frame. "An hour boy, you say you smelled bacon a cook'n more than an hour away?" the old woman grunted in disbelief. "Yes ma'am, that's about how long it took me to walk here I figure, yep about an hour," Michael again replied. "What's your name boy?" the old woman asked. "Michael, my name is Michael Schomeck," he answered. "Well Mr. Michael Schomeck, you come wid me 'cause any boy what can smell bacon more than an hour away, must be needing to eat some bacon real bad, I suppose," the woman said as she slowly turned heading back to the cabin.

As Michael and the old woman walked toward the cabin, he took a long look at the old woman trying to figure her out. She's seventy if she's a day Michael thought, slightly bent over at the waist, Michael couldn‘t tell if she was ailing in her back or watching the ground. Wearing a tattered old gray felt hat, her scraggly hair stuck out from under the brim looking like that of a scarecrow. She wore a faded tan canvas coat and blue jeans that had seen many seasons come and go, and a pair of scruffy leather work boots. A well-worn leather bag hung from her neck with all kinds of bones tied on it with hemp rope. Walking slowly behind the old woman, Michael remembered thinking he could hardly hear her making any sound as she trudged through the heavy grass and under growth. Heck, I can hardly walk through it without falling down. Stepping into the clearing surrounding the cabin, Michael glanced over at the huge black iron cauldron boiling on the fire and thought to himself, “She looks like the witch that led Hansel & Gretel to the oven; I sure hope this bacon’s worth all this.

Stepping into the cabin, the old woman pulled out a chair at the table, reached over and took a tin pan covered with a towel from the window sill and placed it in front of Michael. “Here you go boy, eat up… I hope this is worth all that walk’n you done for it,” said the old woman.

Palmer housing over to a wooden rocking chair sitting in front of the fireplace, the old lady eased herself down, propped up her swollen feet, took a pipe out of her coat pocket, struck a match, lit the pipe and gripped the leather bag in her left hand; then began to talk in a softer and humble way. “Tell me boy, how’d you miss all them man traps I got set in them woods? Ain’t nobody ever snuck up here like that afore. You some kind of woodsman, boy?” “No, I don’t think so. I just got good senses, something like a Bloodhound, when it comes to smelling bacon,” Michael answered with a little chuckle.

Come on over here and sit a spell. I want to know more ‘bout this boy who done showed up wid out me knowing.

Peoples round here calls me Snake Woman. Some of the mean ones calls me Witch Woman. I'm been guessing 'cause I have a way of seeing things other folks don't...like them spirits that walk the woods. I been knowed to cast a few spells on them folks that don't treat me right and bad things been happening to 'em.

I ain't real sure, but I'm somewhere near on seventy-two year old. I been livin' in these here woods, in this here cabin, right near on sixty year now. I was a little girl, no more than ten or eleven year old, when my papa brung me here to live. I never wuz a pretty little girl you see; I had what they calls a lazy eye. On account of my eye, mama didn't want to take me 'round wid her much. Her friends used to laugh and point in my way, when mama took me places. I knowed they was laughing at me. She never said it, but she thought me wuz downright ugly, I reckon. I figured she must a been 'shamed of me. Sometime early fall, must have been 1934 or 5, my papa gathered up my belongings and brung me out here to this here cabin. He told me I was gonna have to stay out here till he could talk mama into letting me come back home."

"My papa built this cabin before the big war. He used it as a hunt'n cabin so it's built real good. It's stood right here through many a storm and never leaked not one time. Anyway... when he brung me here, he made sure I had everything I needed, you know, food, water and my Bible Book. Whenever he'd come to visit, he brung me a sack filled with books and papers to read. When I was in school, I wanted to read everything I could, but after about the 4th grade, I didn't have nobody to help me. I done the best I could try'n to read a bunch of old books left out here 'bout hunt'n, fish'n, and that kind of stuff. I read all of 'em. I read 'em so many a time, I took most of 'em to memory. After a while, I knowed just about everything in 'em, so I used 'em to get my fire started. For long, I burned 'em all in that fireplace over there. That ole water pump right there in the corner works as good right now as it did the first day I come here; she pull from deep water and the water is sweet water too. Papa used to come out to see me every day or two and he'd set here wid me and visit. Me and papa would set right here for hours and read in the Good Book together. Me and papa had us a real good time just read'n and sing'n and study'n over books… right there in front of that fireplace. After a couple of years, I figured mama was happier wid me out of the way, so I settled into the notion that I was gonna live right here the rest of my days. It hadn't been all that bad though 'cause papa took time to learn me how to fish and hunt so I could feed myself. I reckon he figured I was old enough to fend for myself okay, 'cause after a while, his visits come farther and farther apart. Twenty, no maybe closer to 25 year ago, papa's visits come less and less… I ain't real sure why. Then after a while, papa didn't come no more a'tall. I reckon he got sick and died or something, anyway I never seen my papa no more after that. I'd say most of the time, I'm all right living here by myself, but there comes times when I sure do miss my papa. Ain't had nobody to talk to for some time now." The old woman sat and rocked back and forth in her chair and then without a pause turned to Michael and said, "Well boy, now you tells me about you. I needs to know what kinda fella you are if'n you gonna be eating my bacon, you know."

Michael didn't know why, but he opened up and began to talk. And talk he did. Michael spoke from his heart as if he were in confession. He opened up to the old woman and told her things that he had never told another person in his life. He told her about everything he had ever done from the time he was a young boy up until the day he got off the bus from Sandy Dunes. He told the old woman about his insecurities, the fire, his Father, his Mother and about his days at Sandy Dunes. He told her about the gang he was running with, the drugs, the money, everything, everything except the assault on him while in custody. Michael hadn't come to the point where he could bear that demon yet. As bad as he wanted to forget it, he couldn't, and he sure didn't want to talk about it. When he finished talking, the old woman turned and said, "Boy leave me tell you something… you needs some new surroundings. You needs to clear your head out from all that bad juju you got messing with you in there. You needs to learn some new things to put in there and most of all you needs some new friends. If'n you want to stay here with me for a while, I'll learn you some things that will helps you get control of them demons that's messing with your head. The good Lord knows you ain't never gonna get rid of 'em without help," the old woman said. With tear-filled eyes, Michael answered, "Yes ma'am I do." "Well get up from there boy and gives me a hug. From here on out, you calls me "Snake Woman." Michael got up from the rickety table and hugged Snake Woman with all his might. For the first time in his life, Michael felt like someone cared about him and wanted to hear his voice. The hours passed way into the night. Snake Woman needed that same someone.

Grunting and groaning, Snake Woman made a sleeping pallet by the fireplace for Michael's bed. "You get over there and get some sleep, 'cause morning starts real early around here boy," Snake Woman said. Michael settled into the bed and began to nod off to sleep. Drifting off, he remembered a story he heard when he was a little boy about the Black Water River witch, altogether wondering if Snake Woman was that witch.

A story had been told around Seaside County for more than sixty years about a little girl who was put out in the woods to fend for herself near the Black Water River. The story goes that a little girl was born to parents who were so poor that they couldn't afford to feed her and besides that, the little girl was odd. The little girl told folks that she could talk to animals. The strangest part about the little girl's story was that she claimed they talked back to her just like people did. It was rumored that her folks became angry and upset when they learned that the story was being told all around town. Probably the part of their being poor upset them the most. The story went that, at first, her father tried to talk the foolishness out of the little girl's head about animals talking back to her like people. When that didn't work, he tried to beat it out of her. That didn't work either, so one cold winter night he took the little girl to the edge of the Black Water River and left her there in an old shack. When the town's people asked where the little girl was, her folks told them that she had run away and couldn't be found. Nobody doubted their word 'cause everybody knew the little girl was strange. Besides, her parents were "respected" well-known members of the community, plus her father was a Deacon in the church. When the Sheriff got word about little Clara missing, he started a search, yet it didn't last but a couple of weeks. It was told that he had more important things to do than look for some crazy young'un that didn't want to befound anyway. Besides, the family just wanted the whole thing to go away.

For many years, campers, hunters and fishermen reported sightings of a little girl wandering in the woods surrounded by forest animals. The sightings were checked out by forest rangers, game wardens and the local sheriff, but no one was ever able to find the little girl.

Over the years, the number of sightings increased so substantially that the sheriff couldn't ignore them anymore. The sheriff contacted the commanding general on the Marine base and together they formed a search party of more than 300 men.

Neither hide nor hair was spotted of the little girl. Either she wasn't there anymore or was real good at hiding. Since nothing turned up, the search was called off. The tale began to take on horror stories that if witch woman, they began calling her, caught you hurting the animals or messing up the forest, you were in real trouble. It was well known that the only people who went around her were hunters...and they had rifles. The hunters would say, "If you go around her place, you better take her some kind of candy or pipe tobacco to keep her on your side." It was told she would cast spells on you if she didn't take a liking to you, and the spirits would haunt you forever. She would sneak up on you, lead you deep into the tangled forest and cut out your eyes. Then, she'd say, "Now see if you can find your way out wid no eyes."

After spending hours getting to know Snake Woman, the horror stories didn't bother Michael as he slept sound, cozy, and safe by the fire-- more so than he could remember in many years. Michael wiped the sleep from his eyes. He awoke with the smell of breakfast, yet it was still pitch black outside when he looked out the window. "What a wonderful smell to wake up to after a good talk and a good night's sleep, Michael thought as he watched Snake Woman busy at the wood stove. There she was, humming trust and obey for there's no other way... as she pulled a pan of hot biscuits from the oven. A basket of fresh brown eggs, ready to be cooked, sat next to a big plate piled high with bacon.

Without looking around Snake Woman asked, "You gonna lay in that hog wallow the rest of the day or ya gonna get up?" "I'm getting up," Michael responded with a yawn in his voice. "Once you're up and dressed, go out back and throw them chickens a few hands full of feed. You'll see a bucket at the end of the porch high up on a peg-- that's the chicken feed,"

Snake Woman said. "Don't feed them chickens too close to the hog pen. If'n them chickens gets too close to them hogs, we won't have no chickens or eggs no more." "Yes ma'am," Michael replied. "When you gets all that done, you put that old black iron pot on the spit, and stoke the fire under it. Once you gets that fire stoked up and it's burning good, we'll eat some breakfast," Snake Woman said.

"Yes ma'am," Michael said as he pulled the door closed behind him. It took Michael thirty minutes to do his chores. When Michael came back in the door he said, "All done, I'm ready for breakfast 'cause I can't wait for some more of that bacon."

Sitting down to the country feast, Michael reached for a biscuit. As he did, a wooden spoon popped him on top of his hand, "We 'ens don't take out 'round here till we thanks the Maker," with that Snake Woman bowed her head and said the blessing. After praying, she looked over at Michael and said, "Michael if'n you gots thanks to give, do it now." Pausing for a second Michael replied, "Snake Woman, I don't have any thanks to give right now that I can think of…is that all right?"

Without hesitating Snake Woman said, "Well then go ahead and take out boy 'cause we got a long day ahead of us." Michael took a biscuit and a couple of pieces of bacon from the plates in front of him and placed them on his plate. "Boy takes out some of them eggs too," Snake Woman said. "Michael, you to need remember this 'cause when you're dog tired and needs energy, eggs will help you. There's something about eggs that sticks with you and when you're tired they gives you strength." "Yes ma'am, thank you," Michael said as he took out a large helping of scrambled eggs. Michael ate his fill and thought how good the simple country food was to him. After the meal, Snake Woman took the leftovers and covered them with a towel and put them on the window sill. "Well boy, it's time for some learning, let's get at it."

Walking out the door into the darkness, Snake Woman drew the pipe out of her coat pocket, struck a match on the door frame, took a few puffs off of it, and blew out the smoke in a long curly ribbon. As she sat down in a chair made from short pieces of pine and willow branches, Snake Woman told Michael, "Set yourself down right here 'cause the first thing you needs to learn is how to listen. Sit real still and start to listening." "What am I listening for," Michael asked. "Hush up boy! You can't hear nothing when you're talking, anyway you'll knows when you hears it." Sitting in the pitch dark Michael didn't know what he was listening for and was afraid to ask so he sat quietly looking up at the stars. Suddenly Snake Woman asked, "Do you hear that boy?" Michael replied, "I think so." Giving a quick pop to the top of the head from her hand, "Don't think so boy-- either you hears it of you don'ts!" "Yes ma'am." "Listen and hear what I'm telling you right now, don't calls me ma'am no mo boy, you just calls me Snake Woman. You hear what I'm a telling you boy?" she asked. "Yes ma'am" Michael replied. "Now listen when I tells you I wants you to point your ears up into the tree tops," Snake Woman instructed. Michael obeyed by lifting his head toward the tree tops, "No...no...no...don't move your ears up boy-- you needs to *listen* up, not *move* your ears up! Don't make no movement when you listen!" Snake Woman said. "Listen up, you hears that there, hear the breeze gently blowing up high?" "Listen how it's moving the tree tops 'round, hear 'em?" Snake Woman asked a little kinder. "Yes I hear it," Michael replied sheepishly. "That sound tells you what's downwind from you. It also tells you who might be downwind from you. It tells you how fast a scent is moving through the trees; which away the grass is blow'n and which away the river's moving. The wind tells you more than you can get into you head. If you listen real good and you knows what you're listening for," Snake Woman said with a grin exposing hardly any teeth. "If'n you'll listen to me boy, I'll learn you how to listen. But you needs to know this first. What time you're here with me I have two rules. Rule one is I don't take no sass; rule two, the day you don't listen no more be the day you have to go away from Snake Woman," you got that? "I'll be a good student Snake Woman, I'll never sass you. I want to learn everything you'll teach me," Michael answered. "Good boy," Snake Woman said, "Good Boy."

Slowly rising from her chair, "Now boy, we gonna see how much you don't know about tracking," Snake Woman said. "You stays here on the porch and counts to twenty, and then I wants you to come and find me. If you gets lost, wait till the sun come up and walk yourself directly toward the sun and it will bring you straight back to the cabin." Struggling to get out of the chair Snake Woman let out a, "Whew, now Boy you start to count," as Snake Woman stepped off the porch and disappeared slowly into the darkness.

Michael started counting and whispered to himself at the same time. "One, how on earth does this old woman think in her wildest dreams that she can hide from me? Three, I was taught hide and go seek from a United States Recon Marine only we called it search and destroy. Seven, I'll hang back a little bit and not run up on her too fast; that way she won't get discouraged with me, 'cause I know so much. Fourteen, when we get back to the cabin, she'll want to take a nap; and, I'll eat the rest of that bacon that was left over. Fifteen, I wonder what she's got cooking in that big pot all the time. Twenty! Okay Snake Woman, ready or not here I come," Michael said as he stepped off the porch into the darkness.

Michael moved cautiously in the near darkness making his way to the edge of the woods. "The moon's visible so I'll use that light to find her trail," Michael whispered. After walking around the woods for over an hour Michael said, "Well maybe she's a little better than I gave her credit for. I haven't come across any sign of her yet." Another hour went by and Michael noticed the sun was just beginning to rise over the tops of the pines. Michael stopped perfectly still, took a deep breath and took a long hard look around. The woods were beginning to get dark; the wild life sounds he had enjoyed listening to while walking down the road now took on sounds of wild animals that seemed to surround him. "I wonder if she doubled back on me and she's gone back to the cabin...yep I'll bet that's exactly what she did...I better head back that way too."

Michael had only taken a few steps when he felt a tap on his shoulder. Jerking around suddenly Michael looked Snake Woman directly in the eyes. "Where you going boy, you didn't find me yet, did you?" "Whoa!" Michael jumped around startled. Instinctively embarrassed he dropped his gaze and stared down at the ground. "Don't look down there boy; it ain't time to look down there till I tells you to. Now walks right here aside me, it's time for some more learning." As they walked along, Snake Woman talked, "Boy you know why you couldn't find me? It were 'cause you didn't stop and listen right off the bat. When you're on a trail, the first thing you have to do is listening. All God's creatures makes sounds boy. You just don't know what kinda sounds they make yet, but stick with me and I'll learn you. When you knows how to listen, you can track almost anything; or, you can avoid nearly anything if'n you needs to. Next thing you needs to do is to take a good look around. Everything that walks or crawls or flies over God's good earth sept'n maybe a bug crossing hard ground, leaves some kind of sign. If'n you knows what you're looking for, you can track anything," Snake Woman said. Since'n you been up all night hunt'n me, and I've been up all night watch'n you, let's sit a spell and rest up.

"Now boy, look right here, see how the dew is sit'n on this leaf right here," pointing at a fallen leaf. "Now look at this one and see how they ain't the same? See how the dew looks like it's run'n off this leaf? It's trying to tells you something. If'n you knows how to look and listen, you'd learn what it's telling you," Snake Woman said quietly. "It's telling you that I stepped right here when you was looking for me. Little things like that is what you have to train your eye to see. Come Michael, you looks right here and tells Snake Woman what you sees." Michael stepped in front of Snake Woman and stopped dead still; squatting close to the ground he paused for a minute and began to talk. "When I look in this pine straw, I see a slight depression, here and here, and right here, and over here are some more prints that show me that someone walked across this pine straw. Good, now you tell me whose wuz it?" asked Snake Woman. Michael looked at the prints intensely and said, "I believe these are my prints," pointing at a depression. "How you know that boy?" Snake Woman asked. "Because this footprint right here is deeper than those over there. These prints are the ones I made when I was tracking you and these tracks right here are your tracks when you were hiding from me. These are your tracks, I can tell because they're hardly visible. You were walking real soft so you wouldn't leave much of a print," Michael said. "Not so soft that you couldn't find 'em if'n you knowed what you was looking for though," Snake Woman whispered.

"Good boy Michael, I believes this may be the first time you stopped, looked, and listened. See how much you can see when you knows what to look for. Let's get back to the cabin and get some of that bacon Michael. You done real good, boy…real good." Snake Woman said beaming.

As they made their way back to the cabin, Michael would often stop and point out signs to Snake Woman telling her his theory about what they were and how they got there. Although Snake Woman didn't say much, she enjoyed seeing how much Michael had learned in such a short amount of time. Snake Woman knew that Michael had a God-given gift for tracking; and, if she could help him develop his skills, she knew he would be a man to reckon with in the woods before long.

Michael intensely studied Snake Woman's lessons for several weeks; day time tracking, night time tracking, tracking in good weather, tracking in bad weather. Michael, at first, was the hunter; but, as his skills developed, he became the hunted. Michael's talent and skills developed even faster than Snake Woman first thought was possible. It wasn't long before Michael was demonstrating skills to Snake Woman that woodsmen with many years of experience in the woods hadn't learned yet.

Michael was proving to be a natural, his senses were better than good, his reasoning and ability to determine his prey's next move were uncanny; and, Michael consumed every bit of information as he did the country meals that Snake Woman prepared for them each day.

After finishing an afternoon stalk, Snake Woman and Michael were headed back to the cabin when about a mile from the cabin Snake Woman told Michael, "Boy you stay out here and practice your skills while I fix us up some supper. I'll call you when it's ready." "Yes, Snake Woman," Michael replied. Michael walked around the edge of the woods looking for signs, finding them and then tracking them back to see what they belonged to, and how far he could follow them while Snake Woman worked in the cabin. More than an hour passed when

Snake Woman came to the door and hollered, "Michael, supper!"

Michael hooted back, "Coming." As Michael opened the door and entered the cabin, he was surprised to see a cake on the side table along with the other normal supper. "What's this, what's the special occasion?" Michael asked. "It's a party boy… we're celebrating," Snake Woman replied. "Okay I'm up for a party," Michael said. "Ain't you gonna ask me what we celebrating?" Snake Woman asked. "I figured you'd tell me when you wanted me to know." Michael replied. Snake Woman said, "Boy, set yourself down right here." Snake Woman ambled over to the side board, picked up the cake and lit one candle and began to sign Happy Birthday. Michael beamed a smile that would rival that of a Cheshire cat. Michael appreciated the cake but knew it wasn't his birthday. Snake Woman sat the cake down in front of Michael. "Michael, I know you think I'm a crazy old woman, lets me explain. I made you this here cake 'cause you showed me that on this day, you've been reborn into a real woodsman. I do believe you could survive anywhere. You showed me things today that men who been in these woods for twenty years don't know. I'm real proud of you boy, you keep up with your learning, and one day soon, I'll shows you some things that hardly nobody in any woods ever knowed." Snake Woman and Michael enjoyed the good country supper saving the cake for dessert.

As Michael settled into bed, his newly learned skills kept running through his mind. He analyzed each step before taking it… replanted every footstep and stopped…looked and listened before making each move. As he drifted off to sleep, he thought how much more content and happy he was right now than ever before.

NINE

When Michael opened his eyes before daybreak, he was surprised and alarmed not seeing Snake Woman standing at the sink preparing breakfast. Suddenly and almost in a panic, he jumped out of bed. "Where is she…is she all right…? She wasn't in her room. Where can she be? After wild thoughts of something being wrong, he spotted a torn piece of brown paper bag on the kitchen table. When he saw it was a note addressed to him, and before he even started to read, his heart sank in the pit of his stomach with thoughts of the note his father had left on door of his home. Those thoughts quickly vanished as he began reading the note from Snake Woman.

"Good Morn'in Boy. This here is your last test. I done gone to a place in the woods I never took you afore. You gots till sundown to catch up to me. Now, you gotta remember to use ever thing I learned you."

Snake Woman

Michael slowly walked over to his bed and began to get dressed. Pulling on his clothes, the many survival lessons began to run through his mind. As he sat down at the table to tie his shoes, Michael's thoughts and eyes drifted up to the window sill where he saw a plate covered with a towel. Michael took down the plate, lifted the towel finding five or six fried eggs, several pieces of bacon and two biscuits. With the amount of food

Snake Woman had left for him, he knew it was going to be a hard day. After Michael had eaten the last fork full of eggs, used a bite of a cat head size biscuit to sop up the yolks, he washed his plate and then walked to the door.

Michael slowly pushed open the door; but, before setting foot outside, he squatted down really low and tilted his head to the side. If he could catch the moon light at the right angle, he could possibly see a sign that Snake Woman had intentionally left for him. About two feet outside the front door in the dirt, was a half print from a boot heel. Michael knew it was Snake Woman's print from the many, many times he had tracked her through the woods. "There it is, here's where I start," Michael whispered. Michael stepped through the doorway moving toward the single heal print. As he did, he could see other foot prints in the fallen dew.

Michael slowly stepped in the same direction looking for the next sign in the early morning dew. A few yards ahead was a broken branch… a few more steps… two dry leaves facing up with all the other ones covered with dew. Michael trailed very faint signs for another twenty minutes before he picked up his next good sign. He spied a toe scrape mark in some pine straw. "Looks like she dragged her foot before making the second step… she must be getting tired," Michael thought. Fifty yards more, he noticed some bark scuffed off a willow tree that had fallen during a recent storm. "Right here it looks like she walked along the top of this downed tree…yeah, this is where she stepped off… right here," Michael said as he again squatted to listen to the forest. A half mile more was a burned out match and a faint smell of tobacco. "She stopped right here and lit her pipe," Michael said. Moving three quarters of a mile more, there were some crumbs from a biscuit on top of an ant hill. Then it hit him like a ton of bricks. "I'm tracking a woman who taught me everything I know about tracking and she's leaving this much sign…mmm. Either she's taking it real easy on me or she's giving me a bunch of false trails," Michael said out loud. "This is a woman who can walk through a fresh plowed field and not leave a foot print and she's leaving this much sign," Michael said. "She's leaving a false trail…there ain't no way she's gonna take it easy on me 'cause I know her better than that. It's gotta be a false trail," Michael thought. "I'll back track to see if she laid this trail, then again, back tracked and went off in another direction." Michael followed each sign back, making double sure that he didn't miss another trail he may have missed the first time. Michael followed signs until he was almost back at the cabin.

Suddenly, Michael burst out with a huge laugh as he caught sight of Snake Woman sitting on the porch in her favorite chair, smoking on her pipe and grinning a big toothless grin from ear to ear. "Well boy, I'll tell you one thing, you is definitely the real thing…you is a woodsman first class." Michael nearly ran over Snake Woman as he ran back up to the porch to give her a great big hug. "Boy, without a doubt, you is one of the best I ever did see," said Snake Woman. "You is now worthy to learn the rest… now that you really is a woodsman. Come near and listen good Boy, I'ma gonna learn you how to be as hard to catch as smoke. Come over here Boy and let's talk," Snake Woman said. Michael listened carefully taking in each and every word Snake Woman said.

Snake Woman sat quietly, leaned forward and gripped the leather bag in her right hand and softly began to speak, "Michael, you're never alone when you're in the woods. The spirits dwell there, they is the spirits of woodsmen who passed on. A true woodsmen don't never leave the forest, it's figured to always be their home."

"The woods will always take care of you so long as you take care of her Michael," Snake Woman said eerily. "She'll provide you with everything you'll ever need, shelter, water, food and protection. Once a woodsman passes on, they returns to the protection of the woods they loved so much while they was living. They walks the woods and takes care of the forest, the lost, and the animals. When I was a little girl, I was in the woods one day and got turned around and couldn't find my way back home. All I had to do was listen to the voices and follow the mist. Michael, if you ever get lost, remember to look for the mist in the pines, it will always lead you home." Snake Woman said. "How can I tell if I'm a real woodsman Snake Woman?" Michael asked. "You'll know when you hears the voices afore you Boy," Snake Woman replied. "The best time to hear them is in the early morning just before the dawn. Sit and be still as you can, and you'll hears the spirits talking to you from the mist. That's why I gets up early in the morning afore the spirits walk. Michael, they tells me of things that will be, and some things that never was." Snake Woman told him. "You'll know what I'm talking about when you hears the voices Michael. When you hears the voices and understands the message, is when you'll be a true, for real, woodsman Michael." Snake Woman said as she reached over and stroked Michael's shoulder.

"Now boy it's time for you to go out there and find out for yourself. You remembers that bluff that looks out over the biggest of them Crowan Great Lakes?" asked Snake Woman. "Yes ma'am," Michael replied. "You gets yourself there before the sun starts to rise up in the morning. Find the big pine tree grove that lies due east at the head of the lake. Take yourself a set- down right there and be as still as you can. You set real still and listen to the rustle of the pines. Boy, if'n you gets a sign, you come back home and we'll have us a celebration for real,"

Snake Woman said. She then motioned to Michael, "Come here boy and gives me a big hug. You sure do make me proud."

Michael figured it was around two a.m. when he arrived at the western most ends of the Great Lakes. As he worked his way through the thick forest to the shoreline, he couldn't help but think about the task at hand. Michael had always been respectful about the folktales Snake Woman told him but never really believed too much of her stories. Now, Michael found himself following her directions blindly from a position of pure respect that he held for her. Finding the lookout point Snake Woman had told him about, Michael settled down with his back against a large cut off pine tree stump to await whatever was to happen next. Michael sat down and quietly stared out into the darkness; listening to the many sounds all around him. Michael didn't feel fear as one might think, he had come to know and love these woods as his home.

The moon reflecting off of the quiet still water of the lake was as shiny as a polished mirror reflecting a billion stars in the clear North Carolina night. Michael sat quietly remembering everything Snake Woman had taught him. Going over Snake Woman's lessons, he reflected on the many stalks as well as remembering the laughter he had shared with Snake Woman. Michael's heart filled with happiness knowing she cared about him.

The sounds of the woods rang in his ears with amazement, he thought. He heard everything at once it seemed. The crickets were chirping, fish splashing, and an old hoot owl in a tree sounding out his eternal question... *Who*? "It's me Michael Schomeck, that's who," he chuckled. Michael sat still listening without saying another word...details of his life past through his mind as he waited for a sign.

Shortly after the sun came up, Michael began to talk quietly to himself. “What was I expecting?” Michael speculated. “Did I really think I was going to hear voices of ghosts talking to me from the woods… how gullible can one person be? All this juju stuff is messing with my head,” Michael thought. “I’ll bet Snake Woman is having a heck of a belly laugh on me,” Michael assumed. However, Michael stood fast all morning, “I’m going to give this thirty more minutes then that’s it… all over for me. I ain’t gonna wait around here all day.” The hours passed slowly as Michael continued to set one deadline after another yet still refusing to leave. Each deadline came and passed with Michael setting another and then another; swearing each time it would be the last one. Although darkness took over the woods; and, still Michael refused to relent as he recalled that everything Snake Woman had told him was 100% straight from the heart. “She would never tell me something not true,” he pondered. Something inside Michael wouldn’t let him give up.

Michael remembered thinking it was near four a.m. when something woke him. “What was that?” he asked himself. “Did I really hear something or was I dreaming? No wait, there it is again. I definitely heard something that time . . . what was that?” Michael asked again. Suddenly the woods became graveyard quiet. Walking, that’s it; it’s the sound of walking.” Michael opened his eyes wide and cocked his head to the left trying to pick out the exact location where the sounds were coming from. “Yeah, right over there, the sound is coming from right over there; O’ geez, right there where the woods darken at the other end of the lake. Michael figured it was no more than half a mile away “I don’t believe this… I, I can see someone moving over there. Who is it? Good gosh I reckon, right there… I do see someone. Am I really seeing this or am I just tired and my mind and eyes are playing tricks on me?” Michael supposed.

"Well, maybe I want to see something so badly that I'm seeing what I want to... before Michael could finish his thought... "Gee whiz, over there, right over there in the fog at the edge of the lake, I definitely see the figure of a man."

All of Michael's senses were telling him not to believe his eyes. "But how can I not believe what I know I'm seeing?" Michael voiced to himself. Then the figure stopped moving. Michael could see it more clearly now than before. It was a tall man wearing dark tan clothes, a floppy hat, knee high boots and holding what looks like a rifle, yeah, it's a musket or some kind of long rifle. Yes, I can make him out clearly now. It's a man... a man dressed in hunting clothes. But oh my goodness, I can see right through him. My eyes have got to be playing tricks on me. I know what I'm seeing, and I swear I see a man and I can see right through him." Michael sat stunned, totally disbelieving and denying what his mind and senses knew he was seeing.

Without moving his legs, the figure drifted from the shadows toward the edge of the lake and stopped. He took off his hat with his right hand and stretched out both arms until they were parallel with the ground. He then raised his head towards the heavens and softly spoke, "The troubles of this life will be left behind when your life is over here. Live each day as if it were your last day. Never betray your true feelings. Always trust your instincts and most importantly, don't be fooled by the words of evil in the disguise of a friend." The figure floated for what seemed to Michael as five minutes or more. Quietly trying to clear his thoughts, Michael came back from the edge of insanity. "He's praying...looks to me like he's praying." Michael thought. Michael couldn't blink or take his eyes off the figure.

He was afraid if he did the hunter would be gone. Then without warning, the figure rose more than six feet off the ground, lowered his arms and drifted back toward the woods from which he came. As the figure became more and more indistinct, Michael noticed a light mist filling the edge of the woods and then the hunter was gone. Michael sat silently hearing the leaves crackle underfoot of one man walking away, going back into the woods. An overwhelming feeling of peace came over Michael as he realized he had been greeted by a hunter from the past.

It was mid-morning before Michael made it back to the cabin. His head was reeling with thoughts of the vision he had seen. Opening the door, he saw Snake Woman standing at the stove. Again, he felt the peaceful feeling intensify within him. "Snake Woman, have I got things to tell you!" Michael acclaimed as soon as he closed the door.

"Boy, you set yourself down right there and let me tell you something afore you say another word." Michael took a seat at the table and listened attentively. "If'n you got a vision from a woodsman past, it's be your vision and yourn alone. You is not never to tell your vision to no one. You can't tell it to no one on this earth. Your message can only be told when you leave this earth." Snake Woman said solemnly. "You can't even tells me or nobody else," as Snake Woman leaned over and whispered. The only time you gets to tell your vision is when it be your time to pass on. When you gets lifted up, you gets to come back one day and tells your loved one what your vision was and gives them a message, and only then. Remember this boy, if'n when your spirit be known, and if'n the one you gives your vision to ain't no believer, you don't gets to stay in the woods no more. You won't never be that mist in the pines like them woodsmen afore you. So, don't never reveal your vision to nobody." Snake

Woman firmly whispered. "Yes Snake Woman I'll never tell anyone." Michael whispered back.

Snake Woman prepared the evening meal as Michael sat with his back up against the wall close to the fireplace. Before she knew it, Michael had slipped into a deep sleep. Snake Woman didn't wake Michael for supper 'cause she knew the rest was more important than eating for the time being.

When Michael awoke, it was still dark outside so he moved over to his bed to finish out the night's sleep. When he pulled back his old wool blanket, there was a beautiful pair of handmade leather moccasins just under the covers. Michael picked them up and quietly admired the quality of the work. His eyes filled with tears as he sat down on the edge of the bed, then he pulled on one and then the other, they were a perfect fit. Michael rose effortlessly and tip toed around the room, silence... perfect silence... he thought as he stepped lightly around the room. At morning's light, Snake Woman could see that Michael had gone back to sleep with the moccasins still on his feet. This gave her a good feeling. She walked over to Michael's bed and gently nudged him, "Michael wake up son, wake up; I needs to get you to do me a favor." Michael woke up wiping the sleep from his eyes, "Yes ma'am anything." "Get your clothes on and I'll start breakfast. After we eat, I needs you do go into town for me."

TEN

Michael was finishing his coffee as Snake Woman pulled out a jar tucked far back on a shelf. She said, "Here's money I got for sell'n a couple of hogs." She then handed me a piece of paper. "I've made you a list with a few things we needs from town, and I wants you to get a couple of things I wrote down for you." "No Snake Woman, I don't need anything," Michael insisted. "Don't give me no sass boy 'cause you're a woodsman now, so you gonna needs some woodsman things. I wrote them on this here list and I wants you to get everything on this list. You hear me boy, and I mean everything on this list," she said giving me a stern eye. "Yes Snake Woman," Michael obediently replied. Michael picked up the list and an old knapsack before giving Snake Woman a hug, and then reluctantly headed out the door.

The sun was just beginning to break through the trees as Michael started down the long path leading to the highway. Enjoying the cool breeze and crisp morning air, Michael tried out the listening skills Snake Women had just told him about. He was amazed at all the sounds from animals frolicking and playing as they enjoyed the beginning of a new day. About two miles into the trip, Michael decided to make his way to the camp ground and use the camp ground road to get back up to the highway. It was fairly close and an easy walk from the camp ground. Before breaking through the thick woods into the clearing of the camp ground, Michael squatted down and sat at the base of a tree scoping out the area and catching a quick rest before continuing on with his trek. Suddenly, he remembered his box with everything he owned in it was still at the camp site. Michael got to his feet and made his way over to the cabin to see if his things were still where he had fallen asleep that fateful night nearly three months earlier. Fortunately, he found the box sitting right where he had left it. Sliding it out from under the cot, he thought how far he had come since the day he had gotten out of Sandy Dunes. All of a sudden, his senses came alive at once when Michael heard the heavy crunching of a car driving on the gravel road. Whoever it was had stopped right outside the cabin.

Michael felt trapped but then thought to himself, "I don't have to hide… I haven't done anything wrong… I'm not wanted for anything… I haven't hurt or damaged anything …what have I got to worry about?" He stuck his head out the door hoping to catch a glimpse of the car before the driver saw him. Luck wasn't on his side. When Michael looked out, he looked directly into the face of Deputy Daniel Fairlane. Slamming on his brakes, Fairlane jumped out of the patrol car and approached Michael's position. "What in the devil are you doing here?" Fairlane asked in a loud voice as he approached Michael. "I ain't doing nothing," Michael responded. "For a brief second, I thought of running into the woods and disappearing forever, but because I had no reason to run, I stood my ground." Michael said to himself.

"I've been looking all over the place for you Michael! Your parents have been worried to death about you. As for me, all I was trying to do was find your body. They put out a missing person's report on you more than three months ago," growled Fairlane. "Where in the world have you been all that time?" Michael responded, "I've been around. Look Deputy, I tried to go home but my father didn't want me there. He expected 'little Michael' to live by the same bogus rules he imposed when I was a kid. I left that night because I ain't going to live under his rules anymore. I found me somewhere else to live. Look Fairlane, I'm over eighteen and I can live anywhere I want to. I don't ever have to answer to S/SSgt Joseph Schomeck Sr. anymore!" Michael yelled. "There is nothing in my release that says I have to live with my parents. I'm free to do whatever I want too," Michael continued. "As long as you don't break the law," Fairlane snapped. "I warned you not to give me any grief, so now; you are under arrest for trespassing!" Fairlane smirked as he grabbed Michael by the arm. Leading him to his patrol car, Fairlane shoved him over the fender and pulled out a pair of hand cuffs and quickly snapped them on Michael's wrist. "Come on man, all this ain't necessary," Michael pleaded. "I wasn't doing anything wrong; I just stopped here for a minute on my way to town. Fairlane, please don't do this; I wasn't doing anything wrong. I stayed here one stinking night. I didn't hurt anything." Michael begged. "You stayed without permission and that's trespassing. If you give me any more trouble, I'll add resisting arrest," Fairlane barked. "No, I'll come along peacefully; I don't want any trouble," Michael sadly responded. Fairlane put Michael in the back seat of the patrol car, walked around and got in the front seat. Fairlane picked up his radio and called,"313 Seaside County. County communications responded, "Go ahead 313," "I have Michael Schomeck in custody at the Black Water River camp ground. I'll be en route to the Magistrates office," "313, 10-4 zero-seven- fifteen-hours."

Michael shifted his weight to his left side and adjusted the cuffs behind his back to ease the pain of the steel on his wrist. "What happens next Fairlane?" Michael asked. "I take you to the magistrate's office where I swear a warrant out on you for trespassing; then you go to jail-- that's pretty much it. You'll stay in jail until you post bond," Fairlane bit back. Michael asked, "How much will the bond be." "I'm not sure Michael, but if I have anything to do with it, it'll be high, convict, Fairlane said shrewdly.

Michael looked out the window silently the rest of the time during the ride. "313 out at the magistrate's office county." "313, 10-4 zero-eight- twenty- five hours," center replied. Fairlane took Michael out of the back seat and walked him into the magistrate's office. Opening the door, Michael was surprised to see a friendly face he recognized. The magistrate behind the large official-looking desk was Magistrate Joseph Lethridge. Mr. Lethridge had been living in Cape Shore for more years than Michael had been alive. Mr. Lethridge was known by law-enforcement and defendants alike to be a fair and impartial man. Mr. Lethridge would often say, "If something's wrong, just because you're wearing a uniform, doesn't make it right." Michael was hoping for some of that fairness right now. Fairlane lead Michael by the arm and shoved him down in a wooden chair across from Magistrate Lethridge's desk, "Sit your butt down right there and keep your mouth shut till the Magistrate tells you to talk," Fairlane snapped. Mr. Lethridge, in a cool professional voice announced, "Mr. Fairlane, this is my court room. I'll thank you to treat this young man in a civil manner; and, if you cannot, I may find you in contempt of court; then, you may be the one wearing the hand-cuffs, is that clear?" "Yes sir, Judge," Fairlane answered, "Sorry your honor." "First thing I want to know is, has this young man given you any trouble?" asked Mr. Lethridge. "No sir, I haven't given him a chance to," replied Fairlane. "Well then Deputy Fairlane, let's take those hand cuffs off until I think they need to be put back on him." Mr. Lethridge then addressed Michael, "Mr. Schomeck, Deputy Fairlane is going to take the cuffs off of you and as long as you behave yourself, I'll see to it that they don't go back on while you are in my court; is that clear?" "Yes sir, Mr. Lethridge" Michael replied. "Okay then Deputy Fairlane, what are we doing here," Mr. Lethridge asked.

Deputy Fairlane began testifying to Mr. Lethridge, "While I was on patrol at the Black Water River Camp Ground this morning, I caught Mr. Schomeck coming out of a cabin that he had broken into. I approached him and asked what he was doing there. Michael refused to cooperate and tell me the truth, so I arrested him for trespassing." Mr. Lethridge asked, "Was there any damage to the cabin that Mr. Schomeck was coming out of?" "No I couldn't see any," replied Fairlane. Mr. Lethridge continued, "Mr. Schomeck, what were you doing in that cabin at Black Water River camp ground this morning?" Michael quickly thought before he answered, "Whatever I say needs to convince him that I had to have a place to stay," he said to himself. I went in there last night to get out of the cold, your Honor. I didn't have anywhere else to stay and since the cabin was unlocked, I stayed there overnight. When morning light came, I put everything back the way I found it. I tried to tell that 'fine deputy', sorry your honor; I tried to tell Deputy Fairlane but he didn't want to hear anything out of me; so here I am." "Is that what happened Deputy Fairlane?" asked Mr. Lethridge. "Your honor, that's not the way I see it, no," replied Fairlane.

"Okay, here's what we're going to do." said Mr. Lethridge. "Since there wasn't any damage done to the cabin; and, the camp ground is closed this time of year; and, young Mr. Schomeck was in quite a predicament because of the severe cold weather; and, because there are no "No Trespassing" signs posted at the camp ground; I'm going to find no probable cause for Mr. Schomeck to be charged with trespassing." Magistrate Lethridge continued, "Deputy Fairlane, I want you to give Mr. Schomeck a ride back to Cape Shore or where ever else he desires to be taken. This case is dismissed, no probable cause."

Mr. Lethridge, in an admonishing tone said, "Deputy Fairlane, in the future I would spend a little more time conducting my investigation and make sure that a crime has been committed before taking someone into custody." Deputy Fairlane listened to the magistrate's ruling, becoming angrier by the minute. At first, Fairlane was angry with Mr. Lethridge; but, as time went, on his anger migrated to Michael. "Yes sir your honor," Deputy Fairlane responded smartly. "Anything you say sir. I have some paper work to do over at the sheriff's office before I head back to the west. Will it be all right with you Mr. Lethridge for me to do some paper work before I take Mr. Schomeck home, or do you want me to do carry him back post haste?" Fairlane smirked, "Yes, Deputy Fairlane you may go do your paper work but do not take all day about it. You've already deprived this young man of enough time."

Exiting the magistrate's office, Fairlane told Michael, "I have some paper work to do before I go back to Cape Shore. If you want to hang around until I'm finished, I'll give you a ride back. If you don't want to wait, best thing I can tell you is to start walking." Fairlane said. Michael knew Fairlane was peeved and didn't believe he would hang around. Michael thought, you can bet on it… I'll be here when you come out. This may well be the only time I ever get your goat, and your taking me all the way back to Cape Shore will be a sweet well- deserved ride. "Take your time, I'll be around here whenever you're ready to go," Michael said. "I'll wait around here all day just to inconvenience Deputy Fairlane," Michael whispered below his breath.

It was eleven twenty a.m. when Deputy Fairlane walked out of the sheriff's office heading to his patrol car. He was hoping that Michael had given up waiting and then he could leave without having to deal with him. As Fairlane approached the car, the first thing he saw was Michael stretched out on the hood, sunning with his shirt off. Fairlane hollered, "Get your butt off my car." Instinctively, Michael jumped off immediately. "Just hanging out waiting for you like the magistrate told me to Deputy," Michael quipped. "I'm glad you came out when you did, I was just getting ready to go to the Magistrate's office and see if Mr. Joe could get a fire built under your butt, 'cause I ain't got all day to waste you know." Michael said smartly. Fairlane opened the car door and motioned for Michael to get in. Michael jumped in the front seat and laid back comfortably with his hands grasped behind his neck. "This seat sure is a whole lot more comfortable without handcuffs on Fairlane," Michael snidely said. Without saying a word, Fairlane backed from the parking space and pulled the gear shift leaver into drive and headed toward Cape Shore. Michael asked, "Ain't you suppose to tell the communications center you have to take me back home?" Fairlane picked up the radio and advised "313, county, I'm back in the car, I'll be en route back to Cape Shore. I'll be giving this subject a courtesy ride." "10-4, 313 eleven-ten hours," county responded. "Ain't you gonna tell them that Mr. Joe un-arrested me Deputy?" Michael asked.

No words were spoken between Fairlane and Michael on the long drive back to Cape Shore. Approaching city limits, Michael asked, "What's the chance of you dropping me at the Pack the Sack store Fairlane?" "I've got to stop at Cape Shore Police Department for a minute first," Fairlane responded. "Okay, but after that, you'll drop me at the store, right?" Michael asked again.

Pulling into the Cape Shore Police Department, Michael's stomach knotted up when he saw his father standing in front. "What did you do man… you had no right to call him!" Michael yelled. "Your father asked me several weeks ago if I saw you, to make sure to call him. I called him from the sheriff's department and told him I would bring you here. Now you're going to meet with him right now, whether you like it or not," said Fairlane. Michael's father approached him saying, "Somehow I knew the next time I saw you, you'd be in a police car." "Yeah, well it ain't my fault. Fairlane over there made a false arrest on me. The magistrate dropped the charges and made him bring me back here," Michael snapped. "It won't be your last ride in a police car if you don't straighten your butt out," Joseph Sr. said. "I guess you got what you wanted; you've seen me so now what's next?" Michael asked. "If there's nothing else, I'm ready to go," Michael said with disgust in his voice. Just as the words came from his mouth, his mother stepped out of the police department's front door. "Michael how are you son, I've missed you so much," June said as she walked toward Michael. He threw open his arms and embraced his mother. The embracing hug lasted for a long time. During the hug Michael could feel his mother pushing a piece of paper into his hand. Michael took the paper and slipped it into his pocket. "Okay that's enough! We need to talk," snapped Joseph Sr.

Reluctantly breaking away from the hug, Michael said, "What do we have to talk about? When I came home, I got your letter telling me about all the new rules of your house. You made everything quite clear to me. You let me know that if I wanted to stay under your roof, I would obey your rules. I get that. So, I can tell you right now, I ain't gonna live under your roof, and I ain't gonna listen to you or your rules; and, I don't need you. When you let me know you didn't want anything to do with me then…now, that's how I feel about you!" Michael yelled. Joseph Sr. stood stunned. Suddenly Joseph yelled, "June get in the car… I ain't got to listen to this garbage from a punk kid, let's go right now!"

Turning to Fairlane, Michael said, "Well Fairlane, you gonna give me that ride to the Pack the Sack now?" "Get there the best way you can! I ain't taking you nowhere," Fairlane reacted. "Thanks for nothing Fairlane!" Michael quipped.

ELEVEN

Michael walked away crossing Hwy 58. Just before getting to the curb, he reached into his pocket and took out the paper his mother had given him. It had been tightly folded over and over making it small enough for June to palm and slip to Michael without Joseph seeing her. Sitting down on the side of the curb, Michael unfolded the note and began to read.

Dear Michael,

I love you and have missed you dearly. I'm sorry your father treats you the way he does. I do not know why he acts the way he does toward those who love him. If you ever need anything please do not hesitate to call me. I love you,

Signed,

Mother

P.S. This past Friday you received an urgent phone call from a young man who needed to contact you. He asked me to get you this message. Call Tim Blackhardt 252-555-4949 ASAP. Michael, remember I'll love you no matter what.

Love always,

Mother

While reluctantly dialing Tim's number, and waiting for the phone to ring, Michael couldn't keep his mind from drifting back to his time at Sandy Dunes. Tim watched my back and I owed him a big debt for that, Michael thought. Tim was the only person on earth that knew what had happened to Michael that day in the shower stall. Tim had never breathed a word about the incident to another living soul. For this friendship and loyalty, Michael owed Tim a debt that he really didn't know how to repay. Michael had settled on the fact that whatever Tim wanted from him, he was obligated to do, hopefully making them even once and for all.

"Hello, what do you want?" came a rude voice from the other end of the line. "Tim Blackhardt," Michael said. "Hold on. Blackhardt, you have a phone call." Michael heard confusion, cursing and the phone banging against the wall while he waited for Tim to get to the phone. "Yeah, this is Tim." How you doing man this it's Michael, Michael Schomeck, "Yeah man, I know who this is, how you doing man? Where are you?" asked Tim. "I'm home man, Michael paused, "Well not actually home but I am in Seaside County, where are you?" "I'm in New Craven, staying with a guy I rode down with on the bus. He said I could crash at his place for a few days. It's time for me to get out of here...if you know what I mean?" "Yeah, yeah man I do," Michael said. "Well man, tell me how do I get down there from here. I want to see you man," Tim said. "Just get on a bus and go to Kranston Corner. Let me know when you arrive, and I'll try to find somebody to pick you up." Michael responded.

"Do you have a phone where I can call you, it might take me a day or two to get up the money for a bus ticket," Tim said. "Yes, I've got a buddy who stays by the phone all the time. His name is Billy, Billy Fulcher... copy down this number," Michael said. "Yeah, man I'm ready, go ahead with the number," Tim stated. "The number is 919-555-0958. It's a little place up here in Copper Cove where all the kids hangout. When you get to Kranston Corner, call Billy and he'll get me the message. Kranston Corner bus station is only fifteen to twenty minutes from Cape Shore... anyway you call Billy when you're on the way. I'll tell him to expect your call." Michael said. "I sure will man. I'm really looking forward to seeing you again and seeing what kind of trouble we can get in to. I'll be there in a couple of days so be looking for me," Tim said as the phone went dead with the sound of a dial tone.

Michael hung up the phone and slowly came back to reality. "I started out this morning to do some chores for Snake Woman and my whole day is now shot," Michael murmured as he looked up at the position of the sun, and figured it was around three thirty maybe four o'clock. "I'll pick up the stuff for Snake Woman; then stop by and see Billy, and make it back to the cabin before it gets too late," Michael thought as he tucked his mother's note back into his pocket.

Michael took out Snake Woman's list and scanned over it as he walked in Pack the Sack. The list read: five pounds coffee, ten pounds sugar, five pounds dried beans, six cans peaches, three pounds salt, two pounds black pepper, one large bottle hot sauce and ten tins of Prince Albert pipe tobacco. Michael picked up all of the items and paid for them with the bills Snake Woman had given him.

Next stop, William's Hardware Store for: five boxes 12-gauge shotgun shell #8, 5 boxes 12 gauge, 00 buck shot, four boxes Remington 22-250 high brass rifle bullets, 4 boxes 7mm Winchester Magnum bullets, one six inch "Buck Knife" with leather sheath, six pairs size eleven wool boot socks, one pair size eleven Redball hunting boots; one Remington Model 700, 7mm Remington Magnum Rifle. Michael filled the list completely adding in a large knap sack to help him carry all of the items back to the cabin. While packing the items into the back pack, Michael's only thought was to get them back to Snake Woman.

Heaving the heavy back pack onto his back, Michael walked down the road toward Copper Cove. Michael had walked about two miles when Deputy Fairlane drove past him and beeped the horn and waved at Michael as he walked along. Michael almost waved back only he wasn't going to wave with all five fingers. Common sense took over, so Michael threw up his hand and bit his lip as the patrol car quickly disappeared down highway 58. It would be smart to let him get me out of his head.

Although the load was heavy, Michael could hardly feel it as he thought about the incident with his father. I guess I've burned that bridge, Michael thought as he strode down the edge of the road. Just as well, there is no way I'll ever live up to his expectations anyway. Maybe one day, I'll do something that he'll be proud of, maybe someday," Michael uttered. He suddenly realized he was standing outside of the 66 Station.

Throwing open the door, Michael stepped inside and the first person he saw was Billy. He was in the game room sitting in the corner talking on the phone. "I wonder if he's moved since the last time I saw him," Michael thought. Michael slipped off the back pack and laid it at the end of the cash register counter. "Would you mind keeping an eye on that for me?" he asked the clerk. "I'll only be a minute," Michael said as he headed towards the game room. He walked up behind Billy and tapped him on the shoulder. "I'll be off in a minute," he said as he spun around on the stool, "Oh heck, man I didn't know it was you." "I'll call you back in a few," Billy said as he hung up the phone.

"Man, where have you been? We didn't know if Fairlane maybe took you out in the woods and put a bullet in your head or something." "No, man I've been around...you know, just hanging out around the house and stuff." "I need you to do me a favor," Michael said. "Yeah, anything-- just name it" Billy said. Michael continued, "I've got a buddy coming in to the bus station in Kranston Corner in a few days and I told him I'd pick him up. When he knows what time he's going to be in Kranston Corner, he's gonna call me. Will you take a message and tell me when you hear from him?" "Yeah, man I'll do it. You know the bus goes right by the front of the store on its' way to Kranston Corner. If your buddy is smart enough to pull the stop cord, the driver will stop him right outside," Billy said. "Okay when he calls, tell him to get off here and I'll meet him, okay?" "Yeah, man you can count on me, I'll take care of it," Billy said. Michael mounted his back pack and headed out the door. "I'll be back sometime tomorrow to check with you Billy," Michael said as he exited. "I'll be right here," Billy replied.

It was closely approaching sundown when Michael spotted the cabin looming in the dusk. Smoke rising from the chimney, dim lights glowing from behind the windows panes, Michael wondered if there was any way he could stay here and never leave… but he couldn't… I owe Tim, when I needed him; he was there for me… I gotta repay him. This is something I have to do. Stopping twenty five feet from the cabin, Michael hollered out, "Yo, it's me, it's Michael." "Well don't just stand out yonder hollering, come on in," Snake Woman answered. Entering the cabin, Snake Woman could see that Michael was loaded to the gills, "Boy how'd you do with all that load?" she asked. "Oh, Snake Woman, I did just fine. I got everything on your list and picked up a new back pack to help me tote everything, said Michael." "That's just fine boy…you did real good. Now put everything down right here, and I'll see what we got." Michael dropped the knapsack, slung off the heavily loaded new back pack, and laid them at Snake Woman's feet.

Snake Woman started unloading the goods stacking the items neatly on the table. "Here boy, these are for you," Snake woman said as she handed him the wool socks and boots. Michael sat down in front of the fireplace hearth and slipped off his old tennis shoes and tried them on. "Looks like a perfect fit," he exclaimed as he jumped up and strutted around the room trying them out to see how they felt.

"Well, if'n you're going be a woodsman, you have to be equipped with the right gear," Snake Woman said. She then handed him the rifle and knife. "Here boy, these here is for you too." "No Snake Woman, that's too much, I don't expect this." "It ain't for you to expect boy; it's yours because you worked hard and you earned them. You takes good care of that rifle and it will last you a lifetime, and it will take care of you." Taking the rifle from Snake Woman's hand, Michael nestled it in his arms like a new baby. "This is the nicest thing anybody has ever done for me. I thank you very much." Michael said.

Michael was hesitant to tell Snake Woman about the phone call from Tim. Deep inside, he knew the meeting would probably not be approved by Snake Woman. Putting it off to the last minute just before bed time, Michael said, "I got a note from my mother today. It said a friend of mine was trying to get up with me, so I called him and he wants to come down here and see me for a few days. I'm supposed to go back to town tomorrow to find out when he's going to be here." Snake Woman sat silently. "So if you need anything else, you know something that wasn't on your list, I'll be glad to pick it up when I..." Michael was saying. "Hold it right there boy, you don't needs to explain nothing to Snake Woman. If you needs to go, you just go." "When you think it's time to come back, then you come back. Ain't nothing keeping you here, sept'n you. But don't you bring no stranger around here with you. If'n you decides to come back, you comes back alone, you hear?

Holding the leather bag around her neck tightly in hand Snake Woman said, "Michael I threw the bones today when you was gone, and they told me there's a lot of bad juju around you. I thinks that juju is this here boy you been talking about. If you needs to go, just go, but the bones says if'n you get mixed up with that boy, then you be right back in trouble again. Yep, that one will bring a load of bad juju down on your head Michael. Mind what I'm tell'n you Boy!" Snake Woman uttered.

Michael's sleep was quite restless that night, knowing that he was planning to go against Snake Woman, as well as all of his inner senses. "Once I meet up with Tim I'll give him some money to help him get set up. Yeah, that's good, I'll help get him set up with the guys... and maybe they'll give him work, then my obligation is done. I'll speak up for Tim and that's the end of it... I'll be paid in full, and I'm back in the woods," Michael said as he tossed and turned in this bed.

It felt like the longest night of his life. "Paid in full, paid in full," Michael kept telling himself as he walked through the woods toward the 66 station. "I'll get there early enough to talk to Billy. Billy will talk to Buddy... I'll speak up for Tim, and everything will be set, no problems." It was around nine in the morning when Michael opened the door. "Good morning," the sales clerk said with a smile. "Good morning ma'am," Michael responded. "Can you tell me about what time Billy Fulcher usually shows up around here?" "Usually between ten and eleven," she answered. "Ma'am, I'm gonna walk around for a little while. I'll be back in few hours, when Billy gets here, would you please tell him that Michael was here looking for him and I'll be back," Michael asked politely.

Michael decided to walk back to the Pack the Sack. "I'll pick up a thank you gift for Snake Woman… a kind of an apology for putting her in a bad mood yesterday." As Michael walked around the store, he took notice of a fellow shadowing him around. Michael continued to shop, looking over his shoulder, picked up several more items, when suddenly Michael was grabbed firmly by the arm and shoved up against a counter. "Fairlane warned me about you boy, said the security guard. "What's going on?" Michael snapped sharply. "I'm store security and you have property on your person that you have not paid for. I need for you to come with me." Michael was led to a small security room where he was told to empty his pockets. Michael cooperated fully. The guard discovered that everything Michael had on him did, in fact, belong to him. However, during the search, security discovered the Buck knife that Snake Woman had given Michael and decided to cover his own butt for making a false accusation. "I'm going to have to call the Sheriff's Department about this knife," the guard told Michael. Fifteen minutes later Deputy Fairlane showed up. "I knew it wouldn't be long before you'd screw up again," Fairlane said as he entered the security office. "You see Michael, this is a very small county, and the odds are that if you screw up, someone's going to see it, and then that someone's going to call me. I told you I was going to be keeping a close eye on you, so now, your butt is mine," Fairlane sarcastically smirked.

For the second time in two days Michael was in the custody of Deputy Fairlane. "Okay Michael, stand up, turn around, you are under arrest for carrying a concealed weapon; now, let's go see the magistrate," Fairlane said as he clasped the handcuffs on Michael's wrist.

Fairlane walked Michael out to the waiting patrol car and shoved him in the back seat. As Fairlane climbed behind the wheel, he picked up his radio mic and called the county communications... "313, Seaside County," Fairlane called. Go ahead 313, "John, if you will, call over to the magistrate's office and see who's on duty." "10-4, 313, stand by one," came John's voice in response over the radio. A minute later "County to 313." Fairlane responded, "Go ahead Seaside County." "313, Magistrate Santiago in on duty." "10-4 Seaside County," Fairlane replied, "John, if you will, advise Mr. Santiago that I'll be en route to the magistrate's office with one Michael Schomeck in custody." "10-4, 313 Mr. Santiago has been advised." Placing the radio back into the clip, Fairlane peered into his rear view mirror catching Michael's eye and said, "Your luck just ran out Boy. You don't have a friend working at the magistrate's office this time." Fairlane sped out of the parking lot and drove to the magistrate's office as fast as he could. Michael had a sinking feeling in his gut not knowing how this was going to play out at the magistrate's office. "313, county, I'll be out at the magistrates office," Fairlane called. "10-4, 313, eleven-hundred-hours," county replied.

Fairlane removed Michael from the back of the patrol car and walked him into the magistrate's office. "Good morning Mr. Santiago, how are you today?" Fairlane said as he walked Michael through the entrance door. "I'm doing very well Deputy Fairlane, and how are you this morning?" Magistrate Santiago asked, "How can I be of assistance?" Daniel lit right in to telling Mr. Santiago his story, "I received a call to go to the Pack the Sack store at Cape Shore at 9:45 a.m. The manager called the sheriff's office saying a man fitting the description of this young man was walking around the store acting suspicious. When I arrived, the manager pointed this one out to me. I recognized him as being Michael Schomeck, a known trouble maker in the Cape Shore area. I've had a lot of contact with Mr.

Schomeck so I approached him cautiously. When I asked him if he had any weapons on him, he told me that he did not. I searched Mr. Schomeck before questioning him, just for my own protection, and I found this knife... laying the knife on the desk in front of the magistrate. Because he did not inform me of this weapon, I arrested and charged him with carrying a concealed weapon," Fairlane concluded.

Mr. Santiago slid a Bible across the desk toward Deputy Fairlane and told him to raise his right hand. "Do you swear the testimony you just provided is the whole truth and nothing but the truth?" Fairlane replied, "Yes sir, I swear." Mr. Santiago took out some papers and started filling them out. In about five minutes, Mr. Santiago said, "Mr. Schomeck, please stand before me." "Deputy Fairlane has sworn a criminal complaint against you and I find there is probable cause to believe that the criminal act Deputy Fairlane has sworn to did in fact take place. I have found that your arrest was legal, and I have set your bond in the amount of five hundred dollars. Mr. Schomeck, do you understand the charge?" "Yes sir," Michael replied. "Do you have the money to post a bond at this time?" "No sir, I don't." Michael responded respectfully.

Magistrate Santiago continued, "Deputy Fairlane will transport you to the county jail. When you get there, you will be allowed to make a phone call. You can use your call to call anyone you wish. I suggest you call a bondsman. If you are unable to hire a bondsman, you will be incarcerated in the county jail until #1, your court date arrives, or #2, you are able to come up with five hundred dollars to pay your bond." "Do you have any questions Mr. Schomeck?" "No, sir," Michael answered. Okay Deputy Fairlane, he's in your custody."

Fairlane grabbed Michael by his arm pit and walked him out of the magistrate's office and back to his patrol car. He shoved Michael in the back seat and slammed the door. With his chest puffed, he walked around and got in the driver's side. "313, Seaside County, 313 go ahead," "I'll be en route to the county jail with one 10-72 in custody." "313, 10-4 eleven-eighteen-hours. Fairlane shifted his car into reverse and backed from his parking space pausing to look Michael squarely in the eyes, "See, I told you, didn't I," wisecracked Fairlane.

Pulling into a parking space at the county jail, Fairlane advised communications that he had arrived, and would be out at the jail booking his prisoner. Just as Fairlane reached to hang up the radio, he heard the back door slam really hard. Looking around, he saw Michael disappearing around the corner of the court house. Fairlane snatched the mic up to his mouth and excitedly called, "10-33, 10-33 my prisoner just jumped out of the car, he is on foot in the area of the county jail." "Seaside County requests mutual aid from any available cars." Instantly, the communications center began transmitting, "All units 10-33 county car 313 has an escaped prisoner in the vicinity of the county jail. All available units proceed to the area; stand by for the suspect description." "Seaside County 313, advise the description of your escapee on this frequency." "313 to all units be advised suspect is Michael Schomeck, a white male, 18 years old, last seen wearing a green army field jacket and blue jeans . . . also be advised he's wearing *MY* handcuffs!" Fairlane yelled over the radio.

Michael ran as fast as he could looking for a hiding place. As he ran, he could hear the sounds of numerous sirens heading in his direction. Michael also heard Snake Woman's words of stop, look and listen. Michael stopped dead in his tracks and began to look around. Fifty feet ahead was a thicket of woods…that's the spot right there, Michael thought. Michael eased himself into the thicket. Sitting down flat on his butt,

Michael was able to contort his body and moved the hand cuffs from behind his back to in front of him. Bending at the waist, Michael stuck his head into the thicket. He then worked his body through a small hole like he had seen a bear do not too far from Snake Woman's cabin. Once inside the thicket, Michael reached outside the thicket and pulled the branches together erasing any sign of him entering the coppice. Michael worked his way deeper and deeper toward the center of the dense undergrowth and wind-barren trees. Michael thought, "If a rabbit were being hunted, he would find the most dense part of the thicket and settle down, and not move for hours… that's exactly what I'll do." Michael lay down and pulled fallen leaves, pine straw and limbs all around and on top of his body to conceal his shape, as well to help keep him warm.

Day turned to night, dawn turned to dusk and then to the dark of night once again. Michael stayed hidden and did not move all through the day and night. Laying there in a wet muddy undergrowth, Michael couldn't help but remember a conversation he and Snake Woman had laughed about if the law were ever chasing you. She chuckled saying, "Ain't no law ever getting out a clean warm car, and gets them pretty uniforms, and black shiny shoes dirty looking in some muddy hole for nobody. Best thing I can say, if'n you don't wants to get found, you finds the stinkiest, nastiest place you can find…gets real still and quiet, and they will never finds you, even if'n you is right under their noses." In a few days, 'cause they's lazy, they'll quit looking for you; then, you can walks right out wid nobody being the wiser." Never did Michael think he would be actually using that advice, and he felt sure, Snake Woman didn't either.

Interestingly, Michael laid still and watched ten times or more during the day, when police cars were only twenty feet from him; but, none of them ever stopped, and none of them ever got out of their cars to look for him either. With Michael lying flat on his back, he wiggled around a tree root so he could look up through the trees and get a good look at the moon. The familiar sight helped Michael get his mind off the miserable conditions he had to endure in order to secure his freedom. Watching the moon slowly travel across the sky, Michael figured it was around one o'clock in the morning. He hadn't heard any cars in a long time, so he decided it was time to crawl out and take a look around. Crawling back to the edge of the thicket, Michael slowly stuck his head out and laid perfectly still while he looked around to see if the cops were somewhere lying in wait for him to appear. Michael watched and listened for more than fifteen minutes without hearing anything that sent up an alarm. He thought they are probably tired looking for me and have given up. "That worked out just like I planned it," Michael said as he rose to his feet. "Now let's see if I can get out of here and back to the woods where I can feel safe again."

Michael moved quickly but quietly, making sure to stay in the shadows as he started walking back toward Beachwood. Michael stayed off the main streets by using back yards and alleyways. He was constantly and mentally keeping an escape route in mind as he looked around. His first thought was looking for a way to shed the handcuffs and change his appearance. "If I just go about my way and look like anyone else, I can escape the cops, hopefully," Michael thought to himself. Checking the doors on every shed and garage as he walked through the neighborhood, Michael luckily found an open door. "Let's see what's in here that I can use to work on these cuffs," Michael thought as he stealthily slipped through the door. Quietly closing the door behind him, Michael entered the dimly lit garage and headed straight to the tools on the work bench. Hanging on the wall behind the work table, "Just what the doctor ordered," Michael whispered. Neatly arraigned on the wall among the other tools was a pair of bolt cutters. "Perfect, they'll make quick work of these," Michael said. Michael took the bolt cutters down from the wall and stuck one of the handles into a bench vice. He tightened the bolt cutters handle in the vice and place the handcuff chain between the cutting jaws. With all his body weight on the handle, he suddenly heard a loud *SNAP* breaking the handcuff chain. "Oh yeah, just two more cuts," he thought. He placed the frame of the left handcuff in the bolt cutter jaw and *SNAP*...then the other wrist...again *SNAP* and he was freed. Michael turned and took a quick look around to see if there was anything else in the garage he could use. Spotting a red parka hanging on a hook at the back door, he thought, "That may be useful. Michael took the coat down and tried it on for size, "A little big but this will work," he whispered as he slipped on the jacket. Michael zipped up the coat and quietly exited the garage back on his mission.

Reaching Orange Street, Michael decided not to hide his presence anymore, "I'll walk right down the middle of the street... nobody will be looking for an escapee to be this bold. They'll be looking for someone trying to hide. If I stick out my chest and don't look suspicious, they won't even take a second look at me," Michael thought...which proved to be right. Interestingly, a couple of police cars did drive past him without noticing him. Michael's plan was working perfectly until he topped the Morehead/Beachwood high rise bridge and saw two Diamond City Police cars sitting at the foot of the bridge. Never altering his stride, Michael walked right toward the police cars sitting on the side of the road. "What in the world are they doing?" Michael asked himself. They were pulled up real close to each other, you know, the way cops do when they're talking. "I think they're just sitting there talking," Michael thought. With motors running, Michael could see the steam from both cars exhaust pipes rising into the air. “Where can I run if they come after me?” Michael thought as he surveyed the area around where the cars were sitting. Michael reached the foot of the bridge and walked down the side of the road hoping and praying they wouldn‘t recognize him. As Michael walked right in front of the police cars he yelled out, “How about a ride to the beach bridge, it‘s cold out here?” Without hesitating, one of the cops yelled back, “I’d like to help you but it’s against policy…walk faster you’ll stay warm.” Michael chuckled under his breath as he threw up his arm in thanks anyway gesture and picked up his pace. Michael continued walking down the sidewalk until he reached the convenience store at Eighteen Street. It was there Michael noticed some kids about his age going inside, so he stopped and asked for a ride. His luck was still holding out as one of the guys was going to Deep Creek and the other two headed to Marshboro. Catching a ride to either of these places would put Michael only a short walk from his home turf.

Forty-five minutes later, Michael was standing on the side of Sandy Bunker Road, Cape Shore NC. Down the golf cart path a half mile, and then another four hundred yards down a narrow foot path, Michael would be right behind the 66 Station. For half an hour, Michael stood in the darkness behind the station hoping the law was not there looking for him. It was around two in the morning with only a few people left in the 66. Luckily for Michael, one of the hangers-on was Billy. Michael slipped up to the window and knocked qently until he got Billy’s attention. Billy saw it was Michael and motioned for him to stay there mouthing the words “I’ll be right out.” Billy came around the front of the store and staggered over to where Michael was waiting in the dark. “You’ve really stepped in it now boy! The cops have been in and out of this place for the last three days looking for you. Nobody will tell us why or what you did or anything. What did you do, kill the Pope or something?" asked Billy. Michael replied, "No man, nothing like that. You know that no account Deputy Fairlane, well, he arrested me for no good reason and then he took me to the Magistrate and lied to him about everything and he was gonna throw my narrow butt in jail. But he screwed up 'cause he didn't lock the car door when he stuck me in it, so I just let myself out and well...anyway here I am. How hot am I Billy?" asked Michael. Billy was ready with an answer. "Buddy told me to give you this," handing Michael a wad of cash and to tell you to get the devil out of Seaside County. He said you're too hot to be anywhere around us, so you and your friend just need to get gone." "Whoa... me and my friend, who's my friend?" Michael asked. "You know, Tim," Billy answered. "Is Tim here?" asked Michael. "Yeah man, he's passed out in the back seat of my car. We figured we'd look out for him until you decided to show up." Billy said. Billy and Michael walked over to Billy's old Chevy. Bending over looking in through the rolled down back window, Michael let out a yell. Michael completely forgot where he was as he bellowed, "Get your butt out of that rack boy, zero-six- hundred-hours, time to rise and shine."

Tim instinctively jumped up, bumping his head on the top of the Chevy. Tim tried to shake the cob webs from his mind before he realized it was Michael yelling and not Sgt. Jones at Sandy Dunes. Tim opened the door and crawled out of the car saying, "How you doing old salt... long time no see?" "Yeah man, it's good to see you too. Look man, I'm in a little trouble here; and, I really need to beat feet away from here," Michael said as he looked around cautiously.

As they stepped behind the station in the darkness, Michael said, "Billy's gonna look out for you for a few days and make sure you get back on the bus. Here's a few bucks," handing Tim two hundred dollars. "This money will buy you a ticket to wherever you want to go. I'm in some real trouble; and, you don't need this kind of heat just getting out and all… trust me, it's the best thing." Tim broke in, "Hey man, I came here for you. If you run, I run. You're the only friend I have in the world. So whatever we're gonna do, let's get to doing it." said Tim. Pondering the thought only a second, "Okay grab your gear and let's get the heck outta here," Michael said. Turning his attention to Billy, Michael said, "I'll be in contact with you in a few days and see how things are besides I'm gonna need money if I've gotta disappear," Michael said. Billy snapped back quickly, "Well you'll have to get it somewhere else! That's it for us man…we can't do no more for you than we've already done. If them laws finds out that we've been helping you, they'll come down on us hard… and that means we're out of business." We gotta part ways right here and now. The way I see it, any debt we owed you was paid the first day you showed up here. As far as me and Buddy are concerned, you're on your own man," Buddy concluded. Michael turned and started to walk away without saying and word. Billy called out, "Stop man, here's everything I've got," handing Michael a thick pile of wadded up bills. "Make it last as long as you can, I don't know if I'll be able to help you anymore after tonight." Michael took the bills and stuffed them into his coat pocket, "Thanks man, thanks a lot."

Michael stopped briefly at the edge of the road leading into the Crowan National Forest, "Tim, I know a place we can hole up and get our thoughts together about what we need to do. As they walked through the woods, Michael's anguish grew with unsure anticipation. He was trying desperately to figure out how things went from calm and peaceful living with Snake Woman to this awful uncertainty. "She gave me shelter, food and kindness. She taught me how to survive and tried to get me on a path of taking care of myself, and hopefully starting my life over again, Michael said, reflecting on how Snake Woman had taken him in when no one else would. "I can't go back to Snake Woman's. *I should have NEVER called Tim.* She would never, ever approve of Tim and the mess I have found myself in," Michael said to himself. "What do I do...Oh, what do I do? Fairlane seems to be winning this one as my life is quietly falling apart. How did it all go so wrong?" Michael said sorrowfully.

"Follow me and be as quiet as you can, 'cause we can't bring any more attention to ourselves. If I start to run, don't wait for me to tell you to run, you just run. If we get separated, find a place to hide and stay still and be quiet. I'll come back and find you when everything's clear." Michael instructed. "Whatever you say, Daniel Boone," Tim answered.

Michael and Tim talked quietly as they walked deeper and deeper into the woods. They reflected on their time together at Sandy Dunes when they were two 'against the world'. Tim boastfully reminded Michael that he would always have his back and nothing had changed. Not wanting to go there in thought, Michael agreed in silence.

"What you think Michael? How we gonna get this one behind us?" asked Tim. "The way I see it, we only have two choices," Michael responded. "We can either stay here and hide; or, we go somewhere that no one knows us and start over," Michael replied. "You know if we try to stay here, we'll have to live like dogs…running and hiding all the time…that just ain't no way to live. If we leave, we have to have money…some real money…not that chump change like Billy gave you tonight." Michael said. "Where we gonna get that kind of money?" Tim asked. "Banks have that kind of money," Michael answered.

"We've got a bank right down the road here. It wouldn't be that hard to take." Michael continued. "It's a small town with only three cops on the whole police department. It would take careful planning, but you and me could do it." Michael said. Michael and Tim walked and talked for more than an hour before coming to a small clearing in the woods. "It's just a little bit farther Tim; and, I'll guarantee you no one will look for us this far in the woods. We'll be safe here." Just another twenty minutes we'll be there. "Okay, we're here," Michael spouted. "We're here? You mean this is it?" Tim repeated. "Dog gone, the explorers that discovered the Mississippi River didn't walk this far. What in the world is that?" asked Tim as he pointed to what seemed to be a rundown house. "That's where we're going to spend the next few days," Michael replied. "It's dry, has a good roof and we can make it warm pretty easily. It's a perfect place for us while we're trying to figure out what our next move will be." As they drew closer, Tim could see in the moonlight it wasn't as bad as he first thought. It was a very old house and most all of the paint had aged off it. The weeds were grown up almost as high as the boys' heads. The property was deep and wide and appeared to have been a very large yard.

"Tim, you stop right here for a minute, and I'll go check out things to make sure we're alone. I'll come back and get you in a few minutes, stay here and be real quiet." Before Tim could respond, Michael disappeared into the tall weeds and darkness. It seemed like a lot longer but in about fifteen minutes, Michael returned to where Tim waited anxiously. Crouching next to Tim, Michael whispered quietly, "Everything's clear . . . this is real important so listen real good. I need for you to step where I step. Try not to disturb anything!" "When you take a step, pick your foot straight up before you move it forward, and be careful not to move anything as you step." Tim said, "Okay, just take it easy man; I ain't all about this woodsy owl stuff you know." "I'll take it slow," Michael replied.

Michael led Tim the long way around to the house ending up close to the back door. Michael walked over to a rusty old set of bed springs leaning against the side of the house. He lifted the springs away from the house revealing a crawl space. "You go first, then once you are under the house, hold the springs with that stick and I'll crawl in," Michael told Tim. Once they were under the house, Michael let the springs down over the crawl space and led off toward the center of the house. Tim reluctantly followed quickly and quietly, "Any spiders or snake under here Michael? You know, *I don't like spiders and snakes and that ain't what it takes to love me*, Tim sang jokingly as they crawled along. "Why sure there is. I've always been told that if you don't bother them, they won't bother you. Just keep moving." Michael chuckled. "How can you see what you're doing Michael? You have turned into an owl, I can't see a thing." "Just follow my voice Tim," Michael whispered.

Michael stood up underneath the house and lifted a sheet of plywood that was covering a hole in the middle of the floor. "Here, hold this up while I climb in. Once I'm inside, I'll hold it up for you," Michael said as he crawled up through the hole. "Okay I've got it, come on up Tim," Michael said. Once Tim was inside, Michael laid the plywood gently down covering the hole. "Okay we can relax now," Michael said as he sat down on an old worn out sofa in the middle of the room.

"Where are we man, I can't see a thing?" asked Tim. "Please tell me that this ain't no bat cave! Oh my heavens, what just landed in my hair? You sure this ain't some vampire cave? All I'm waiting for now is for someone to bite me on the neck!" Tim said in near panic. "Just sit right over here," leading Tim over to a ratty old sofa. "Believe me when I tell you, "It'll take your eyes about ten minutes to get used to the darkness, then you'll be able to see better, trust me," Michael said. "What is this place, man? How'd you know about it?" asked Tim. "Over the past three or four months, I've spent a lot of time in these woods and this one of the places I found. There ain't a handful of people in the whole county that knows that this place exists," Michael told Tim. After a few minutes, Tim was beginning to get his night vision. "Oh yeah, I see this place ain't half bad now. All we need is one of them interior decorators to come in and fix it up...you know, a little paint, wallpaper and some curtains and we could be happy little beavers right here," Tim joked.

"We can't stay anywhere in Seaside County long," Michael said. "We'll be okay for a week... maybe two, but then we'll have to move somewhere else. No place goes unnoticed forever... even a place this deep in the woods," Michael said in a low tone. "Come on man, follow me and I'll show you where you can bed down for tonight." Michael led Tim to a room near the back of the house. "There's an old bed in here. It ain't in real good shape, but at least, you won't have to sleep on the floor. If you have to use the bathroom... there ain't one. Just use this gallon jug. If you got to do the other, you know your numbers, right; then you'll have to get up and go into the woods." Michael told Tim. "No this will be fine. As crappy as this place is, it's still better than Sandy Dunes, ain't it?" Tim asked. "Yeah, compared to Sandy Dunes, anywhere free is good," Michael said. "Go ahead and get settled in. I'm going outside to check our back trail and make sure we didn't miss anything."

Tim sparked up, "Hey man, where'd you learn all this woods stuff? You didn't talk about none of this kind of stuff when we were at Sandy Dunes." Michael answered, "I learned it from an old woman I met named Snake Woman who lives in the woods by the black water of Black Water River. "Yeah man, sure you did. I'll bet she had a big black kettle where she'd brew up some love potion and cast a love spell on you. How many of them voodoo dolls did she have?" Tim said laughing. "Be careful what you say about Snake Woman. She just might be in that dark corner over there listening to every word," Michael said as he reached down and picked up a pine straw and tickled Tim behind the ear. "Whoa, what the heck was that?" Tim said as he jumped a foot off the floor. Michael said, "She's for real man, I promise you! "You're serious, aren't you, Michael?" "Look, if it ain't none of my business, I won't ask you anymore questions. Just tell me to mind my own business, Tim said. "We'll talk about all that tomorrow, settle down and get some sleep. I'll see you in the morning," Michael replied.

Michael was awake and standing lookout as the sun began to rise. Tim woke up somewhere closer to nine o'clock. When Michael heard Tim stirring, he asked, "You okay?" Tim responded, "Yeah I'm okay. I shared my bed with a dead rat and a billion bed bugs, but yeah, I'm all right," as Tim put his feet on the floor and stretched his arms out as wide as he yawned. Michael walked over to Tim's room and leaned against the door frame, "I've given it a lot of thought, and I think the best thing for you to do, is go back up to the store and catch the next bus to anywhere but here. Nobody knows you Tim, and you ain't the one wanted by the law. There's no reason for you to get caught up in this mess on my account," Michael said. "Hold it right there!" snapped Tim. "If you want me to go, I'll go; but, before you ask me to leave, let me say something. Michael you're the only friend I got. If I leave here, I'll end up on somebody else's couch, no job, no money, no future. How long before you figure I'm in the exact fix you're in right now?" Tim asked. Michael responded, "You're my best friend too, but if you stay, we've gotta keep moving. It won't be long before someone finds us. I ain't sure why this Fairlane guy hates me so much, but he does. He won't quit till he has me locked up for life. We have to make a decision about how bad we don't want to get caught. I'm telling you right now, I ain't never going to jail again, ever!" Michael said seriously. Tim, without hesitation said, "If it comes down to you or me being put back in jail, I want you to know right now that I will kill the man who tries, and not give it another thought." "Okay then, it's all or nothing," Michael said.

TWELVE

"I've come up with a plan. We're gonna hit the bank in Cape Shore. It's gonna take a lot of planning, training and recon. We can do this. Since nobody knows you, you'll be in charge of getting the information we need before we can do the job. If everything goes as planned, we could get enough money from this one job that we could live comfortably for a few years," Michael told Tim. "When do you think we'll be ready?" Tim asked. "If we can gather all the intel we need . . . maybe as early as next Friday. You with me, or what?" Michael asked. "I'm with you big Boy, I'm one hundred percent with you," Tim agreed.

"Come into the living room and I'll show you what I've come up with so far," said Michael as he turned and walked over to the couch. Picking up a drawing Michael had made up on an old newspaper, Michael began to talk, "This will take a lot of planning and one of the first things we need to do, is gather our supplies. I've made up a list of things we'll need. You'll need to go to several places to get them so no one can piece together what we're doing. I counted the money Billy gave us last night, and we have just short of seven hundred dollars. We'll buy what we can; and if we run short on money, we'll steal the rest. Are you ready to do this?" asked Michael. "Yeah man, I'm in like Flynn." said Tim.

"The first thing we need to do, is go to the grocery store and get enough grub to last for a couple of weeks. Only get canned stuff for now… you know, spam, sardines, pork & beans, peanut butter, jelly, some cokes, chips and that kind of stuff. Don't get anything that has to be cooked, heated or refrigerated… remember, everything has to be ready to eat. Next, go to the Community Dollar Store. I've made a list of things you can pick up from there. We need black shoe polish, two wrist watches with count down alarms, two black ski masks, a pair of G.I. Joe walkie-talkies, some AAA batteries for the walkie-talkies and two pairs of black leather gloves. On the gloves, get the military style 'cause they have to fit tight. Next, take a twenty dollar bill and go to Cape First Bank across from the police station and see if they'll change it for you. They'll ask how you want it. Tell them you'd like to have it in two dollar bills if they have any. Tell them you're collecting them and you'd appreciate it if they could do that. They'll probably have to go into the vault to get them; so, when they do, notice if the vault door is locked or if it's just pulled closed. Look around but be careful not to move your head too much. I'll show you how to do that to locate the cameras. Once you locate the cameras, commit their locations to memory. As soon as you leave the bank and in the clear from anyone, immediately draw everything you can remember about the inside of the bank on this paper." Michael then handed Tim a small note pad. Michael continued, "Be careful not to bring suspicion on yourself … be friendly and polite. Once you've done the drawing, walk over to the pay phone next to the hamburger place. Make note of the time. Dial 911; tell who ever answers the phone that you just saw a man enter the bank and you think he had a gun under his coat. When they start asking questions, just hang up and go inside the hamburger place and have some lunch. Sit up front next to the windows so you can see out. From there, you should be able to see the front of the bank and the police department at the same time. Use one of the wrist watches to time how long it takes for the police to get to the bank, once you hang up the phone. Remember everything you can about what happens next. Once everything is over, just sit still. Don't be in a hurry to leave. As a matter of fact, when everything is over and back to normal, go back and get some ice cream. It's important for you not to look out of place or appear to be in a hurry," Michael said as he finally took a breath.

"Tim, sit right here and go over this stuff until you can do every task on this list without even thinking about them," Michael firmly stated. "What about the bank? How we gonna do the bank?" Tim asked. "Don't worry about that right now. I'm still working on a plan, but once I get all the bugs worked out, I'll go over everything with you," Michael answered. "Now get yourself ready to make your trip to town. When you get back from town, if I'm not here, don't worry. I've got a couple of places to check out. I believe I know where I can pick up some guns if a fellow I use to know still lives in the same place," Michael said. Michael laid everything down on the table in front of the couch and took a long pause, "Tim you really want to go through with this?" Michael asked. "You bet your life I do," Tim replied. "Okay just remember one thing...if we do this there's no turning back, once we make our first step." Taking a giant step forward, "You mean like this one?" Tim asked. "Yes, like that," Michael said. "Yeah, just like that one."

It was seven twenty p.m. when Tim returned from town. He followed all of Michael's survival instructions...make as few tracks as you can, don't move anything you don't have to, and watch your back trail. Pulling himself up through the hole in the floor, Tim thought, "We're really going to do this. We're really going to rob a bank." Michael was not at the house, so Tim unpacked the supplies, separating the food stock from the clothing and equipment. He then sat down on the sofa looking over the notes he had written during the day. Tim squinted in the dim light attempting to decode what he had written; but, he really didn't need to read the notes because he had memorized his every move. He recalled how long it took the cops to respond to the bank threat, the locations of the cameras, the number of employees, and everything else. Sitting in the dark he thought, "I'll start figuring a plan for the bank, and when Michael gets back, we'll take my ideas and his ideas and put them together to come up with a *killer* plan.

Michael stopped two hundred yards from the old log cabin he had learned to love and known as home. He was trying to figure out in his mind what his next move would be. As he watched the cabin, he could see the front door open as Snake Woman walked out on the porch, and sat down in her old chair. Seeing the glimmer of a match, Michael could see Snake Woman light her pipe and begun to rock back and forth in her favorite chair.

All at once, Snake Woman rose from the chair and stared out into the woods. Michael's first thought, was that she had spotted him, but no, she was looking toward the North and he had approached from the East. Michael hunkered down in the brush as he kept a weather eye on the cabin. Michael heard a faint voice call from the woods, "Yo! Snake Woman it's me, it's Fred McDaniels. Yo! Snake Woman. It's me, it's Fred McDaniels." "Come on in Fred McDaniels," Snake Woman hollered back.

Michael was able to see the dimly lit figure emerging from the woods. It was a slightly built man wearing a Smokey the Bear hat approaching the cabin. Moving with all the prowls of a mountain lion, Michael eased closer to the cabin so that he could hear the conversation between the man and Snake Woman. Michael timed his foot movement with the strangers to cover any sound he made while moving closer to the cabin. Michael and the stranger's feet stopped movement at the exact same time. The stranger stopped a few feet from the front porch. Michael had made it to within twenty yards of the porch. Squatting behind a clump of bushes, Michael was nearly invisible.

"Snake Woman how have you been my friend?" asked Fred. "Tolerable, Fred McDaniels, just tolerable, and how about you, how you been?" Snake Woman asked politely. "I have been doing right good for an old man," Fred replied. "Fred McDaniels, what did you bring me this evening?" asked Snake Woman. "I brought you some good Ocean community bee honey, Snake Woman. I got this out of my own hive and there ain't none better between here and Elizabethian City, and I'll guarantee it." "Bring it on up here and have a seat on the porch Fred McDaniels," Snake Woman said. Fred drew closer to the porch and sat on the top step at Snake Woman's feet. Reaching into his front coat pocket, Fred pulled out a plug of tobacco along with his pocket knife. Cutting off a chunk, he held the plug out offering some to Snake Woman. "No Fred McDaniels, I've got my pipe." Snake Woman said. "All right Fred McDaniels, what you doing out here in these woods this time of the evening?" Snake Women asked. "I'm looking for a fellow. He's a young boy named Michael Schomeck," Fred said. "This boy is wanted by the Sheriff for escaping from one of the deputies," Fred said. "What's this boy do to get himself locked up in the first place, Fred McDaniels?" Snake Woman asked. "He was carrying a concealed weapon in the Pack the Sack," answered Fred. "What kinda weapon him be toting, Fred McDaniels?" Snake Woman interrupted. Fred said, "He was carrying a Buck Knife." "Buck Knife ain't no weapon!" Snake Woman said. "Well, maybe it is and maybe it ain't, but that ain't why I'm here, Snake Woman." "Well then, why you here Fred McDaniels?" Snake Woman asked impatiently. "I'm here because I believe that you know that boy, and I believe he's going to get in touch with you, if he hasn't already. I need you to give that boy a message," Fred said politely. "What message you wants me to gives this boy if'n I sees him, Fred McDaniels?" Snake Woman asked. "If you see him, tell him that if he turns himself in, I will see to it that he is treated fairly and I'll help him anyway I can," Fred said. "Is that boy gonna have to go to jail if'n he turns himself in to you, Fred McDaniels?" Snake Woman asked. "I ain't gonna lie to you Snake Woman 'cause you've been my friend for too many years for that. Even if this boy turns himself in, he's still got to go to jail. But he'll only have to stay there until he can post his bond," Fred said. "How much he's gotta pay for a boy who gots caught wearing a Buck Knife, Fred McDaniels?" Snake Woman asked. Fred replied, "I don't know for sure Snake Woman, but I've heard some say that his bond will be at least one hundred thousand dollars." "One hundred thousand dollars for carrying a Buck Knife in the Pack the Sack seems to be a little high to me Fred McDaniels," said Snake Woman. "I know Snake Woman, but he's also wanted for the escaping." "Fred McDaniels, I ain't seen that boy, but if'n I do, I'll tells him what you sayin," Snake Woman said. "That's all I can ask you to do." Fred replied.

"Do you need me to do anything for you while I'm here?" Fred asked. "No Fred McDaniels I don't need nothing. I'm all right," Snake Woman answered. "Fred McDaniels, I 'preciate the honey," Snake Woman said. Without saying another word, Fred rose to his feet and walked into the darkness of the woods. Snake Woman continued to sit on the porch smoking her pipe for thirty more minutes. Michael stayed perfectly still not flinching a muscle. Snake Woman slowly got up from her chair and walked over to the front door. She stood there listening to the woods for a minute before stepping inside the cabin. Hesitating at the door, Snake Woman waved her arm in Michael's direction and quietly said, "Come in here boy." Michael got up slowly and walked over to the cabin. Opening the door, Michael quickly slipped inside and closed the door behind him. Snake Woman had taken a seat at the table, "Come right over here boy and sit yourself down. I figure you heard what Fred McDaniels said, so I won't tell it back to you. Now it's your turn to tell me your side of this story," Snake Woman said quietly. Michael started at the beginning and never paused until he had told her about his sitting in the woods listening to her and Fred McDaniels talking. Snake Woman asked, "What's you planning Michael? What you gonna do now? If'n you goes to jail, you'll get out afore long, won't you? I've got a little money saved up and I'll help you all I can," Snake Woman said. "I can't go back to jail." "Tim and I have a plan to get some money and leave. He knows people up in the mountains that will give us a place to stay and we'll just go up there and stay until everybody gets tired of looking for us. Maybe I'll be able to come back one day," Michael said holding back the tears in his eyes. "Boy if'n you run, you'll have to run for the rest of your life, and running ain't no way to live," Snake Woman said. "I'm sorry but I can't stay here in Seaside County. If I do, they'll catch me and put me back in jail. I'd rather be dead than be locked back up in a six foot by nine foot cage," Michael said. "You're right boy, that ain't no place for a woodsman to be. You have to do what you think is best for you. But afore you go, sit yourself right down there. I gots some things for you." Snake Woman said as she walked into her bedroom. Returning a few minutes later, Snake Woman laid down the moccasins, the rifle and the ammunition she had bought only the day before. "These things are yours Michael, 'caus'n you'll need them now more than ever afore," Snake Woman said. "Michael, you been a real joy to me these here past few months. I wish you'd been wid me from the 'ginning. I love you boy." Michael got up from the chair and walked over to Snake Woman where he fell to his knees, hugging her with all his might. Michael knew that when he left the cabin he may never see her again. Michael whispered in Snake Woman's ear, "Thank you for everything you taught me. I will never forget you, I love you." Michael didn't want to let go and Snake Woman knew it. "Okay boy, if'n you don't get moving, you'll get caught out in the daylight, and you don't needs no body to see where you been, it's time for you to go now," Snake Woman said with her eyes filled with tears. Michael wept softly as he released his arms from around Snake Woman's waist. Michael turned his face toward the door so Snake Woman couldn't see he was crying. Pausing before opening the door Michael said, "I love you so much." "I love you too, Michael," Snake Woman replied as he pulled the door shut.

Buddy Thompson had lived in the same house since he was a boy. Buddy often bragged about how many guns his dad left when he ran off during the middle of the night and Buddy had taken claim to them, "Rifles, pistols, shotguns; you just name it I've got it," Buddy would say, "and the best thing about it, is they're all mine and they didn't cost me a dime."

Michael prayed that this wasn't just another cock and bull story that Buddy told to make him look like a big shot. Sitting in the woods, and taking a look around, Michael could see a few lights left on in the house, but no movement. Michael thought as he sat and watched the house, "Please let this be one time that red headed stepchild liar told the truth. Let's go check it out," Michael whispered. Making his way quietly to the house, Michael walked around peeping inside to see if anyone was home. Looks empty…let's give this door a try as he put his hand on the door knob… a slight turn and pop… the door opened right up. Buddy's words came to Michael's mind on the night of the fire when he said, "They make this so easy," "Yeah he was right, they make this so easy," Michael said as he stepped inside the house. He took a quick and quiet look around to make sure he was in the right house. When Michael saw family photos on the wall, he said, "Oh yeah, no doubt about it, this is Buddy's house. Here are some pictures of his ugly red headed self with his Mom. I'm in the right place; now let's see if I can find all those guns I heard Buddy talk about so much." Michael quickly scanned each room taking a quick look around; first to make sure he was there alone, and then looked for the weapons. Entering what had to be Buddy's room, Michael could see shoes thrown in the corner and a big pile of dirty clothes in the middle of the floor, and a few girly posters on the wall, "yeah, this has gotta be Buddy's room," Michael thought. Yeah, it had to be Buddy's room. It was dirty, un-kept and smelled bad, just like Buddy. "First, I'll look in the obvious places, you know, under the mattress and in the closet," Michael muttered as he methodically searched every nook and cranny. Taking hold of the corner of the dirty mattress, Michael lifted the corner cautiously, "BINGO" a cache of weapons! Michael reached between the mattress and box springs and quickly removed three hand guns and a half dozen magazines. Looking around for something to put the guns in, he grabbed Buddy's pillow and gave it a quick shake dumping the pillow on the floor and used the case as a ditty bag. "One, two and three," Michael counted as he dropped the guns and magazines into the pillow case. Michael dropped to his knees and looked under the bed…“aha… yeah,” Michael said as he reached under the bed and removed a .22 caliber rifle. Not exactly what I’m looking for, but maybe we can use it for something, I’ll take it just in case,” Michael said as he stuffed the gun in the bag with the others. Michael moved to the closet hesitating only a moment before peeping inside, “Oh my gosh what a mess,” clothes piled half way up the wall. “Yeah, here we go, looking in the back of the closet covered with dirty clothes. “What’s this? Oh heck yeah, a Mini 14…*Jackpot*! Now that‘s what I‘m talking about,” Michael said as he picked up the rifle and stuffed it into the bag. On the top shelf, Michael found a stash of ammunition for several of the guns and a supply of extra magazines for the Ruger. Michael took everything; boxes of ammo, magazines, shotgun shells, a cleaning kit dropping them into the pillow case not even taking time to make sure the ammo was for the guns he was taking. “Eight or ten magazines for the rifle and several hundred rounds of ammo just goes to show you, even Buddy the liar, can tell the truth once in a while,” Michael said as he looked for another pillow case to stash more ammo in. Just then Michael’s heart nearly stopped. “Seaside County to 311, 311 go ahead Seaside County.” Michael’s first thought was “I’m caught,” as he looked around quickly to see if the police officer had the drop on him. Spotting a police scanner sitting on the window silll, Michael laid his back against the nearest wall and slid quietly to the floor trying to catch the breath that had just left his body. Sitting still only long enough to regain his composure, Michael got up, walked over to the window, picked up the scanner and clipped it on his belt. “This may come in handy when it comes time for us to keep up with the police on our tails,” Michael said as he continued searching Buddy’s room.

Finished in Buddy's room, Michael went into the kitchen. "Let's see, what's for dinner?" Michael thought. Picking up an empty plastic grocery bag from the floor, he opened the refrigerator door. "What do we have in here?" Spotting a bucket of CFC Chicken, Michael broke into a tune, "I feel like chicken tonight," Michael put the bucket of chicken into the bag along with a six pack of beer, quart of milk, and five sodas. Then, he helped himself to the cabinet by the stove for a jar of peanut butter, a jar of grape jelly, a can of mixed nuts, a piece of a bag of potato chips, and half a dozen cans of pork & beans. "Don't forget to look for a can opener," Michael said as he continued foraging. Pulling out a kitchen drawer, Michael took a handful of forks, knives, spoons, and yeah, there it is, a can opener. Over the stove, Michael found a Coleman camp stove but no fuel. "Why would anyone have a stove if they ain't got any fuel? There must be some fuel here somewhere." Michael whispered as he ransacked the cupboards. Michael looked under the kitchen sink, and there it was, a gallon of stove fuel. "I knew if I looked long enough, I'd find some." Michael said. "I really hit the jackpot here," Michael said to himself as he piled the bags of goodies near the back door. Michael's internal clock kept telling him it was time to go, but he decided to make one more sweep in case he missed something. As he looked around, he observed a homemade board behind the door for keys. It was one of those projects preschoolers do. You know, labeled and painted with little butterflies and flowers. "I'll bet Buddy made this himself when he was a kid," sniped Michael. House Keys, Buddy's Keys, Mom's Keys, and Barn Keys they read. "How sweet," Michael said as he removed each key from the board. "Who knows, maybe I'll have need for these," Michael said dropping them in the pillow case. Taking another look around the kitchen, Michael pulled out a drawer marked 'BILLS' hoping for money. What Michael saw wasn't money, but was worth more than all the money in the world could buy. There in the drawer was a stack of envelopes bound with a red rubber band with Buddy Thompson's name written in bright red ink. The return address read, Seaside County Sheriff's Department addressed to Buddy Thompson. Of course, this caught his eye and piqued his curiosity immediately. Michael couldn't stop himself, so he took out the stack of envelopes and opened one and began to read. The heading on the letter read: Please find enclosed your final check in the amount of five hundred dollars and no cents for information that provided leads to the apprehension and conviction of Michael Schomeck for the crime of Felony Arson. Michael took each of the six letters from their envelopes. "5, 10, 15, 20, $2500.00 dollars," Michael said as he dropped to his knees. "Buddy started receiving reward checks almost as soon as I was convicted. That liar got twenty five hundred dollars from the Sheriff's Department for providing information that lead to my arrest and conviction. I don't feel so bad about robbing your butt now you sorry scoundrel. Buddy, you can consider this a down payment on what you owe me, old friend," Michael said with a feeling of total betrayal. "But don't worry Buddy; I'm not finished with you yet. Before I'm done, I'm gonna give you many more chances to clear your conscious about what you did to me," Michael said quite detrimentally.

With trembling hands, Michael gathered up the loot and weapons and got out of the house as fast as he could. "Wow, what a haul! I'll bet there's eighty... no, closer to a hundred pounds of stuff in these bags, as he heaved them up balancing them on his shoulders.

THIRTEEN

Michael slipped into the woods starting the long trek back to the safe house. "I hope Tim was able to complete his mission today. If he did, we're one big step closer to pulling off the job and getting the heck out of Seaside County," Michael said to himself as he slowly walked through the woods. As he walked, he couldn't help but think about; and, begin planning the revenge he would exact on Buddy for turning him in.

As Michael trod through the woods on the way back to the safe house, his emotions wrestled within him. The weight of the heavy load didn't compare to the heaviness he felt deep in his soul. Michael had become what he didn't want to become. He was now angry enough to spit nails; and, more determined than ever to do whatever necessary to disappear. His thoughts centered on planning the bank job and evening the score with Buddy. With adrenalin pumping and emotions high, the long walk seemed shorter than ever. "Wow, I'm almost there. I can see the old house just a couple of hundred yards ahead," Michael thought. Before Michael reached the house, he tried to clear his head so he could concentrate on his plan. Michael looked up at the moon's position and determined it must be around 11:00. "Tim should be back by now," he thought.

Michael let out an owl hoot call toward the house...no answer. "Maybe Tim ain't got back yet," Michael thought. Either it's him or someone else here 'cause here are some new signs that weren't here this morning. Bending over cautiously examining the foot prints in the moon light, Michael thought, "These are Tim's foot prints all right...I'd know his gait anywhere." Michael slowly moved in closer to the house until he could peek through a crack in a boarded up window near the living room. Michael could see Tim sitting on the couch listening to a portable radio. Michael knocked hard on the side of the house. Tim jumped up and tiptoed over to the window looking out to see who was out there. Michael squatted down out of Tim's sight, just outside the window. When Michael saw Tim peeping through the crack, he jumped up and hollered. The prank nearly caused Tim to have a heart attack. Michael couldn't quit laughing. "Very funny, very funny," Tim said with a fake smile. "Now that you've scared ten years off my life, I guess it's okay for you come on in. Go to the front door and I'll let you in," Tim told Michael. Michael nodded in recognition as he started toward the front door. "Good job Tim," Michael said as he entered the house through the door. "Coming in the front door sure beats the heck out of crawling under this house every time we need to get in. Only one thing...once we're inside, we must make it hard for anyone else to come in," Michael said. "You mean something like this," Tim said as he picked up a log about four feet long and wedged it between the door and the entrance wall." "Yep just like that," Michael replied.

"Wait here by the door for a minute. I've got some stuff stashed out in the weeds," Michael said before he disappeared into the tall weeds. Retuning only a few minutes later, Michael handed Tim two grocery bags. "Man, what you got here? You've got to be kidding me... you brought dinner, that's great," Tim said with excitement. Michael then threw one of the loaded pillow cases in the door behind Tim, with the other one draped over his shoulder as he walked through the door. The boys moved all the bags over to the sofa. Tim was excited to show Michael that he had completed his assignment. Michael sat down and took a deep breath. "Go ahead Tim, tell me about what you found out today. I'll sit right here and catch my breath," as Michael fell back on the sofa.

"Here's the stuff you told me to pick up," Tim said as he began taking the items out of the bag and stacking them on the rickety old coffee table. Michael examined the items as Tim talked. "When I got to the bank, it was somewhere near eleven o'clock," Tim said. Michael took one of the watches off of the table and handed it to Tim. "Here take this and put it on so next time you'll know exactly what the timing is." Tim took the watch and at the same time Michael said, "On my mark it will be exactly eleven forty eight p.m. Now, set your watch to that exact time." Tim held his watch at the ready and waited for Michael to speak again. "Mark," Michael said. Tim set the wrist watch to exactly eleven forty eight p.m. then strapped the watch on his wrist.

Tim continued giving Michael the run down about what he had accomplished in town today. "I went in the bank and talked to this old lady...her name was Sandy, she's the head teller. I made some small talk with her to show her I was friendly. I thought for a minute she was gonna give me her number, I think she liked my muscles. Anyway, I asked if I had to have an account to change a twenty dollar bill. She told me no and was happy to help me. I told her I was just starting to collect two dollar bills and asked if they had any. She was very helpful. She asked the other tellers if any of them had any two dollar bills but none of them did; so, I asked her if they could be keeping them anywhere else." She said, "You stay right there, I'll check in the vault." Sandy walked over to the manager's desk. He's located behind a four foot high rail to the north end of the bank just at the end of the tellers' windows," Tim said as he reached over and pulled out a piece of paper with a sketch of the interior of the bank, and handed it to Michael. "She told him what I was looking for, so he told her to look in the vault. With that, he took a key out of his top desk drawer…the key was on a bright red round key marker. He handed it to Ms. Sandy… she walked over to the vault… put the key in the wire door and opened it. The vault is located in the north west end of the bank at the end of the tellers' counter," Tim said as he pointed to the sketch. "Michael, I could see the whole inside of the bank, and most of the outside from right there in front of the tellers' counter," Tim said. "I did what you said while Sandy was in the vault. I looked around real careful not drawing any attention, and I think I spotted all the cameras," Tim said proudly. "But before I took my second scan, I heard the door to the vault close, so I turned my attention back to Ms. Sandy. As soon as she locked the vault, she took the keys back over to the manager. He just pulled open the desk drawer and she dropped the keys in the drawer. She then walked back over to where I was waiting, with a big stupid grin on my face; you know…'cause I was so dog gone excited to get some more two dollar bills for my new collection. She counted out ten two dollar bills and handed them to me. I put on my best oh golly gee gosh face, thanked Ms. Sandy and left just like you told me to. I remembered everything I could so I could draw it out for you just like you said. I wanted to get it on paper while the info was still fresh in my head." Tim said as he laid other drawings on the table in front of Michael.

"I then walked to the phone booth…waited until I saw somebody walk in the bank… watched for somebody to walk out at about the same time, and then I called 911. I could see the time and temperature clock in front of the bank…it read 11:26 a.m. Michael, did you know it don't cost you any money to call

911? I even made sure my two dimes didn't have any finger prints on them while I waited for the operator to tell me to drop twenty cents for the call, but she never told me to drop any money. After I dialed 911, the next thing I know, I was hearing a voice saying *911 Emergency, what is your emergency*? Michael, to tell you the truth, it caught me a little by surprise. There I was waiting to drop the twenty cents, and all of a sudden, I'm talking to the emergency operator," Tim said beginning to ramble. "Tim, *please*...heaven's sake...that's enough about the twenty cents!" Michael rushing him along said, "Go on with what you found out." "Tim continued, "I used a fake voice, you know, like one of them Harker's Island fishermen do. I said I was coming out the bank up here at Cape Shore, and as I was walking out, I bumped up against a man going inside, and I think he had a gun or something under his jacket. The voice on the other end of the phone started asking for my name, so I hung up the phone. I dropped the two dimes back in my pocket and walked away. Then the phone started ringing. Michael, it must have rung thirty times. I didn't know what to do so I answered it," Tim said befuddled. "You did what?" Michael roared. "Wait a minute... it's ok... the man on the phone asked if I had just used the phone to dial 911. I told him no, that I was sitting in my truck eating lunch, and the darn phone wouldn't stop ringing so I answered it to make it stop. The emergency operator asked if I had seen anyone around the phone. I told him I saw an old fisherman on the phone a few minutes ago but he left. Then I said, look man, I only have thirty minutes for lunch. I don't know anything and I've got to go back to work. The voice said okay, thank you sir for your help and they hung up the phone. Then I went into the hamburger place and ordered a sandwich, fries and a drink. When I got my food, I sat right in front in one of those window seats, just like you told me. I kept a good look out, but there won't anything much going on anywhere around the bank. But then all of a sudden, I heard this siren. I couldn't really tell which way it was coming from, but a few seconds later, it pulled into the bank from the Diamond City direction, I guess that's east, ain't it? Anyway, the time was eleven forty five exactly. It took the cop fourteen minutes to get the call and make his way to the bank. Don't you think it took him a long time, Michael?" Tim asked. "Yeah, it did Tim," Michael answered. "We can get a lot done inside that bank in fourteen minutes. What did the cop do once he got there?" Michael asked. "Michael you ain't gonna believe this. That cop pulled up right to the front doors... he gets out...no gun drawn...no looking around and then...the nut just walks right into the bank. He only stayed in there for a minute or two. I'll bet they get false alarms there all the time, and he just knows that one of those teller ladies has set it off by accident again." "Good, that's exactly what we want him to keep right on thinking too," Michael said with a smirk. "Then what?" Michael asked. "Well, like I said, after one or two minutes, the cop comes out and gets in his cruiser, drives across the street to the police station, gets out and goes inside." "Michael, did you know the police station was in view of the bank?" asked Tim. "Yeah sure, I knew that," Michael answered. Tim asked, "Well...I gotta ask, ain't that cutting it a little close?" "It's close, but I've got a plan to deal with that if it becomes necessary," Michael answered.

"Oh yeah there is one more thing," Tim said. "I brought you a cheeseburger and some fries but the drink didn't make it 'cause the bottom of the cup fell out and I threw it away, so you'll just have eat without a drink." Michael interrupted, "How would that burger go with a cold beer," asked Michael as he pulled two beers out of the bag, sitting them on the table. "And there's more where they came from too. I have CFC, beans, chips," speaking excitedly as he pulled the items from the bag. "A stove, some gas, candles, cokes, eggs, bread and on and on and on," Michael stopped talking but kept pulling items from the bag. "Wow man, you really made a haul... what else you got?" Tim asked. "Let's see what else you brought to the party," Tim said as he reached for the stuffed pillowcase. "HOLD it right there!" Michael snarled as he snatched it from his grasp. "You ain't very smart Tim. Boy, you're about as dumb as a box of rocks. If this job is to go off like it's supposed to, it's up to me to teach you everything! Lesson number one...don't ever reach into a bag unless you KNOW what's inside. There just might be something in there that will bite you! You understand?" Michael snapped.

Michael carefully reached into one of the pillow cases and pulled out the hand guns. "What we have here is a 9MM Beretta and a Colt 45 automatic, and last but not least, a Smith & Wesson Model 19, .357 magnum." Michael said as he handed Tim the Beretta, "Here, see how this fits your hand." Tim carefully took the gun and looked it over. "Is it loaded?" Tim asked squeamishly. "Oh yeah!" Michael responded..."Fifteen rounds in the magazine, one in the pipe, sixteen rounds total." "Tim my boy, that means once you start shooting this baby, you can fire sixteen rounds before you have to reload. And here's three extra magazines with fifteen rounds in each mag...that gives you a total of sixty one rounds." Tim watched Michael in amazement as how he handled the guns and seemed to know so much about them. With Michael's mood, Tim was almost afraid to ask but decided to anyway. "How is it you know so much about guns man?" Tim asked. "You know my *father* was a marine! All that time at Sandy Dunes, I read everything I could about weapons and police tactics. It was just something I found interesting. You know, guy stuff," Michael responded with a better tone. Tim felt a little better that Michael had calmed down a bit, but was still not sure what was going on with him. He just knew he was hot and cold...and he had no idea when he might be scalding.

"We'll start your lessons on how the Beretta works and everything you need to know about it in a few minutes," Michael said. "I'm keeping the Colt; the Beretta's yours. My father has a Colt just like this. The S&W we'll keep as a backup, you know... just in case we need it," Michael said as he laid the S&W next to him on the sofa.

"Now, let's take a look at the BIG GUNS. Michael then slowly picked up the shotgun immediately pulling the stock into his right shoulder. Simultaneously, his left hand instinctively grabbed the forearm. Quickly, he ratchetted the forearm to the rear and forward again, making a thunderous clank of steel striking steel. Tim sat helplessly in fear as Michael raised the shotgun barrel pointing it directly at his face. For the first time, Tim witnessed the evil that obviously had taken control of Michael. Leaning forward, Michael pressed the tip of the shotgun barrel firmly against Tim's forehead and pulled the trigger...click! Michael broke out in a wicked laugh as Tim sat there in shock, mad, and scared to death. Tim hollered, "What are you doing man? Are you crazy? That wasn't funny! You're about three bricks short of a load, man!" In hysterical laughter, Michael kidded, "You should have seen you face! I'll bet you peed your pants. I was just fooling with you, man. Here, have another beer." Michael pitched the Remington 12 gage shotgun to Tim. We'll saw the barrel off really close, so it'll be easy to wheel around while you're sitting in a car. "How does that feel to you? You like it?" Michael asked. "Yeah, sure thing, just so it ain't pointing between my eyes," Tim replied. Michael then picked up the .22 automatic rifle. This one just ain't got a lot of fire power; but, we can use it to hunt up some squirrels or rabbits or something like that when the food runs out. Now...I saved the best for last... drum roll please, Mr. Bandmaster!" Michael exclaimed. Tim started drumming with both hands on the broken down coffee table. Michael pulled out the Mini-14. "What we have here is a Ruger Mini-14 .223 cal. assault rifle. This weapon takes a thirty round magazine and will shoot just about as fast as you can pull the trigger!" Michael stated with an uncommon thrill. "This will be our main gun when we do the bank." Michael said. "If anybody gets in our way, they'll have to face the full wrath of what Mr. Ruger can spit out...and I'll tell you this...anybody on the receiving end, will be having a very bad day," Michael said with a sinister look in his eye.

Michael picked up the other pillow case and dumped it out on the coffee table. Out came a boat load of extra magazines, shotgun shells, rifle ammo, a few boxes of .22 ammo, and a bunch of mixed loose bullets. "Looks like we've got the bullets... if we ain't got good sense." Tim said.

"Let's leave this mess alone and have some supper," Michael said as he reached for the bag with the cheeseburger and fries. The house got really quiet during supper. Silence filled the room. Tim looked over at Michael and said, "Man, we're really gonna do this, ain't we?" "You can bet your life we are," Michael affirmed. "Oh yeah, there's one more thing. You won't believe what I found out today about my old friend Buddy," Michael scoffed in a demonic voice.

The morning sun was just beginning to rise and Michael was already hard at work getting the equipment ready. "All the 9mm rounds are in this bag, shot gun shells here, .45 ACP in this bag, 22 cal. right there and all the spare magazines are in the bags with the correct bullets," Michael muttered to himself as he continued to work.

He chuckled thinking about Snake Woman when he heard Tim finally stirring about. "She would holler out at me with, "You gonna lay there in that hog wallow all day?" Michael recalled fondly. Michael made two stacks from the items Tim had picked up: ski mask, gloves, watches, tape, walkie-talkies and the scanner. Michael started putting fresh batteries in all the equipment. As he placed the batteries in each one, he would turn them on and check to make sure they were working properly. Although everything was working perfectly, Michael gave them all a second check.

Michael stuck his head in Tim's room and asked, "Everything all right in here?" Tim, still in bed answered, "Yeah, I'm up, just…give me a minute." "Make it quick," Michael said. "Today we start training for the job." That was all Tim needed to hear. He sprang from his bed like a child on Christmas morning. "I'll be in the living room when you're ready," Michael said.

Five minutes later Tim strutted into the living room, snapped to attention and reported, "Tim Blackhardt reporting for duty, ***Sir***! I'm ready, willing, and able to get this party started." "Well, sit down right here and let's get started," Michael said as he picked up one of the weapons and began Tim's first lesson. Working closely with Tim for the next eight hours, Michael taught Tim the workings, both inside and outside, of all the weapons they had at their disposal. Over and over, Michael had Tim show him what he had learned by repeating each action. He taught Tim how to load each weapon, how to cycle the actions, how to unload and reload quickly, how to clear a jammed or misfired round, how to disassemble and reassemble each weapon, and the proper handling and point of aim for a quick kill shot. Michael tried to teach Tim everything he knew. Tim proved to be a good student; learning quickly, and retaining the information. “You know, I do remember my daddy teaching me most of this stuff when I was growing up, I just had to re-remember that I knew it,” Tim said owning his dim wit. “Okay, let’s see how good a teacher I was. Show me everything I just taught you,” Michael instructed. Tim picked up each weapon showing and telling Michael what he had learned with military precision. After more than an hour of practice, Michael was impressed at how Tim had retained what he had shown him. “Like I said, you’re a darn good student. Now we’re gonna work on tactics,” Michael said as he picked up the Mini-14 shouldering the weapon. Pay attention Tim, this is important. I’m going to demonstrate how to properly clear a room.

Michael and Tim worked well into the dark on drilling tactics. “Tim, come over here. I want to go over the plan with you one more time. Tim stood over Michael’s shoulder attentively, as Michael went over everything step by step, for the sixth time of the day. “Do you have any questions ‘cause now’s the time to ask?” Michael inquired. “Nope, no questions…I‘ve got it, I‘m ready.” Tim responded. “Today’s Tuesday, so if everything goes as planned, we’ll hit the bank Thursday at noon. The bank will be good’n fat with money for check cashing on Friday,” Michael asserted. “Okay, let’s have some grub and get to bed…we’ve got a big day ahead of us tomorrow. We still got a few things to pick up and some old ‘*friends*’ to say goodbye to. Ain’t no way I can leave before seeing Buddy Thompson one more time,” Michael avowed.

It was before sunrise the next morning when Michael walked into Tim’s room and shook him awake. “Get up Tim, time’s wasting! We got too much to do today to lay around in bed half the day, if we’re gonna be ready for Thursday.” “I’m up, give me one minute…I’m up,” Tim growled.

Michael had a couple of candles lit and a can of soup warming on the stove when Tim finally made it to the living room fifteen minutes later. "Sit, I'll bring this over to you," Michael said picking up the can of soup. Handing Tim the soup, Michael said, "I want you to go back to town and run through everything one more time today. Don't try to cash any money in this time, but everything else needs to be done exactly the same as the other day. Hang out at the hardware store for a while. Pick up some more grub at the grocery store and remember to stay focused. Keep a good watch on the bank and the police station. Around four o'clock, call 911 with another story about the bank," Michael instructed. "You think they'll fall for that false call mess again Michael?" asked Tim. "What other choice do we have? If they don't send the cops, that's to our advantage cause they ain't taking the alarm going off seriously; and, if they send the cops, we get to time their response time again. How do we lose?" asked Michael.

"What you gonna be doing today?" Tim asked Michael. "I'm gonna pay my old friend Buddy Thompson a little visit," Michael said. "Hey man, don't go over there and start no trouble with that boy. We can't afford for you to get your butt locked up, or get into some other trouble today, of all days." Tim said. "No, I ain't gonna get in any trouble. I'm gonna go get us a car." Can't do a bank job without a car, can we?" Michael asked.

Fifteen minutes later Michael was out the door, thirty more Tim was right behind him; both boys were on a mission. The sun was just coming up as Michael squatted down at the base of a tree about two hundred yards behind Buddy's house in the woods. "From this vantage point, I can see everything moving in the whole neighborhood," Michael said to himself. About the same time, a light came on in the kitchen at Buddy's house. Buddy's mom must be getting ready for work, Michael thought. More lights came on in the house...one in the bathroom...one in the living room, "Yeah she's getting ready for work," he believed. Michael decided to close his eyes and take a quick nap while he waited. He had only been asleep for about thirty minutes, when he heard the back screen door slam; Michael woke up immediately. A few seconds later, Michael could hear an engine turn over several times and finally start. "Sounds like she needs a tune up to me," Michael thought. A few seconds later...there she goes...out the old barn... down the dirt path, and out of sight.

Michael listened as he heard Buddy's mom drive away out of ear shot. Michael waited an additional five minutes making sure she didn't turn around and come right back. Michael rose to a standing position, "I'll move a little closer and see what I can see." Michael whispered to himself. He quietly moved up to the south side of the house. Hesitating only a moment, Michael slowly and cautiously walked around the house, peering into the windows to see if anybody was still home. When he reached Buddy's room, he could see a big lump in the middle of the unmade bed. Michael thought, "That could be Buddy, or it could be just another pile of dirty laundry... one's just about as useless as the other."

Michael crept up to the back door without a sound. Reaching into his pocket, he retrieved a key labeled Buddy's House Back Door. Slowly inserting the key into the lock, Michael turned the key unlocking the door with a quiet *click.* Michael slowly turned the knob and pushed the door open just wide enough for him to slide inside. Michael walked softly to Buddy's room where he stood by the door looking in and thinking. Michael stood glaring down at Buddy for several minutes before putting on a serious face. He then softly crept over to where Buddy was sleeping and pressed the .45 against

Buddy's forehead and nudged his shoulder. Buddy's eyes opened and immediately recognized the weapon pressed to his head. "What's, what's going on man? You don't need to do that to me. Come on Michael. Lower the gun. You, you really don't need that... we're friends," Buddy earnestly plead. Michael laughed and said, "Oh man, don't pay any attention to this, I was just funning with you," as Michael pulled the gun away from Buddy's face and stuck it back into his waistband. "Sorry Buddy, I didn't mean to scare you, but I need to ask you a favor and I couldn't see you anywhere else, you know, with the law looking for me and everything," Michael snickered. "No, Michael it's all right," Buddy stuttered. "You just scared the crap out of me, that's all. Are you all right where you been staying? You know they're still looking for you, don't you?" Buddy asked. "What's the deal with the interrogation, man?" Michael said, "I feel like I'm talking to Deputy Fairlane, not to one of my long lost best friends." "No man, I'm just concerned for you, that's all," Buddy said sincerely. "Yeah, I know, that's why I came here like I did, because I couldn't trust anybody else but you, Buddy," Michael retorted. "Seriously man, I need your help," Michael pleaded. "Anything, anything you need, just name it." Buddy said. "What can I do for you? You need money, food, what?" Buddy said nervously. Michael answered, "I need your car." "My car! Man, I ain't giving you my car! The only car I have is that old Chevrolet," Buddy said. Michael snapped, "That'll do." "Man, you can't take my car," Buddy snapped back. "Hey, wait a minute! Somebody robbed my house a few days ago. You know anything about that?" asked Buddy. Michael countered, "What kind of a friend would I be if I robbed your house, especially after all you've done for me?" Buddy stood up and puffed out his chest in an attempt to intimidate Michael. Michael took a step back and brushed back his jacket revealing the butt of the Colt 45. "I hoped it wouldn't come to this, but if you try me, I'll kill you, Buddy," Michael said coldly. Buddy began to shake noticeably. "Well what's it gonna be? You gonna give me those keys, or am I gonna have to take them off your body? The choice is yours to make," Michael derided. With shaking hands, Buddy reached over into a pile on his night stand and picked up the keys. Handing them to Michael, Buddy asked, "Am I gonna get my car back when you're finished with it?" "Oh yeah…sure… Buddy, just as soon as I'm finished with it. I'll make sure you get what's coming to you," Michael replied. "And one more thing, keep this little arrangement we have just between you and me. By that, I mean don't report your car as missing or stolen or anything like that to your friends over at the Sheriff's Department," Michael added. "What friends at the Sheriff's Department? Buddy remarked." Michael reached over and pulled open the drawer where he had found the reward envelopes. Taking out the stack of envelopes, Michael said, "All these years, you've been selling drugs right under the cops' noses, and they never busted you, or even took a second look at you. They've been allowing you to deal. I knew you weren't that smart the first time I met you. You know, now it all makes sense to me. You inform on your competition… the cops let you continue to operate without hassling you. What a perfect arrangement. You got in bed with the cops when you turned me in… and in return, you sold your soul; and, turned against every friend you ever had.

Let me ask you something, Buddy, does Billy know you're a rat? This is the deal. I'll use your car for a couple of days, and after that, I'm out of Seaside County forever, and you'll never see me again." "But there is one thing that I can guarantee you before I go. If you do anything to interfere with my plans, you'll never live to regret it. I'll consider the use of the car as payback for the years I spent in lockup because of you ratting me out," Michael firmly stated. Buddy's voice quivered as he responded, "I had to do it Michael; they were going to put all of us in jail. Fairlane wanted somebody to pin the fire on and he wanted you. He said if I didn't cooperate, we were all going down. Michael, you've got to believe me... if I had to do it again, I'd take the fall myself... I'm really sorry."

"Go ahead and take the car. I won't say nothing to nobody. You keep it as long as you need it," Buddy added. Without saying a word, Michael turned to leave, "Hey man, wait a minute... take this," as Buddy reached into the drawer of the night stand and pulled out an envelope. Here's some money to help you out. I know this don't make up for much, but at least it will give you some traveling money. Michael, if you need anything, let me know, and if I don't have it, I'll get it for you somehow." Michael took the envelope, shoved into his jacket pocket and said, "This don't make up for nothing, Buddy! I was locked up for four long years while you and yours were allowed to run free. You still owe me!" By the way, Michael continued, "Give this a thought... I could have just as easily snuck in here, slit you throat, and took those keys and money rather than ask you for them." Buddy dropped his gaze and stared at the floor for a moment. It was partly in shame, and partly in fear of looking Michael in the eyes. Before Buddy could raise his head, he heard the back door close as Michael pulled it closed behind him. Buddy sat down on the edge of the bed fumbling through the pile on the night stand looking for a cigarette. Placing the shaking cigarette between his lips, Buddy hung his head and began to sob uncontrollably.

FOURTEEN

Michael unlocked the car door and jumped inside the Chevy, sliding the key into the ignition. He gave it a quick turn and the engine sprang to life. Revving the engine a few times, Michael reached up for the gear shifter, pulled the handle to *D* and slowly eased down the driveway.

Zero-eight-twenty-five hours, Michael turned down the CC Road just off of Hwy 58 and proceeded down Seaside County's longest dirt road. From Hwy 58 to the Ten Mile Road, the CC Road was just short of twenty seven miles long, and Michael knew it like the back of his hand. "I have to pick the perfect spot to stash the car," Michael whispered casting his gaze from side to side, as he slowly drove down the dirt road.

The dry sandy dust floating into the dry air made Michael realize how easy a car could be seen driving down a road like this. Suddenly Michael said, "That's it… right here. This road is just what the doctor ordered." From the main road,

Michael could see the side road went into the woods about two hundred yards, before it made a hard left turn, paralleling the main road for about two hundred yards. "If we stash the car right there, we can set up camp, and see everything coming from either end of CC road. If we camouflage it right, they'll never be able to see us. It's perfect," Michael thought. It's close enough to the old house, yet not too close for someone to put two and two together, and figure out the house and car is somehow connected, should they stumble across the car.

Michael pulled the car far enough down the road so it wouldn't be seen by someone driving by. Michael backed the car between some heavy bushes, leaving just enough room for him to squeeze out of the driver's side. He then walked from the area to survey it. He felt confident they could hide the car, set up camp, and have easy access to it. "All we need to do now is cut some evergreens and put them on top of the car. It will then be almost invisible!" Michael said, as he admired his hiding location when the job was done. "I'll head back to the house and gather up some supplies, and be back at camp before Tim gets back," Michael thought.

Michael glanced down and checked the time. It was ten-hundred-forty-five hours when he broke out of the woods, about thirty yards from the back door of the old house. Michael stopped just long enough to take a quick look around before approaching the house. Everything looked clear, so he eased up to the house. He gathered up the shovel, rake, saw and hatchet. He put the hand tools in his knapsack along with some of the spare food and water, and headed out to prepare the camp site. "The more I do now, the less we'll have to do later," Michael said as he picked up the knapsack and slung it over his shoulders. Dropping down through the hole in the floor, Michael was on his way back to the car. He could mark another task off the list he had prepared the day before.

Tim got back to the house around six thirty p.m. slumping down on the sofa. Tim dropped his head in his hands, gave out a big sigh, took a deep breath, and stated, "We're really going to do this! We really are going to do this!" His words became more intense and louder each time he would repeat what he realized was happening. "Yeah Man!" Tim yelled at the top of his lungs. "We're ready, and we're really going to do this!" Tim stood up suddenly and slapped his hands over his mouth. "What in the heck am I doing...anybody outside could have heard that," Tim said as he rushed over to the window hoping nobody was hearing him.

"Where in the world is Michael?" Tim asked. "I hope he didn't go to Buddy's and get in some sort of scuffle with that peckerwood that landed his butt in jail. I wouldn't put it past that turd calling the cops on Michael if there was any trouble." Tim looked at his wrist watch... it was seven-thirty-five p.m. "I'm not gonna wait for him anymore. I'm gonna eat something, and he'll have to fend for himself when he gets here," he said to himself. Tim walked over to the counter and picked up the bag he had brought back from town. Tim took out a cheeseburger, grabbed a beer, and went over to the sofa to eat. Just as Tim sat down, he heard Michael's hoot owl call. In about 10 seconds, Tim hoots back giving Michael the clear signal. Tim went to the back door and removed the wedge so Michael could come in. "Another fifteen minutes and it'll be dark... good thing you came home while you still had some light left," Tim said as he held the door open for Michael. "You're starting to sound like a woodsman saying stuff like that," Michael quipped.

Michael slapped Tim on the back, as he replaced the wedge in the door frame. "Well Timmy, did you get everything done today?" Michael asked as he lit a match and held it to the candle." "10-4 Mr. Schomeck, I did," Tim responded. "Let me grab one of those burgers and we sit down and go over what we accomplished today." Michael said.

Michael picked up the bag of burgers and walked over to the sofa where he joined Tim who had already begun to eat. Leaning back, Michael popped the top on a can of beer. "Okay, tell me about your day, then I'll tell you all about mine," Michael said. They reviewed what each had done until the early hours of the morning. Quietly, Michael said, "If you feel good about things so far, we'll do a dry run tomorrow." Silently, Tim looked Michael directly in the eyes and nodded. "We'll drive the entry and exit routes, check the timing one more time, and if everything goes to plan, Thursday will be the big day," Michael said as he held his beer can up and toasted Tim to their success. Tim just sat there with no response looking at Michael in disbelief. "Well Tim, that's your cue. Right about now, I'm expecting you to say, yeah Michael, I'm ready, let's do this thing." Tim still not speaking just sat there perfectly still. Michael said in a much louder, frustrated tone, "Hey, Tim, you with me or what? You need to snap out of it!" Hesitantly and reluctantly, Tim responded, "Sorry man I just kind of drifted off there for a minute." "Get your head out of your butt! I've got to have you one hundred percent in the game, if we're going to do this," Michael said. Questioning Tim's hesitation, Michael asked, "Tim are you capable of doing this with me or not? I need a definite answer." "Yeah man," Tim replied. "I was just thinking about the last thing my Mama told me. She told me that one day I'd end up a criminal, if I lived long enough. I was just thinking how proud she would be of me knowing that I'm finally going to make it happen." Michael responded, "Don't worry about that crap, if everything goes like we planned it, by this time next week, we'll have so much money we won't have anything to worry about for a very long time."

"Michael, what we gonna do come Thursday after the job is done?" Tim asked. "For the first few weeks, we're gonna have to lay low and stay off everybody's radar. After that, if we can keep from getting caught or killed, I guess we'll split up the money and go up to the mountains."

"Tim, if this place is as rich as I think it is, we'll just about be able to go or do anything we want to," Michael said. "I'll tell you one thing, Michael. If they catch us, I sure the devil ain't going back to Grantsville. There ain't nothing there for me, and there never was!" Tim snapped. The way I see it Michael, you've been the only one I could ever depend on for a long time. You are the only family I have anymore," Tim said. "Man, I feel the same way about you," Michael said in kind. "It's getting late and I guess we've done about as much as we could for one day. It's probably best we turn in and get some sleep, tomorrow is gonna to be a heck of a day," Michael said.

Michael laid back on the sofa looking at the patterns of the peeling paint made on the ceiling and thought about tomorrow. A million things went through his head…all the plans as well as all of the 'what if's'. Michael rehearsed the approach routes and the escape routes, working them over and over in his head, until he knew he couldn't improve on them anymore. Every question he asked himself was answered quickly without hesitation. "I'm ready," he thought, hoping Tim was as prepared as he was.

Zero-seven-hundred hours Michael went to wake Tim but there was no Tim to be seen. "Hey, you in here?" Michael asked. "Yeah, man," a voice called out from the other room. "I've been up most all night going over the plans. I couldn't sleep a wink, so I got up and made some coffee. I've been working the plans over and over in my head. Michael, I'm 100% ready. You see, I just had to work some things through in my own way," Tim said sheepishly. "It's all right man. I knew I was pushing a lot at you mighty fast. You just need to know that if things go wrong on Thursday, we'll have to rely on our training to get us through; because if the bullets get to flying, we won't have time to think about how to react. I understand you needed to work it out in your own way," Michael said with empathy. "And, one more thing Tim...there ain't another person on earth I'd have do this with me other than you... By the way, you can take that to the bank! If this won't so serious, that would have been funny," Michael said as he gave Tim a shoulder bump. Tim responded, "I'll be right there beside you to the end Michael, and you too, can count on that," Tim assured him this time.

Michael followed Tim to the kitchen where the coffee was brewing. "Smells good man," Michael said as he leaned over and sniffed the aroma of the coffee. With excitement, Michael asked Tim, "Hey man, what do you think about us going over to the camp where the car is stashed, and going into town and having some real breakfast?" "You're kidding, right? Man, you know we can't be seen in town," Tim replied quickly. "Who says we have to stay in town? We've got a car now, so what the heck! We need to chill out a bit and it wouldn't kill us if we rode over to K-town and picked up a few things we need. Let's take care of business first, and if it's not too late, maybe we'll head to K-town," Michael said. "You had my attention when you mentioned breakfast," Tim answered. Michael walked in the lead heading toward the new camp. After walking about thirty minutes, Michael said, "We're here... how do you like it?" "We're where?" Tim asked. "We're here at the new camp... you know the hideout... our new home for the next week or so,"

Michael answered. “Stop playing games with me Michael. I’m already stressed out up to my ears, just tell me where the heck here is.” “Here, is right here! “What looks like the woods is our base camp. You are standing right smack in the middle of it!” Michael came back. I’ve been coming here for the past few days preparing it. Over here, under all that brush, is where you’ll find a tent pitched for our dry sleeping quarters. Come walk with me. Only 20 feet from here is a natural stream with clear spring water. I dug out two bunkers, with yours on the west side of the camp and mine on the east. They are deep enough to stand in and fire on anyone coming from either direction on CC Road. Use the natural undergrowth to cover yourself should you hear someone approaching. Follow me over here and tell me what you see,” Michael instructed Tim. “I see a dense thicket of branches and undergrowth. What am I supposed to see?” Tim asked. “You got it Man! That’s exactly what you should see! Michael answered. “I found an old shrimp net and strung it up in the branches over the top of the car. Then, I chopped some evergreens and stuck them all over in the net. The net drapes down in front of and behind the car so it can’t be spotted by helicopter or plane, Michael told Tim while showing him around camp. “Dog gone Michael, you’re dangerous! I walked right up on this here mess and couldn’t tell a thing. You are good! Tim said. “From now until we can come out of hiding this will be our home away from home,” Michael said. Tim interrupted, “Why can’t we just stay back at the house? I‘ve kinda come use to living inside.” “Because, if we need to run, we want to be able to get in the car and get out as fast as we can,” Michael replied. “The old house will be our fall back point if everything goes wrong here: and, if we have to run, it will be our rally point.” Michael continued. “Besides we can load all our gear in the car.

If we need to, we can pull down any dirt road, and we'll be able to find a place to hide or sleep for a few hours."

Michael sitting down on an old milk crate said, "Tim the way I see it, right after the job we'll have to lay low, maybe for about a week or so. After that, if they ain't caught us, then we've got a pretty good chance of getting away with the whole thing." "What then Michael?" asked Tim. "Let's say we get away with it, you know the bank job. What do we do next?" Tim asked. "At first, we'll have to split up. If everything goes to plan, about the only thing the cops are gonna know about us, is that there are two of us. The cops will be looking for two people traveling together, Michael said."

FIFTEEN

"We'll need a place where we can leave messages for each other. Then, in a few weeks, when the heat is off, we'll meet up. Do you know a good place up in the mountains where we can meet up?" Michael asked. "Yeah man, there's an old train depot they turned into a shopping center in Highland that I'm real familiar with. I got a friend who works at a shoe store there that I trust. His name is Jimmy Sparks. We're old friends from a juvenile stretch that me and him did together up in Morganton," Tim said, feeling somewhat proud of his contribution. "Okay, that will be the plan after the job… we split up the money, and in a couple weeks from Thursday, we'll meet in Highland," Michael said. When you get to Highland, get up with Jimmy and tell him to be looking out for me. Tell him what I look like, and give him my name. When I get in town, I'll make it my first stop looking for you. Make sure you tell him how I can get up with you, so we can hook up." Michael said. "What if one of us don't show?" Tim asked. "Then I guess the other will check with your friend every day for one week; and, if we don't hook up in that time period, the other will have to assume that the other one has been killed or caught." Michael said seriously.

Neither of the boys slept very well, as they were thinking about how important the day was going to be toward finalizing their plans. "Let's try on these disguises," Michael said as he handed Tim a paper bag. "I made these up for us to wear for our drive around town today," Michael said. As Michael pulled his disguise out of his bag, he asked Tim what he thought. "I got me this old hat, a wig and some sunglasses. If I'm lucky, they ought to keep anyone from recognizing me." "What did you get for me?" Tim asked. "I got you a shawl, a blue wig and a yellow dress. I'm dressing you up like my ole lady," Michael said in a serious tone. Both boys were laughing like little 10 year old children. "No man, I'm just busting your chops…I got you a hat and some sunglasses. Besides you're way too ugly to be my ole lady," Michael said laughing.

"Tim, since you'll be doing the driving during the job, I want you to do the driving today," Michael said seriously. "Although I know the area a ittle better than you, I want you to get used to how the car handles. You can learn the streets better if you're doing the driving. Don't worry about memorizing everything right now, 'cause we'll repeat the route several times until you can drive it without having to think about where you're going."

As Michael and Tim rode down the highway, both boys were starting to feel tense but still chuckled about their disguises. "You know that's not a bad look for you Michael," Tim said. "You might want to keep those glasses for when this is all over." "Yeah, I'll think about it," Michael responded. "Hey I'll keep and wear mine if you do the same," Michael said. "No thanks I think I'd rather wear that wife outfit you were telling me about than to wear this mess," Tim was saying when Michael broke in.

"Turn left at the traffic light," Michael told Tim. "Okay, it's time to get serious… no more bull from this point on. Once you make that left turn, slow down and merge in with east bound traffic. Drive real slow as we drive past the bank, I want to get a good look around. Slowly, slowly," Michael said as Tim motored past the bank. Michael's head was on a swivel looking back and forth and from side to side looking down both sides of the roadway. Michael made oral and mental notations as Tim drove slowly down the highway. Looking to the right side of the road, Michael said, "The police department is right there." Got it." Tim responded. Michael counted out loud, "One…two cars parked in back parking lot… that means there's only one cop on duty… our luck's holding up. Once you pass the bank, turn right on the first paved road." "Yes Sir!" repeated Tim. "Go down to the end of this road and turn around and head back toward the highway." "Yes Sir, got it," Tim affirmed. Tim followed every direction with military precision. "Now, when you get alongside that house on your left, slow down…like real slow. Let's see how good we can see the front of the police department from here," Michael said. "Yeah that's perfect, from here we can see everything, there's the front of the bank and right there is the front of the police department. Man, we can see everything… this is a perfect observation point," Michael said assuredly.

"Okay Tim, drive to the highway and make a right… I'll show you the getaway routes," Michael instructed a very attentive Tim. Without saying a word, Tim made the right turn and headed east on highway 24. "Make this left right here… pointing at the intersection just ahead. This is Sandy Bunker Road which takes us back to Highway 58. Go to the end of this road and turn right onto Hwy 58. That takes you back to Deer Creek Road, and two miles on the right, you're back at the CC Road…from there, you're on the road back to the old house or to base camp, get it?" Michael asked. "I've got it down pat, Big Boy!" Tim responded loudly. "Okay, let's do it again, but this time, we'll time our every movement." Michael said. For the next three hours Michael worked with Tim, making sure he knew every entry and exit points to and from the bank. Finally Tim spouted, "Enough is enough, I've got it...I've got it! Give me some credit, Man! This town is so small... believe me Michael, I've got it."

Tim, it's nine-thirty...what you say we drive to Kranston Corner and have a beer and a pizza?" Michaels asked. "You read my mind partner," Tim responded. The boys drove west on Hwy 18 towards Kranston Corner for some much needed R&R.

While driving to Kranston Corner, Michael couldn't help thinking about everything he was about to give up once they did the job tomorrow. He had a terrible feeling of loss. He also knew in his mind that the only thing he was really was going to miss was Snake Woman and the woods. "I wish I had met her long before I met Buddy Thompson," Michael regretfully pondered, while Tim fiddled with the radio, trying to pick up a clear station.

It was one-fifteen pm when the boys crossed the Lowland County line and entered the city limits of Kranston Corner. "There's a military surplus store about a mile ahead on the right, let's stop and see what they have that we need," Michael said pointing toward Uncle Sam's military Surplus Store. Entering the doors, Michael grabbed a tote basket and walked around examining and handling the military equipment. He picked up a pair of black BDU's, black tee shirt, boots, a black belt, and a load bearing vest with magazine pouches, then called out to Tim. "Tim come over here and take a look at this stuff. Pick up some of that black face paint and get a pair of those boots," Michael instructed. "I've got you some BDU's. Anything else you need?" Michael asked. "If you need anything now's the time to get it. Tim moved real close to Michael and whispered, "How about a couple of these bags to tote everything in…you know, the money." "Yeah, good idea… they may come in handy," Michael answered.

After around thirty minutes of shopping, Michael said, "Come on man, let's get this stuff up to the register and get out of here." Tim gathered up the gear in his arms and took it to the cash register and piled it on top of Michael's stuff. "You boys find everything you needed?" asked the old grizzly clerk. "Nope, where do you keep them hand grenades?" Tim joked. "You boys going hunting or you gonna rob a bank with all this stuff?" asked the clerk. "Yeah, that's it old dude… you hit it right on the nose… we're going to rob a bank," smirked Tim.

"What a bunch of smart aleck kids! Can't joke around with these young'uns…should'a just kept my mouth shut," the clerk said to himself. Michael paid for the gear and thanked the old geezer for his help. They left feeling confident they had what they needed to complete the job. Throwing the supplies in the trunk, Michael said, "Well, that's one more mission accomplished. Let's go get that beer and pizza now!"

"This place right here looks promising… Hot Pizza and Cold Beer…what else do you want? That's just what I was looking for, how about you?" asked Tim. "Yeah man, that's fine. Pull in and let's give it a look-see," Michael replied.

Swinging the front door open, Tim noticed the place was empty, except for an old bartender who looked like something the wolf threw up, and some old red headed bag that Tim was sure had been rode hard and put up wet on many occasions. "How's the beer?" Tim asked as he approached the bar. "Cold," answered the bartender. "Well, then set us up with a couple of cold ones, we'll decide if we want to stay for the pizza," Tim replied. Michael and Tim took a booth in the corner and spent the rest of the afternoon and early evening having a few beers and quietly talking over plans. For a few hours, they relaxed playing pool and laughing at their silly jokes. It was if life would be like this forever, when Michael looked at his watch and realized it was almost 9:00 pm. "Hey Man, it's getting late. We can either stay here, get good'n drunk, and call the whole thing off, or we can go get a good night's sleep for the big day. What do ya think Tim?" asked Michael. It was if Michael was hoping Tim would give him a way out of what his gut was telling him was not going to end well. Tim picked up his beer, turned it bottoms up and sat it down on the table, turned to Michael and said, "Well, I reckon it's time we get going then." Michael stood up and pulled on his jacket. "Okay Tim, let's go," Michael said.

Heading home, Michael said, "Stop at the first gas station you get to and top off this beast." "Michael, we've got more than half a tank... we got plenty of gas," Tim responded. "I know how much gas we've got, but do you really want to run the chance of running out tomorrow? We won't get the chance to stop for gas if the cops are chasing us and shooting their guns at us, will we?" Michael sarcastically asked. "You're right, sorry," Tim responded. Tim thought to himself, "You just do the driving stupid and Michael will do the thinking... that's worked fine so far... there's no reason to change it now... just shut up and do the driving!"

It was nearly 10:00 pm when the boys rolled back into the Cape Shore city limits. Turning toward Tim, Michael voiced, "I guess we've got time to give the route one more drive through before we call it a night." "Whatever you say, Boss," Tim quickly responded. Driving the route for the tenth time of the day, Tim commented, "Man, I've got this. I could do this with my eyes closed, sitting in the seat backwards." Michael snapped back, "Yeah, but could you do it with a bullet hole in you while you're trying to stop the bleeding and with the cops in hot pursuit?" Hesitating a second before answering, Tim said, "Yeah, I could do that, no problem!" "That's what I wanted to hear, that's exactly what I wanted you to say," Michael said laughing. "Okay, that's enough let's go home," Michael said.

Arriving back at base camp, Tim backed the Chevy into its hiding place, and turned off the engine. The boys sat silently for a few minutes, then Tim asked, "Don't leave me in suspense any longer, what time we gonna get started tomorrow?" "We're gonna do it tomorrow morning. We'll hit them at ten-hundred hours just after they open the doors." Michael added, "Whatever you need to do to get your head ready, go and get to it. There ain't no backing down from here." The boys quietly got out of the car and without talking, began covering the car with cut limbs. "Tim, I'm gonna go for a walk in the woods. I'll be back before sun-up. If you can Tim, try to get you some sleep, you'll need to be sharp tomorrow," Michael said. "Okay I'll try but don't take any bets on it," Tim responded. "I'll see you in the morning," Michael said as he walked off into the darkness.

Tim huddled in his sleeping bag with his eyes closed but was never able to fall asleep. His mind was too busy thinking and rethinking everything about the plan for tomorrow. Tim, still lying awake, heard walking in the woods. He could hear someone nearing his location. Tim was startled when he saw it was Michael returning, as it was almost sun rise. Tim had not realized he had lain awake all night with how things might go. "Daybreak was approaching and that meant the big day was here," Tim anticipated.

"There's about an hour before the sun rises. Let's me and you walk over to the house and make sure we didn't leave anything they could use to identify us." said Michael. "Might as well, I ain't getting no rest lying here," Tim said. Tim slipped out of the sleeping bag, pulled on his shoes, and quickly joined

Michael as he walked down the trail. On the way to the house, Michael asked Tim questions about what he was going to be doing during the job. Tim answered each question without hesitation and with perfect response. "Great job Tim, you've got it all together but," starting to jog Michael asked, "Can you tell me what your job is while you in a run?" Tim began to recite his job responsibilities as they jogged. "Great, how about if we were in a full run, could you tell me what your job was then?" Michael asked as he broke into a run? "Heck no, I can't tell you my responsibilities…I can't even breathe…how can I tell you anything…when I can't breathe," Tim said gasping for air. "I didn't think so. You're huffing and puffing like the big bad wolf after those little pigs," Michael laughed. "I just wanted to see how far I could push you, Michael continued." "Push me, I'll show you how far you can push me," Tim said as he ran up behind Michael and grabbed him by the belt, pulling Michael along for eight or ten steps. "Okay, that's enough," Tim said as he stopped dead in his tracks, and dropped to the ground out of breath. "You got me, Man, I ain't never smoking another cigarette, I think I'm dying!" Tim struggled to get out.

Stopping about a hundred yards from the old house, the boys waited long enough to take a good look around. "Everything looks clear to me," Tim said. "Yeah, me too. Let's go in," Michael said. The boys spent a little over an hour cleaning up the old house. Making sure to remove everything they had taken in and returned everything back to the way it was when they first entered the house. Picking up a bag of trash, Michael said, "We'll dig a hole and stash all this stuff in the woods. That way, no one can trace us back to the house. Who knows, there may come a time when we need to use this old house again; and, I don't want anyone to know we used it the first time. She was good to us when we needed her, so it's only right we leave her back like we found her," Michael said respectfully.

Throwing the last shovel full of dirt on the trash bag, Michael looked over at Tim and said, "If we're gonna do this thing, I reckon we need to get ready." Michael reached into the tent and dragged out the two duffle bags and placed them on the edge of Tim's sleeping bag. While unpacking the bags, Michael made two piles. "This pile's for you and this one's mine," Michael said. As Michael finished unloading the last bag, he stood up and started taking off his clothes. Michael picked up a plain black tee shirt and pulled it on over his head. He then picked up the BDU pants and slipped them on. Tim followed suit, mimicking Michael's moves. Michael sat down on the blanket, slipped off the brown boots Snake Woman had given him, and pulled on the shiny black combat boots. "Hand me that face paint, Tim." Michael said. "Here you go. What exactly do we do with this stuff?" asked Tim. "We use it as part of our disguise," Michael responded. "We'll use this black paint all around our eyes like this," showing Tim how to apply the face paint. Then, when you put your ski mask on, nobody who sees you will be able to tell if you're white or black, or a woman, or a man, under those clothes," Michael explained.

"Once we're full dressed, everything that could be used to identify us will be covered with something; either clothes, gloves, ski mask or face paint," Michael explained. Tim took the face paint from Michael and continued to follow his lead, dipping his finger in the black paint and making a ring with it around his eyes. They checked out each other, making sure each one was covered. "Okay, it's time to get armed up," Michael said, as he began to take weapons out of the remaining bag, neatly arranging them on the edge of the sleeping bag between the boys. Michael picked up each weapon examining them carefully by removing the magazine, unloading the weapons, working the action, and making sure the magazines were filled to the top. With the weapons passing inspection, Michael reloaded and placed them neatly back on the sleeping bag.

"Okay, we're ready, come over here, and I'll give you your weapons," Michael said. Tim stood over Michael as he handed him his weapons. "This is your main side arm," Michael said handing Tim the 9mm Beretta. "Remember you have sixteen shots and here are two extra mags." Tim took the pistol and tucked it into the back of his waist band. "No, put that weapon on your right hip, that way, you don't have to lean forward to draw it!" snapped Michael. He then handed Tim the sawed off shotgun. "You'll place this beside your right leg. It shoots seven times before you need to reload. I've loaded a round in the chamber, so don't point it at anything you don't want to kill; and, don't forget you have to take the safety off before you can shoot it. Put the extra shells in your top *right* pocket," Michael said emphatically. "Why do I have put them in my top right pocket, I'm left handed, shouldn't I put them in my left pocket?" Tim asked. "You keep them in your right pocket so you don't have to take you hand off the trigger. Besides, if you're dead, I'll know where to find the extra shells on your body if I need them," Michael answered abruptly. "Sorry I asked," Tim replied. "Put the .22 on the floor at the edge of the front seat, then if push comes to shove, you can cause a lot of ruckus with this little thing," Michael added. Handing Tim the scanner, Michael said, "Stuff this in the gap between the seats, and turn it up as loud as it will go. If anybody calls the cops, and it goes out on the scanner, we'll be one of the first to know." "Any questions about any of the weapons?" Michael asked. "No questions," Tim responded. "Any questions about anything?" Michael asked. "No questions," Tim responded. "Remember, if shooting starts, aim carefully; squeeze the trigger and count your shots. If you count your shots you'll know when it's time to reload your weapons." Michael said. "Got it!" Tim responded.

Michael stood up and slipped his load bearing vest over his shoulders. Sliding the extra magazines into the pouches Michael said, "I hope the cop on duty today is at the café flirting with the waitress. I sure would hate to have to open up on his butt with all of this fire power today." Tim picked up the rest of Michael's gear and handed it to him tentatively.

"We're really, I mean, really going to do this, ain't we?" asked Tim. Taking the last rifle magazine from Tim's fingers, Michael slid it into the vest, looked Tim directly in the eyes and responded, "Unless there's something really upside down when we get to the bank; yes, we're really going to do this," Michael answered agreeably. Tim picked up his ski mask and put it on top of his head like he would a cap. Before he had time to pull it down completely, Michael said. "Don't put on your ski mask yet, man. Take it off the top of your head. We don't want anyone to get suspicious before we get too close to the bank. We're going to be wearing our other disguises until we get close by." "Yeah, yeah... I knew that... I was trying it on for size," Tim said nervously clearing his throat. "Hand me that .357," Michael told Tim. Tim lifted the S&W off the sleeping bag and handed it to Michael. Michael pulled up the edge of his vest and concealed it there. "A little insurance just in case everything goes wrong," Michael laughed. He then bent over and picked up his last piece of weaponry, the Ruger Mini 14. Michael slapped a magazine in the well, racked the bolt to the rear and released it quickly driving a .223 round from the thirty round magazine into the empty chamber. Clicking the safety to the on position, Michael said, "I really hope we don't have to use any of this crap today."

"Time check?" Michael speaking to Tim. "I have exactly zero-nine-ten and forty five-seconds." Tim adjusted his wrist watch and said, "Check, I have exactly zero-nine-ten and forty-five seconds." "Set your count down timer to ten minutes and leave it there," Michael said. Tim set the timer to ten minutes, "Check," said Tim. "Okay, Tim, we're ready," said Michael, "Let's get the car out and check the oil, water, tires and gas." Tim pulled away some of the hedge concealing the car, jumped in and fired up the Chevy. Pulling it out of its hiding place, Michael motioned for Tim to pop open the hood. Tim did as instructed. Michael checked under the hood while Tim walked around the car making sure the tires were aired up properly. He checked the ground for any unusual oil spots, and generally looked for anything that might hinder the performance of the car during their getaway. "Everything looks good to me," Tim said loudly. "Everything good under here too," Michael said as he slammed the hood closed.

Michael walked around to the passenger side, opened the door and calmly took his seat. Tim stood outside the car for a second before opening the door and sliding behind the wheel. Patting the gas petal two times, Tim twisted the ignition key and fired up the engine. Slipping the gear shift knob into drive, Tim slowly eased down the dirt road until reaching the CC Road. Tim stopped for a second checking both directions for traffic before making a left turn heading towards Deer Creek Road. "Put on your hat and sunglasses," Michael said as he did the same. "Try to stay cool, and I'll tell you when to put on your ski mask," Michael said as he positioned the Mini-14 across his lap.

Reaching White House Fork Road, Michael said, "Listen real careful now Tim, don't do anything that will bring attention to us once we're out on the highway. If we get stopped for speeding or making a turn without a turn signal, or anything else, all our plans, all our dreams…everything is over, and we're done before we get started." "Don't worry, man, I've got everything under control. I ain't gonna let anything stop what we've got to do today. There's no turning back now," Tim said confidently in a calm voice.

SIXTEEN

Approaching the intersection of NC Hwy 18 and NC Hwy 58 at Cape Shore, Michael turned to Tim and said, "Okay Timmy this is it, when we make this left turn we're 100% go... put on your mask now." Michael reached over and held the steering wheel while Tim slid the mask on over his face. With Tim's mask in place, Michael pulled on his. "Oh heck, the on-duty cop is at the police department! What we gonna do?" Tim asked in a near panic. "Stick to the plan," Michael said. "As soon as you pull up to the steps, I'm gonna jump out. As soon as I put my feet on the ground, start your timer and back the car right up to the front doors. If I ain't out when your timer goes off... come in shooting!" Michael said seriously. "I've got your back Michael, don't worry!" Tim replied. "Okay, here we go," Michael said as Tim pulled into position with the passenger door directly in front of the bank's door. "Start your timer now!" Michael barked. "Check," Tim responded as he hit the countdown timer. Tim's watch read ten hundred hours exactly. Dropping his right hand, Tim's hand rested gently on the shotgun laying beside his leg. Unconsciously, Tim lifted his hand and reached over and adjusted the volume on the scanner to high.

Michael paused outside the front doors...glanced in getting the lay of the inside of the bank. He leaned back and kicked the front doors open with a quick snap from his foot.

Stepping through the doors, Michael clicked off the safety of the Mini 14, and loudly shouted, "This is a holdup, everybody who don't want to be dead, better get their hands in the air!" Picking out the first camera location, Michael pointed the rifle at it, and shooting from the hip, let a three shot burst go, knocking out camera number one. Turning to his left, Michael quickly fired a second burst from the Mini 14 shooting camera number two. It exploded ripping it into a dozen pieces, sending shards of the camera over the tellers' counter striking one of the, frozen with fear, bank clerks in the face. With a slight swivel of Michael's hip, he shot the last camera off the wall in a hail of automatic gun fire. The noise of the automatic weapon fire inside the small bank was deafening. Michael quickly leaped over the counter, landing like a cat where he leveled the mussel of his rifle at the tellers, ordering them to lay on the floor behind the counter. "Get your hands behind your heads and don't move! If anybody sticks up their head, they ain't gonna have a head no more! Is that clear!" Michael shouted. "Yes," they collectively responded with quivering crying voices. As Michael moved toward the vault, he immediately saw the rapid blinking of a red light, indicating that the silent alarm had been set off. Michael wasn't surprised as he anticipated they would do that. He then glanced over at the bank manager, who was still seated at his desk with his hands in the air. Michael aimed the weapon at the bank manager and yelled, "Give me the keys to the vault!" "The vault is on a time lock. I…I can't open," the manager answered. Michael hit him square in the face with the butt of the rifle, knocking him out of his chair and onto the floor. Michael pulled out the middle desk drawer and began looking for a single key on a red key marker. Spotting it within a fraction of a second, Michael picked up the key and walked to the vault. Quickly turning, Michael pointed the Mini 14 at the manager's head and said," If you move or if you try to escape, I'll kill you." The manager nodded silently as he sprawled out on the floor covering his head with his hands. Michael inserted the key into the vault door, gave it a yank, and the vault door pulled open and swung freely. Jerking out the duffle bags from under his vest, Michael started filling them with stacks of money that lined the shelves of the small vault. Glancing at his wrist watch, Michael saw the countdown timer on his watch; he had been in the bank for six minutes.

Joseph "Joe" Williams, Cape Shore Car #357, had worked for the Cape Shore Police Department for nearly five years. Prior to that, he was with the Beachwood PD for five years. Moving to the Cape Shore PD wasn't much of a transition for Joe. Both were small towns with similar duties. The difference was that, most of the time, officers worked their shift alone at the small CSPD.

Day shifts were usually filled with routine. Zero-seven-hundred hours, put up the flag in front of the police department. Zero-seven-thirty thru zero-eight fifteen, perform school traffic. After school traffic, go to the local's restaurant, have breakfast and a few cups of coffee, and rub elbows with the local power brokers. Depending on who's working, flirt with a waitress or two. Other than answering citizen complaint calls, you're pretty much free until fifteen hundred, when school lets out.

Joe had been working the day shift the entire month and things had pretty much been normal. Today's shift started just like all the others; but, before the end of this shift, Joe would have to make a decision that would keep him second guessing the rest of his life.

Zero-eight-thirty-two, Joe pulled into the police department to do his morning paper work. He had just begun filling out some forms, when county communications gave him a radio call. He was to phone a complainant on Loblolly Drive about a stolen lawn mower. Joe picked up his radio and called in, "Cape Shore car 357 Seaside County, I'll be out at the police department making that 10-21 regarding that stolen mower." "357, 10-4," replied Seaside County. Joe called the complainant, wrote up an incident report and told the complainant how the police department would keep their eyes open for his mower and hung up the phone. It had been a slow morning, so Joe decided to take it easy for a few minutes before going back out on the road, beginning his morning patrol work.

Joe walked into the police lounge, reached down and turned on the television. Pulling off his gun belt, Joe thought, "I might as well relax for a few minutes, ain't much going on right now anyway." Settling down in a recliner, Joe murmured to himself, "Wonder who's on Regis today?" After only a few minutes, Joe suddenly felt the urge to go to the toilet. Grabbing his walkie-talkie and pistol, he stepped into the toilet to take care of business. Joe had only been in there for a few minutes when..."Seaside County to Cape Shore Car 357." Reaching for his walkie-talkie, Joe thought, " ain't this always the way it is..."357, go ahead county." Seaside County rang out over the scanner, "357 are you still at the PD? If so, can you 10-21 the communications center?" "10-4," Officer Williams replied. "County, I'll 10-21 in about five minutes; I'm 10-99 at the police department." Only a few seconds elapsed and again county communications called, urgently, "357, it's 10-18 that you 10-21 the communications center ASAP!" "357, be advised we just received a 10-90 at Cape First Bank." "10-4, Seaside County," 357 replied, "Probably a false alarm," Joe assumed. I'll be 10-17 ASAP." A few seconds later, Officer Williams called, "Seaside County can you 10-21 the bank and see if they have a problem or if it's another false alarm? They've been having trouble with that alarm for the last week or two. I'm 10-6 at this moment and it will be a few minutes before I will be able to respond. "357, 10-4, ten-zero-seven hours, stand by I'll 10-21 the bank," communications replied. "Seaside County, 357." "357 go ahead," Officer Williams answered. "I am unable to get anyone at that location to answer the phone." "10-4," Officer Williams replied. "I'll be 10-17 to that location in two minutes." Finishing his business, as soon as humanly possible, Joe pulled up his trousers and swung the door open. Reaching for his gun belt with one hand holding his walkie-talkie and pistol in the other, Joe ran to the front door. Pausing to finish putting on the belt, Joe peered out the front window looking toward the bank. "I can't see anything unusual," he said to himself, "Probably another false alarm."

Pushing open the door, Joe paused and once again, looked toward the bank before jumping in his patrol car. Starting the patrol car, Joe dropped the gear shifter into reverse then reached for the radio microphone. "357 Seaside County I'm 10-17 to the bank." "Seaside County be advised I am unable to see anything unusual from my location," Officer Williams reported. "I'm just going to drive over and make sure everything's okay inside." "10-4, 357 ten-hundred and fourteen-hours," Seaside County responded.

Tim seated in the Chevy with the engine running, was on pins and needles waiting for Michael's return, when he heard the communications center dispatch the Cape Shore Police to Cape First Bank. Without a second thought, Tim picked up the shotgun and laid it across his lap, a loud snap accented the sound of the safety being placed in the fire position. Raising the sawed off barrel just to under the windows ledge, Tim glanced down at his wrist watch, geez' he thought, "Michael's been in there for nine minutes but it seems more like an hour."

It was just at this moment Tim spotted a tall blonde haired police officer walk out the front door of the police station. Tim noticed before getting into his patrol car the officer stopped and looked in the direction of the bank. "Oh, darn, here he comes!" Tim said in panic. Tim watched the backup lights come on and the car swing from its parking space. Moving forward now, the car made a right turn into traffic and headed directly to his location. "You're gonna be sorry," Tim whispered as he took a firm grip on the stock and forearm of the shotgun now poised to be thrown up into firing position. Watching the left blinker come on, Tim could see the officer reach over and pick up the radio microphone. As the officer spoke over the radio, Tim heard him say, " 357 Seaside County I'm 10-23 at Cape First Bank." "10-4 357." Seaside County answered, "Zero-nine-fifteen-hours." Tim raised the shotgun over the window's ledge aiming it directly at the police officer who was now pulling into the parking lot where he sat anxiously waiting.

Suddenly, over Tim's left shoulder, he was deafened by the sound of automatic gun fire. His head followed his reflexes and jerked his gaze over his shoulder seeing Michael standing on the top steps of the bank firing the Mini 14 full-auto mode into the patrol car. Whipping his head back in the direction of the patrol car, Tim began to fire and pump the shotgun rounds into the patrol car, as fast as he could fire them. "One, two, three," Tim counted as he fired non-stop at the patrol car, "four, five, six, seven." "Reload, reload, reload," Tim shouted as he reached into his pocket grabbing fresh shells and loading them into the shotgun. In disbelief, Tim watched the car explode into pieces as it absorbed shot after shot being fired from Michael's weapon. "10-33(Emergency) 10-33(Emergency) Shots fired, shots fired," went out screaming over the radio.

As Officer Williams turned into the parking lot of the bank, he was immediately besieged with a deluge of automatic gun fire coming from the direction of the bank. At this point Joe made a fateful decision to abandoned reason, and crawled over the radio console, into the passenger side floor board, you know the area you usually put your feet when you ride in the passenger side of a car. Because of his training, Joe knew this was a spot that puts the car's engine block, the heaviest steel on a car, between him and the relentless gun fire he was receiving. "I have made myself into the smallest ball ever been!" Joe said. With no one behind the wheel, the patrol car slowly rolled to a stop twenty feet from the front doors of the bank.

When Michael saw the police officer was no longer visible, and offering no resistance, he bent over and picked up the duffle bag at his feet and threw it toward the rear of the waiting getaway car. He then grabbed the other bag and heaved it over his shoulder as he resumed firing on the helpless officer. Holding cover fire on the police car, Michael calmly walked to the waiting car and tossed the bag into the back seat. He then walked to the rear of the car and straddled the second bag just long enough to insert a fresh magazine into the now empty Mini-14. Snapping the magazine in place, Michael racked a round in the chamber and held covered on the now stalled, steaming patrol car, while he grabbed up the other bag and tossed it into the back seat.

Totally composed, Michael held his rifle on the patrol car as he walked around to the passenger side of the car. Tim covered the patrol car with his shotgun while Michael climbed in through the window. Tim felt a tinge of terror and disbelief as he held his shotgun on the gunshot riddled patrol car. He became even more frightened when he realized there was absolutely no movement coming from inside the car. His heart pounded so hard he thought it was going to explode. For the first time, Tim had regained rational thought. Michael had entered the bank ten short minutes earlier and now his realization came in loud and clear, "We've just killed this cop… now we're really in deep trouble." At this very moment, Tim knew there was no turning back.

Sitting on the window ledge of the car, Michael covered the disabled patrol car with the Mini. 14. Leaning inside the car Michael shouted at Tim, "What the heck are you waiting for, let's get out of here!" Tim slammed his right foot down on the gas pedal and raced out of the parking lot. As Tim turned left onto NC Hwy 18, he heard calls going out over the scanner. "Seaside County to all available units 10-33…10-33…10-33… respond to Cape First Bank, Cape Shore 10-90 in progress. Repeating, all cars 10-90 in progress Cape Shore, Cape First Bank. Shots Fired, I repeat, shots fired!"

Deputy Aaron Hill was in his personal vehicle traveling west on NC Hwy 18 in the vicinity of Bogie Field, when the first call went out about the bank alarm. Deputy Hill was returning home after testifying in a court case earlier in the day in Beachwood NC. Deputy Hill was in uniform and had his walkie-talkie with him so he was able to hear the traffic that was taking place on the radio. Although Aaron was off duty at the time of the incident, as soon as he was able to get clear air, he called out, "317 Seaside County, I'm at the Eastern Cape Shore City limits, do we have a description of the 10-90 vehicle?" Seaside County responded, "Standby 317." "Seaside County 357." "Seaside County 357." "Seaside County 317, I have no contact with 357 at this time. I cannot advise a vehicle description at this time." "317, 10-4 Seaside County…you may want to go ahead and dispatch the Cape Shore Rescue Squad to the 10-90 location and have them check on Cape Shore Car 357." "Seaside County 317, 10-4 doing so at this time."

In a panicked voice, Aaron said, "317 Seaside County, I'm behind the suspect vehicle at this time. Be advised the vehicle is a 1969 Dark Green Chevy Impala NC Reg. NNL-4922. We have just turned onto Sandy Bunker Road headed toward NC Hwy 58. Seaside County, I am able to observe two occupants in the vehicle at this time. I'll give you more information as soon as I have some." "Seaside County 10-4," came the reply.

Inside the getaway car, Tim had the scanner turned up as loud as it would go. Michael was busy reloading magazines and checking the status of all of the weapons. "Listen man…listen… they're talking about us!" Tim shouted. "Look behind us man, do you see any cops?" "No there ain't no cop cars nowhere that I can see!" Michael yelled back at Tim. Tim shouted, "Wait a minute, man, look right there, see that big blue truck! He's talking on a walkie-talkie. It's a cop, man… that's got to be a cop." "You just drive the car… I'll take care of him," Michael said as he slipped his upper body out the window of the speeding car and positioned himself on the window ledge facing to the rear. Reaching inside the car, Michael grabbed the Mini-14. Shouldering the rifle, Michael took careful aim at the truck and Bam...Bam!...Bam!...firing three single shots in rapid succession. At the same time, Michael heard the sound of bullets zipping by his head. "He's shooting back at us!" Michael screamed. Michael took a deep breath and carefully aimed and squeezed off several burst of fire into the front of the truck. Almost immediately, steam began to pour out from under the hood of the truck. The steam poured out so thick that Michael could no longer see the officer seating behind the wheel. "I'll teach you to shoot at me," Michael hollered, as he unleashed a fury of full automatic rifle fire at the officer. Michael thought how weird it was as he watched the .223 rounds strike the truck altogether knocking off little chunks of the vehicle, with each bullet strike. Feeling the bolt lock in the open position, Michael knew he had fired the last round in the magazine. Michael reached for a fresh magazine while watching the distance between the two vehicles getting farther and farther apart.

SEVENTEEN

As the getaway car rounded the next curve, Michael could see the driver of the steaming gunshot riddled truck pull over to the side of the road and roll to a stop. "317 Seaside County, my vehicle is 10-7...he shot it all to pieces. I am unable to pursue any further." Seaside County, "317 are you 10-4? Do you need medical assistance at your 10-20?" Deputy Hill paused for a few seconds before answering, "No, Seaside County not at this time. I have some glass in my face, but no I'm okay. I don't require medical assistance at this time." "Seaside County 317, 10-4. 317, give me your location and I'll have a wrecker and backup in route to your location ASAP." "317, Seaside County, 10-4. I'll be by the big blue dodge truck, sitting on the side of the road by Star Valley Golf Course, that looks like a giant piece of Swiss cheese. I'll stand by at this location. County, have you been able to make contact with 357." Seaside County replied, "317, negative, no contact at this time, standby on this frequency and I'll advise as soon as I have 357's condition."

"Cape Shore Rescue Nine, we're 10-23 at Cape First Bank. We'll advise you of 357's condition as soon as possible." A few minutes later, "357 Seaside County." County replied, "357 go ahead" "357, Seaside County be advised, I am 10-4. Sorry I couldn't get back to you, but my car radio is shot all to pieces. I'll be 10-6 at the bank regarding this investigation."

"Seaside County 357, 10-4 be advised, I have contacted Chief Swain, he will be 10-17, his 10-26 is ten minutes." "10-4, Seaside County," responded Officer Williams.

Michael staunchly told Tim, "Just as soon as you round this curve, I want you to slow down and drive like you're taking your mama to church. Keep your mask on and put on your hat. Take it real slow and easy, and let's see if we can get back to the hideout." Tim followed Michael's instructions without reservation. Turning onto the CC Road, Michael said, "Stop next to that big piece of chain link fence for just a minute." Stopping as instructed, Michael got out of the car and dragged the long piece of chain link fence out of the ditch and hooked it to the trailer hitch on the back of the car. As he got back into the car, Michael said, "Okay go ahead but drive real slow. If that chain does what I think, it ought to wipe out our tracks pretty good." Tim eased his foot off the brake proceeding forward at about 5 miles per hour. Ten minutes later they turned on the side road leading to the base camp.

"Stop right here," Michael said. "I'm gonna get out and make sure our tracks are covered. You drive on to the camp and put the car in hiding. I'll be there as soon as I make sure there are no signs that will lead anyone in here to us." "Okay," Tim responded as he drove away. Tim was just putting the last tree limb in front of the car when Michael came out of the woods from a completely different direction than Tim had expected. Tim jumped back and said, "Man, you need to signal me or call out or something when you do that crap, I could have killed you." Michael replied under his breath, "Yeah, right, if anybody was going to kill anybody, it would be me killing you, not the other way around." Then Michael said aloud, "I guess I was just caught up in the adrenalin and didn't think about warning you." "Don't worry about it man. I guess I'm a little amped up, too,"

Tim said as he leaned his back against a tree and slid down the trunk to the ground, drained.

"Let's sit here a minute and catch our breath. You got the scanner?" Michael asked. "Yeah, it's right here between the duffle bags," Tim said, while holding up the scanner. Michael reached out and took the scanner from Tim's hand and adjusted the volume so they could hear it clearly, but left it low enough so no one outside the camp could. "How much do you think we got?" Tim eagerly asked. "I don't know for sure, but I took everything they had. You know, the stuff in the vault, not the stuff in the drawers," Michael said. Tim squawked, "Why not the stuff in the drawers? There was probably another twenty five or thirty thousand dollars in the drawers, man! You should have taken everything they had," Tim said with irritation. "I didn't take the money in the drawers because that's where they put the dye packs," Michael snapped back harshly. With a look of confusion, Tim asked, "What's that?" "Don't tell me you don't know about dye packs, genius. Well then, let me send you to school...the bank puts exploding dye packs in a secret pile of money in the cashier's drawer. If the bank gets robbed, the clerk slips the dye packs in with the other money that's being stolen. When you get a few hundred feet from the bank, the dye pack explodes. The die explodes with bright blue and yellow dyes. The dye gets all over the money and all over whoever is carrying the money. That makes the money no good to anybody; and. leaves you walking around with bright blue and yellow dye all over you. The dye is permanent. Please tell me you know what permanent means." Michael continued. "It means you can't wash it off. You can't wash it off with soap, and you can't clean it off with chemicals. You just walk around with it all over you until it wears off. You still with me on this, Tim? In the meantime, you're walking around telling everybody, look at me,

I'm the jackass who robbed the bank. That's why I didn't take the money in the drawers. Did I make it plain enough for you? Do you have any more questions, Timothy?" Michael asked very condescendingly. Tim didn't answer, he just sat thinking this was the first time Michael had ever spoken to him in such a harsh, humiliating manner.

Michael sat and listened intensely to the scanner making mental notes about where the officers were setting up road blocks, and what they were doing to find the armed robbery suspects. Tim remained silent for more than an hour, before Michael asked him if he was all right. Tim sat up straight and replied, "Yeah man, I'm all right. I was just thinking about the last time my Dad talked to me the way you just did. It won't pretty. We went out in the back yard, and neither of us went back in the house until I showed him that I won't nobody for him to talk down to like that. I was big enough and strong enough to give him 'a what for' to earn his respect. Maybe it's time for me to earn a little of that same kind of respect from you, Michael," Tim snapped. Michael came back, "Look Tim, if I was out of line and said something I shouldn't have, I'm sorry. We ain't got no reason to fight, we're rich men. If we keep cool and don't get caught, we can live real good on this money, right here for a long time." "No man, we're all right. I guess I was still a little jazzed up, that's all. Forget it ever happened... forget I said anything," Tim said, as he picked up a bottle of water and took a long drink. "When we gonna count it?" asked Tim. "We'll have to wait until we're sure the cops ain't closing in on us and then we'll count up." Michael said. "Yeah, I guess it wouldn't be too cool if we had all that money laid out all over the place, and the cops rolled up on us, and we had to run and leave it," Tim laughed. "I'll tell you one thing," Michael said, "I fought to take this money, and if anybody tries to take it back, I'll fight to keep it." "Yeah, and that goes double for me too," Tim added.

The boys settled into camp for a long wait. Tim took out what was left of the burgers and fries and split them up for supper. It was just getting dark when Michael sat up straight and took a long look down the CC Road. "Tim...psst...Tim. There's a car coming down the road. Grab that shotgun and take a position down there by that big fallen tree," Michael whispered. Michael grabbed the Mini 14 and assumed a prone position behind a fallen tree, twenty five yards to the right of Tim's position. Tim grabbed the shotgun and moved silently to the position where Michael instructed him to go.

Keeping the car under constant surveillance, the boys watched the car round the curve more than a mile east of their positions. As the vehicle approached Michael's position, he was able the see clearly that it was a Sheriff's patrol car. Michael clicked the safety off on the Mini 14 with it cradled in his arms preparing for anything that might happen next. The car was traveling under five miles per hour now with the alley lights shining brightly from both sides of the car. Tim glanced over at Michael, waiting for a cue to how they were going to respond. Michael calmly gave Tim the signal to sit still and wait before engaging the patrol car with gun fire. "Wait, wait, wait," Michael whispered as the car drew nearer and nearer to their positions. Slowly the car drove right alongside where the boys were waiting, and then on past their positions without stopping. "Whew!" Michael let out a low sigh of relief looking over at Tim. Michael gave him the hold your position hand signal, as he observed the car drive out of sight. Tim remained perfectly still waiting for the all clear signal. Watching the car drive out of sight, the boys stayed in the ready position for ten more minutes, just in case there was a second car backing up the first one, or in case the first one doubled back.

After fifteen minutes, Michael gave Tim the all clear signal and motioned for him to meet back at the camp. "That was a close one, wasn't it, Michael?" stated Tim. "Yeah it sure was, it was real close for that Deputy. He will never know how close he came to losing his life down a dusty old dirt road in Seaside County today." Michael responded.

The next two days passed without incident. On the morning of the third day while eating a can of beanie weenies for breakfast, Michael asked, "Tim, what you say we take the money over to the old house and count it?" "Yeah, man, now that's what I'm talking about!" Tim replied with excitement. Tim got up and dragged some limbs away from the car. He then reached into the back seat and grabbed one of the bags, and then the other dropping them next to the car, while he worked quickly replacing the limbs. "I'm ready if you are," Tim said as he threw one of the bags down at Michael's feet." "I'll take this one and here's one for you," Tim said as he heaved his bag over his shoulder and headed down the path toward the old house. Michael grabbed up his bag and took down the trail having to hurry to catch up with Tim. "Hey, take it easy there hammerhead, don't be in such a big hurry, we ain't out of the woods yet," Michael said in a loud whisper. Trying to slow Tim's feverous pace was useless, Michael thought, as he scanned ahead of the trail. " If we come across anybody on the trail at this speed, we'll be on them before we know it, we really need to slow down, Tim," Michael said again. Walking fast enough to keep up with Tim they were up on the old house in less than thirty minutes.

"Wait right here and rest for a minute, while I go check the house and make sure everything's clear," Michael said as he tossed his duffle bag at Tim's feet. "I'll sit right here and wait, but hurry up; I don't know how long I can hold out," Tim said as he squatted down on the duffle bags. "You gotta be beat also, Michael." Tim added. "Right, Michael? You gone? How in the heck does he do that? Nary a sound, and poof, he's gone. He just disappears like thin air," Tim whispered to himself.

Michael had been gone nearly thirty minutes when he returned to Tim's location. Dropping down on one knee, Michael noted, "Everything is clear now, but somebody's been to the house. I can only estimate how long ago he was there; but, most likely, it was the same day we saw the Sheriff's car on the CC road. I found a cigarette butt that burned for about five minutes before somebody stomped it out. The tread on the shoe that smashed it looks like a cop's shoe. It's pretty clear they only looked here one time. You feel lucky about going in there and doing the count or what?" Michael asked. "Yeah man, I feel lucky; let's go to the house," Tim responded. "All right, let's get moving then," Michael said as he slung a duffle bag onto his shoulder. "If you're waiting on me, you're backing up," Tim said as he grabbed up his bag and fell on Michael's trail.

"Drag that old table over here," Michael instructed. Tim grabbed the edge of the old coffee table and dragged it to the sofa. "Let's get started," Michael said as he unzipped the duffle bag and dumped the money out on the sofa cushion next to him. Tim followed suit, "Wow, look at all that cash!" Tim spouted. "There must be a million dollars there," Tim said as he stood with his mouth gapping open. I just want to roll around in it. Have you ever seen that much money in your life?" Tim gushed. "We'll never know till we get started with the count, will we?" Michael said, as he grabbed a handful of the banded bills and started sorting them into like piles. "All this money is banded so stack them in piles of hundreds, fifties, twenties, tens, fives and ones," Michael instructed. When we get everything sorted, we'll add everything up and divide it into equal shares," Michael told Tim. "10-4 boss man," Tim responded.

It took the boys more than an hour to sort the bills out into piles. "What do we do now, Michael?" Tim asked. "Well, now we add up the piles and see how much we have, then we divide it by two, and we'll each have equal shares," Michael answered. "If it's all right with you Michael, you'll have to do the adding and dividing, I never was too good at math and I trust you'll give me a fair split," Tim said sheepishly. "Yeah man, I'll take care of it. This is how we'll do it...we'll just split everything into two even piles. This one will be yours and this pile will be mine," Michael said as he started sorting the money.

The old coffee table was piled over a foot high from end to end with stacks and stacks of cash. Michael left a small space down the middle of the table to separate Tim's pile from his. After placing the last stack of cash on Tim's side of the table, Michael leaned back on the sofa and took in a deep breath, and said, "Pick a side." Tim stretched out both hands and placed then on top of the stack of bills directly in front of him. Michael then told Tim, "Okay, everything on that side of the table is all yours, I'll take what's on the other side."

Tim dropped to his knees in front of the table staring at the money in disbelief. "How much you think we got there?" Tim asked. "The best I can figure, we've got about $375,000 each!" Michael replied. "I ain't got to be no math whiz to know how much money that is...that's a butt load!" Tim spouted. "Man, we're rich...is it all right if I have my share now?" asked Tim. "Yep it's yours, you do with it whatever you want," Michael answered.

Tim hesitated a minute and asked, "What you gonna do with yours?" Pausing for a minute, thinking about the question,

Michael answered, "I'm gonna take about $10,000 with me now Then, I'm gonna bury the rest of it somewhere back there in those woods." "Bury it... you're gonna bury it... why bury it?" Tim asked. "Because if they catch me, they won't find all that money on me; and I figure without the money, I don't think they can convict me for the bank job. Besides, if they do catch me and I can manage to escape again, I'll know where it is. I'll be able to come back and pick it up before I go on the run again," Michael said. "That's not too bad of an idea, but I'm gonna take mine with me," Tim said. "Well, it's yours... you do whatever you want to do with it," Michael reiterated. Michael picked up one of the empty duffle bags and tossed it to Tim. "We've been here long enough; we probably need to get back to the camp," Michael said as he picked up the remaining bag and started putting his part of the money in it. "Yeah, I guess you're right; we don't want to get caught with our pants down now," Tim answered. Tim, still kneeling down in front of the table, started pulling the piles into the bag with his forearm. "Stay here for a minute and I'll check things out real quick," Michael said, as he dropped through the hole in the floor. "I'll be waiting for your signal," Tim responded. "Hoot, hoot all clear," Michael signaled. Tim heaved the duffle bag across his back and dropped through the hole. As he crawled across the ground, Tim thought how heavy the money was on his back, but it was a burden he was more than willing to bear. Although the weight of the money he was packing was burdensome, the trip back to the camp seemed like

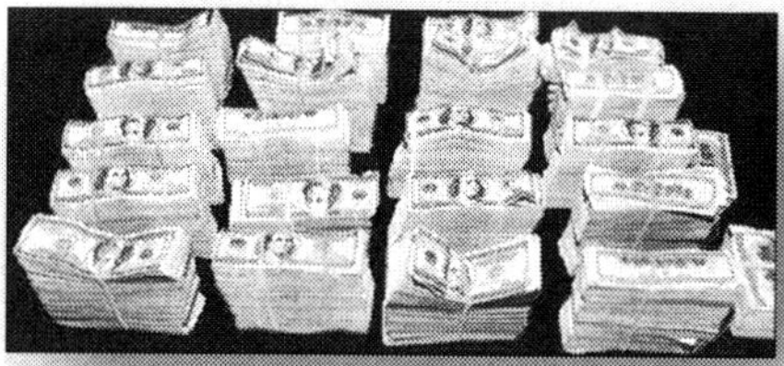

a hop, skip and jump from the old house. Within a few minutes of returning to camp, the boys were in bed using the duffle bags as their pillows.

The boys fell asleep with little effort, as they were close to exhaustion. Taking turns keeping an eye out, neither of the boys had slept soundly nor for any length of time for a few days. For now, this very moment, everything in their world was good.

EIGHTEEN

It is now one a.m. on the morning of the fourth day. Michael has kept his ear to the scanner listening for any conversation about him, Tim or the robbery…there is none. The road blocks that had been so quickly posted had been canceled. Michael hadn't seen any air traffic that appeared to be looking for him or Tim. From all the information Michael could gather from the traffic on the scanner, things were back to the same old routine. "I think they're tired of looking for us," Michael whispered to Tim. "We'll wait one more day and if we don't hear anything about us on the scanner, Thursday night we'll see about getting out of here." "I'm ready for that! Here we are sitting on all this money, and to tell you the truth about it, these beans and sardines are getting a little old!" Tim responded. "I'm ready for some real food; you know a steak or some of that good seafood you told me about when we were at Sandy Dunes. You know Michael, we can go to any restaurant we want to… order anything we want to eat, and we ain‘t even got to look at the side of the menu with the prices on it," Tim expressed. "Yeah man, if we can get out of here we‘re definitely gonna be able to afford the good life," Michael replied. We'll keep a good ear on the scanner today, and if everything's cool, we'll get out of here in the next day or so," Michael said beaming.

The boys took turns listening to the scanner for the next two days, "From everything I hear over the scanner, it looks like they've given up the hunt for us. I think it would be safe for us to break camp and get out of here this evening, after it gets dark," Michael said. "Yahoo!, Tim hollered, "Man those are some beautiful words to me. I've been waiting for you to say that for the last two days!" Michael continued, "Nobody around here knows who you are, so it ought to be easy for you to get us a car, without anybody taking much notice of you. You'll need to leave camp around five o'clock and head for town. It will be getting just about dark by the time you make that walk to Cape Shore," Michael continued.

"Go to the Pack the Sack parking lot; there should be right many cars there this time of day. If you look around a little bit, I'm sure you find one with the keys left in it. Don't take the first one you see though, pick one that's kind of plain...you know, one that can blend in. It's real important to make sure whatever you get don't stick out, nothing flashy!" Michael continued, "Once you find a car, drive over to the drug store and take a license plate off of a parked car and swap it with the one on the car you get. That will keep the cops confused for a few days. I'll take our gear and put everything in the woods one mile past the Filmore 66 station on the right side of the road. With me, so far Tim," Michael asked. "As you drive north on highway 58, look for the big yellow sign on the right side of the road; it's a bill board advertising Silver Valley Golf Course. Pull off right next to the sign and I'll meet you at the car. That's a lot to remember, you think you got it all." "10-4 good buddy, I've got it," joked Tim. "This is no time for joking or clowning around; I need to know you got it, Michael said sternly. "Yeah man, I been with you so far, I got this," Tim came back.

Looking at his wrist watch Tim stood up and stated, "I'm gonna head on into town…what…uh…what about my loot?" "Don't worry, I'm gonna have the money and guns with me when you pick me up," Michael replied. "You've got nothing to be concerned about; I'll be there waiting for you when you get there, trust me," Michael said. "Oh heck man, that ain't what I meant…I…I meant do you need some help breaking everything down?" Tim said. "No man, I've got this; you go ahead and get started to Cape Shore," Michael answered. Michael watched until Tim was out of sight, then got busy breaking the camp down. Michael worked with military precision as he loaded Buddy's car with all of the gear he thought they could use on the road. After working around the camp site for over an hour, Michael took a branch and wiped out every footprint and sign that showed him and Tim had ever been there. Pausing long enough, to take one last look around, Michael whispered, "I've got one more thing to do before I'm finished with Seaside County!"

Saying that, Michael stuck his hand deep into the duffle bag sitting beside him on the front seat, and pulled out a stack of hundred dollar bills. Pulling back the edge of the carpet underneath the car seat, Michael stuck the stack of bills under the carpet then smoothed it back out, making the mound of cash almost invisible. "Let Buddy explain to them laws how that got there," Michael said with an evil quake in his voice, as he hit the key and started the engine of the Chevy. Michael shifted the car into drive and slowly rolled away from the camp that had served to protect and hide him and Tim for the past week. Within thirty minutes, Michael was sitting on the side of the road next to the Silver Valley sign…another ten minutes and all the gear was unloaded and stashed in the woods behind the billboard sign.

Michael hopped back in the car and drove straight to the 66 station. Parking the car among a dozen of other cars in the parking lot, Michael dropped Buddy's keys in the glove compartment, quietly closed the door, and walked down the road unnoticed.

Michael arrived at the rally point within thirty minutes and patiently waited for Tim's arrival. Forty minutes later, a fairly new dark blue Ford F-150 4 x 4 pickup truck pulled off the road exactly where Michael had instructed Tim to meet him. Chrome Mag Wheels, huge off road tires, and the stereo blasting Sweet Home Alabama, A quick on-off flash of the head lights signaled Michael it was Tim. "I guess that's his idea of plain... something that doesn't stick out . . .redneck," Michael mumbled as he ran out to meet the truck. Making sure Tim was the driver of the vehicle; Michael ran back into the woods and emerged a few seconds later carrying a double arm load of money and the camping gear from the base camp. "Why don't you come give me a hand with the rest of this stuff?" Michael asked. Tim jumped out and followed Michael into the woods. With both boys carrying the equipment, they were able to bring the remainder of the gear in one trip. Tossing everything except the money and personal weapons in the back of the truck, Michael yelled, "Okay, make a U-turn and head back down towards Cape Shore." Tim slammed the gear shift into drive and did a burn out turning the truck around headed in the opposite direction.

"Stop at the first pay phone you get to," Michael barked. "Right on," replied Tim. "What you gonna do?" "Just wait, you'll see," Michael answered. "There's one over there on the right," Tim said as let off the gas and pulled over to the pay phone. As soon as the truck rolled to a stop, Michael jumped out and walked around to the phone and dialed 911. "911, what's your emergency?" the operator asked. Using a dialect and slang of a southern down-easter, Michael answered, "I stopped at that 66 station up here in Copper Cove, and I saw this feller park a car 'round behind the place, and I might be wrong, but that car looks a lot like the one you people was looking for the other day. You know, the one that crowd used up here to rob that bank. I didn't see nobody 'round it, but I see a car back there. Hey, let me ask you something… ain't there a reward or something for this here information?" The dispatcher repeated back the information, "Okay sir, you're telling me that there is a car that matches the description of the car used in the armed robbery the other day at Cape Shore and it's parked behind the Filmore 66 at Copper Cove." "Is that correct sir?" asked the emergency operator. "Yep that's about the size of it. Hey man, what about that reward… how much am I gonna get… you know, if this is the car you people are looking for?" "Hold one minute sir, I'm going to switch your call to a deputy over in investigations," said the operator. "I'll hold for a minute but I ain't got all night," Michael replied. As soon as the hold signal came across the phone, Michael hung up. Walking quickly around the back of the truck, Michael jumped in and said, "Okay let's get the heck out of here, this place is gonna be crawling with cops in about ten minutes." Tim hit the gas and sped down the highway spinning the tires and throwing gravel and sand like a rooster tail from a speed boat. "I'd like to be sitting in a tree watching Buddy's car when the cop's get here," Michael laughed heartedly! "You ever heard that saying, revenge is a dish best served cold," Michael asked Tim. "Ain't sure, what does it mean?" Tim asked. "Well, let me just say, my good ole friend Buddy just got a whopping big plate of it!" Michael exclaimed.

"What we doin' now Michael?" asked Tim. "You're gonna take me to Kranston Corner, and I'm gonna get me a car, and then, we're gonna go our separate ways for a little while,"

Michael answered. "You know Michael, I almost hate for all of this to come to an end," Tim softly lamented. "It ain't coming to an end Tim, we're just starting fresh again," Michael responded. "Listen Tim, we can take this money and buy us a nice place up on the side of a mountain somewhere and live there real comfortable for a long time, if we have a mind to. If we get tired of that, we'll buy us some first class IDs and we can go wherever we want too. As long as we keep our cool and don't be too obvious with the money, we can live real good for a very long time," Michael concluded. If we can't flaunt this money in front of our friends, you know, people we trust, how come we did it in the first place?" Tim asked while laughing. Michael sat silently shaking his head. "You know I'm just kidding around, don't you Michael? Where's your sense of humor, man? Chill out!" Tim added. "I'm just ready to blow off some steam and enjoy life for a change, and not worry about how to get the money to do it." "Yeah, that sounds real good, but let me remind you; we ain't out of the woods yet." warned Michael. "There's a lot of people out there looking for this money. We can't let our guards down yet. We've gotta keep watching our backs and be careful," Michael stressed to Tim. "Besides, there are way too many folks out there who would like to collect a big reward for turning us in. Once we get up in those mountains, where nobody knows us, then maybe we can kick back a little and enjoy what this money can do for us. But until then, we have to lay low and be on guard," Michael explained.

Driving down West Boulevard, Michael told Tim, "Put me out at that movie theater up there on the right. I'll get me a car and meet you back at that gas station," Michael said as he pointed to a station on the side of the road. "Wait there for me, I shouldn't be more than fifteen minutes or so, I'll meet you there and pick up my gear. After that you know the plan…we meet back in Highland in two weeks, right?" Michael asked. "Yeah, right, just like we planned," Tim answered. "Pull in at the theater and let me out," Michael instructed. Driving between the parked cars, Michael suddenly opened the truck door and leaped from the slow moving vehicle. Tim continued to drive slowly exiting the parking lot and turning back onto Lejeune Blvd.

Michael crouched down in a low walking position and walked slowly from car to car looking in each one to see who had been dumb enough to leave their keys in their precious car until...BINGO. "Here's one with the doors unlocked, yep, keys in the ignition. They just make this too darn easy!" Michael said quoting his ole pal Buddy Thompson. Michael quickly opened the door and slipped behind the wheel, slumping down low in the seat, Michael reached up and twisted the key, firing up the engine. Michael grabbed the floor shifter and eased it into drive. Leaving the lights off until he turned back on the highway, Michael had removed the car without being noticed and was on his way to meet with Tim.

Five minutes later, Michael pulled in next to Tim, who patiently waited at the station. Tim didn't notice Michael's new ride right off because he was trying to tune in to a radio station on the truck. Michael opened the his car door, got out, and without saying a word, started pulling his gear from the truck bed transferring it into the trunk of the dark green, 1984 Ford Mustang he had just picked up. Tim looked in the right rear view mirror and noticed Michael unloading the gear, so he got out and walked around to the back of the truck reminding Michael, "Don't forget you've got a few things up front." "No man, I won't forget," Michael said as he opened the truck door and removed several guns and a large black duffle bag filled with the cash from the bank job. "Well, I guess this is goodbye for now, old buddy," Michael said with a break in his voice.

“Yep, I’ll see you in two weeks,” Tim said. “Two weeks,” Michael replied as he slipped behind the wheel and started the engine. As Michael put the car in reverse he gave Tim a wink, backed out and drove away, blending into traffic on the boulevard headed east.

Michael had only driven about a mile when he glanced down at the gas gauge and noticed it was nearly empty. ”Why couldn’t I have stolen a car with a full tank?” he asked himself. “Well I have no other choice, I’ve gotta have gas,” Michael said as he pulled into the next gas station he came upon. Stepping out of the car, under the brightly lit gas bay lights, made Michael feel like all the eyes of the world were on him. After pumping in only ten dollars’ worth of gas, Michael threw a ten to the clerk through the security window and was quickly back in the car and down the road. “I’ll stop in some little town that hasn’t got so many lights later on and fill her up,” he told himself as he drove back toward Seaside County.

Against his own better judgment, Michael was returning to the scene of the crime area. There is no place on earth I know better than Seaside County, and if I’ve got to lay low and hide out for a week or two, there’s no place I’d rather be than home.

NINETEEN

Parking his new ride in among the vehicles waiting to be repaired at WO Motor Company, Michael slung the money laden duffle across his shoulder, picked up his Mini 14 and walked toward the edge of the woods. Stopping briefly before crossing the road, Michael looked up and down the highway making sure he hadn't been seen before stepping into the woods, and then disappeared quickly into the thick pines.

Dawn was just beginning to break, when Michael caught a whiff of wood smoke in the air. Without having to think about it, he knew it was Snake Woman's cook fire he smelled. Michael cautiously and quietly made his way up to the cabin, making sure everything was clear before approaching the door. Stepping up on the porch, Snake Woman pushed open the door and said, "Welcome home boy. I got your breakfast ready for you, come on in the house." Michael stepped inside and softly pushed the door closed. "Sit yourself down right here boy and let this old woman take a look at you." Michael took his place at the table. "I wanted to see you one last time before I left," Michael said. "I knowed you wuz coming, I was up early this morning and I saw you walking in the mist." "No ma'am, it couldn't have been me, I just got here a few minutes ago," Michael said. "Boy, don't you go telling me what I seen and what I don't seen, I knowed I seen you in the mist! At first, it took me to fright 'cause I knowed that only those who has passed walks the mist, but I knowed it was you, I seen you clear as day. Only you was telling me that you would be returning to me soon and that you had made your place in the mist. I don't know what it means, Michael. I just don't know what it means," Snake Woman said puzzled. "Now here you are back home like the prodigal son." Michael interrupted, "I have to leave Seaside County and we've decided to go up to," Snake Woman stopped him. "Don't go telling me or nobody else where you going." We're going, you say, you and that Tim boy? I told you that boy was trouble, bad juju, bad, real bad, you should' a stayed clear of that one," Snake Woman said. "Michael, you can stay here as long as you want. There ain't been nobody here looking for you since Fred McDaniels come 'bout three week ago. I don't expect they'll come here looking for you no more," Snake Woman continued. "I can't take that chance. I've done some real bad things since the last time I saw you." Michael said as he lowered his gaze in shame.

"Me and Tim needed money to leave with, so we pulled a bank job in Cape Shore about a week ago. There was trouble and shooting and well to keep it short, they want to find me and Tim real bad," Michael said sadly. "Did you kill anybody, Michael?" Snake Woman asked. "I don't know for sure; there was a lot of shooting," Michael answered. "Anyway I just came to say goodbye and see you one last time before I leave. I'll never forget you and...I...I love you, Snake Woman." As Michael finished these words he slipped out of the chair into the floor and leaned over and hugged Snake Woman around the waist like a small child hugging his mother, and softly began to sob. Snake Woman held Michael and rocked him in her arms, comforting him, not wanting to let him go.

Michael spent the next few days with Snake Woman re-living the memories he had made with her. He recalled the many many lessons she had taught him. Before morning light on the fourth day, Snake Woman woke to begin her day just like she had done for nearly sixty some odd years. Walking through the doorway, she glanced over to the pallet next to the fire place where she had left Michael sleeping, and was stunned and saddened to see that Michael was gone. Snake Woman walked slowly over to her chair at the table and slumped down sadly. Suddenly she spied a note leaning against the old rusty box on the kitchen shelf above the table. Snake Woman reached over, picked up the note, unfolded it slowly and with tear-filled eyes silently began to read.

Dearest Snake Woman,

Time has come for me to move on. I'll never be able to thank you for the loving spirit you shared with me. Your caring and loving ways have taught me more than I can ever express. I learned more about life from you than I have from any other person I've ever knew. I knew if I didn't leave before you awoke, I may never find the courage to leave. I couldn't live with myself if I brought trouble down on your house. Maybe someday they'll forget about me and leave me alone, and I can return to my only true home. Remember one thing, I'll never forget you. I buried the money in the woods, I didn't tell you where, cause you probably already know. I took enough to get me by for a while. If they don't catch me, I'll come back one day and pick it up. If I don't come back, it'll mean they caught me, and if that's the case, I won't ever come back. Snake Woman, I can't go back to jail, I'd rather be dead than ever be locked up in a cage like I was for those four years. If that's the case, I want you to have the money, there's enough there that you won't want for anything else as long as you live.

Your loving son,

Michael

Snake Woman dropped her arm beside her leg and the note slipped from her fingers. Snake Woman leaned forward in her chair cradling her head in her hands and quietly wept. In her mind, Snake Woman knew this was the last time she would ever see or hear from Michael.

Michael knew he had to maneuver back to where he had left his ride while it was still dark. He walked to the garage where he had stashed the car. The clock on the dash said four-twenty-two a.m. Michael fired up the engine and pulled out onto Highway 24. After driving several blocks, Michael reached over and pulled the head light switch into the on position. Michael looking forward and then into the rear view mirror, with no cars in sight, Michael hit the accelerator speeding up to the posted speed limit and held it there as he motored toward Marshboro. Suddenly, car lights rushed up behind him. It appeared to Michael to be a police car of some type. Nervously, he kept at the same speed. Michael wasn't sure what to do at this point, realizing that if he stayed on the open road in a stolen vehicle, he would surely be facing more police vehicles. Before reaching the bridge at Marshboro, Michael decided to turn off at Dawson's Marina. The patrol car went on past. "Whew, Michael thought, looks like I dodged that one." As he sat pondering what to do next, he decided to see what might be ready and easily available at the yacht basin. Michael stuffed all he could, including his Mini 14 into his duffle bag and walked down the floating dock until he spotted a nice 26 foot cuddy cabin with sleeping quarters, head, and kitchenette. "This will be perfect, sure hope the key is in the ignition," Michael said to himself. He boarded the boat, threw his duffle in the forward cabin, walked back to the pilot house and luckily the key was right there in the ignition on one of those orange floating key rings. "Now, what kind of nut would leave keys to a yacht in the ignition?" he asked himself. "Anyway, I'm sure glad he did!" Michael said feeling a little relieved. He cranked the engines, admiring the low droning sounds. Moving out to the deck, he quickly slipped the boats moorings; then took the helm and shifted the lever into forward and quietly idled away from the dock toward the ICW.

Heading south on the ICW, about 30 minutes out of Marshboro, Michael dropped anchor to make his plan. He searched through cabin cabinets until he located a chart bag. There he found a chart marked with fuel docks and restaurants all the way south to Florida. "Mmm...I could live in Florida. Never been there before, so I know nobody will know me," Michael thought, feeling free out on the waterway.

After three months in the Florida sun, Michael was looking handsomely tanned with blonde surfer-type hair. He had come to know some of the local shore birds, which sorta made him nervous. He didn't want to become too close to anyone.

Being on the lam, Michael decided to move to a more inland location with more trees where he trusted his survival skills. As he walked along the side of the road, all of a sudden, two police cars with blue lights flashing and sirens wailing, came at him, one from the west and one from the east. With nowhere to run, Michael stripped off his jeans and shoes and nose-dived into the swamp. "I'll take my chances with the alligators. At least I won't have to go back to jail," Michael thought as he positioned himself in the thick sawgrass of the Florida Everglades.

Three days later, after near misses with alligators, airboats, helicopters, and planes, Michael crawled out of the swamp. The traffic had stopped. "Well, I guess they figured I was supper for a gator, and have quit looking for me," Michael said as he flopped his waterlogged body on dry land.

Hungry, wet, and no money on him; once again, his expert survival skills kicked in. "I've got to get back to the boat, but I can't be walking around with no jeans," Michael said. "Let's see if one of these Flamingo colored houses has easy access. If the garage door is open, I'll bet the back door is also unlocked," Michael thought. "Jackpot! Bet I can find some designer jeans just my size, a nice Johnny Hiltfinger pullover, and a pair of penny loafers. Always wanted a pair of those so I could put a penny in the slot," Michael said as he searched through the man's huge walk-in closet. "Can you believe this? It's my lucky day... size 9 shoes with tassels, some cool khaki pants in my size, and a sharp Butter and Cut pullover just waiting for me," Michael said as he quickly got dressed. He took a carry-on bag from the closet, scurried to the kitchen, and filled it with goodies from the fridge. "I gotta get out of here fast and back to the boat," Michael told himself. Wearing his new duds, he strolled along looking quite normal in the ritzy neighborhood. He was about 30 minutes from the old hurricane damaged pier where he had docked the boat. "There she floats! She's been good to me the past few months. I wonder if anybody is even looking for it. After all this time, they probably just collected the insurance money and bought an even bigger yacht," Michael hoped as he stepped aboard. "Something doesn't feel right," Michael paused. It's been three days since he had been there. Although all his gear, money, guns, everything was still right where he had hidden it, that eerie feeling Snake Woman used to talk about when she'd say, "there's bad juju 'round this place, ain't no place to be, boy. Best, you gets far away from that juju you can," she'd say. "I gotta go with my inner gut on this one," Michael thought. It's time to get to the

mountains anyway; and, I can't get there in a boat," he chuckled. Michael gathered up his belongings, took hold the rail and hoisted himself up on the rickety pier. He took one last look at his "party barge" as he walked away from her, saying, "You've been good to me ole girl…sure gonna miss you."

Michael stood in the shade of a tall Palm tree, sipping on an Italian ice, looking around for the perfect opportunity to pick up a car for his long trip to the mountains of North Carolina. As luck would have it, or Snake Woman had thrown the bones, an older slow-moving gentleman pulled up to the gas pump driving a newer model Chevy truck. He filled it up to the brim and went inside to pay, leaving it running with the air conditioner wide open in the hot southern sun. Within 30 seconds, Michael had thrown his gear in the back of the truck, and quickly slipped behind the wheel, put it in drive, and off he went. Michael glanced back and could see the old man's back as he waited to pay the clerk. "Wow, that was easier than I thought," Michael said as he drove out of sight. The heat had become much too hot for Michael to stay in Florida. And, he wasn't referring to the weather.

TWENTY

As he drove up Interstate 95 to North Carolina, his thoughts went to Tim. "Wonder what he's up to now. He probably thinks I've been jailed or killed by now," Michael thought.

The sun began to set and the miles clipped by without much notice. He had so much running through his mind; he was in Georgia before he knew it, then South Carolina. "Maybe I need to switch up vehicles before I reach North Carolina," Michael gave thought. "They just might be looking for this one by now," Michael said as he pulled into a busy shopping center parking lot. Michael rode around the lot looking for a new ride. "Something easy, something plain," Michael thought. About half way through the first parking lot, Michael spotted a set of keys hanging in the door lock of a bright red Jeep Wrangler. "I hate to let that one go, but there's something about a red car that I just don't like," Michael murmured to himself as he drove on past. "I'm looking for something with a little less flash." Michael parked the truck between two vehicles at the GoMart which was close by a pizza place. He sat watching the pizza place just waiting to see if someone would leave their car running while they ran in to get their pick-up order. Sure enough, in less than five minutes, an older model brown Chevy pulled in the fire lane. This guy jumped out leaving the motor running and went inside. Michael was sitting on go! "Kinda looks like an old highway patrol car," Michael thought as he opened the door and quickly slipped behind the wheel. Barely raising his head above the dash to see out, Michael pulled the gear shift into drive and eased the Chevy the quarter of a mile to where his truck was. Michael pulled the emergency flashers knob and stopped right behind the truck. Working quickly, Michael transferred the gear and guns from one vehicle into the other and bid his old ride a fond farewell as he flipped off the flashers and pulled into the exit lane from the mall. Two minutes later, Michael was in a new car barreling down the highway toward the Tarheel State.

When Michael reached the North Carolina line, his emotions were like being on a fast moving roller coaster. He felt comfortable when he thought about Snake Woman, yet he knew he was still running. "Just like she told me, 'if'n you run Michael, you be running the rest of your life and that ain't no way to live, Boy.' "Snake Woman was right about everything, Michael sadly thought. "Anyway, I can't think about that right now. I'll soon be approaching Highland where I'm to meet up with Tim.

Feeling a little more at ease as the miles clipped by, Michael pulled the Colt .45 out of his waist band laying it beside his leg before reaching over and turning on the radio. "All I need now is some good traveling music, and down the road I go," Michael said as he belted out the words to Radar Love blaring out over the speakers.

The road sign said Highland next five exits. Michael glanced at his wrist watch; it was one-forty-seven p.m. Taking exit number three, Michael stopped at a Union 76 station for gas and directions. Fifteen minutes later, Michael was pulling into the parking lot of the Old Railroad Depot in downtown Highland.

Michael sat in the car cautiously looking around for anything or anybody that appeared suspicious. Getting out of the car, Michael paused and looked at his reflection in the car window just long enough to make sure the Colt .45 in his belt was covered by his jacket. Blending in with the crowd, Michael was in the middle of the old depot within minutes. "Now to find that shoe store," Michael said to himself. "Dog gone, this place is huge…there must be four or five shoe stores in here…I should have gotten the name of the place from Tim," Michael thought. "I'll just have to try each one until I find somebody working in one named Jimmy," Michael said as he walked through the mall. Michael's luck was holding out because on his second stop, he met Jimmy Newton, the self-proclaimed long time good buddy of Tim.

"Yeah man, I talked to Tim yesterday, and he told me to keep an eye out for you," Jimmy told Michael. "He told me if I saw you, to give you this phone number and tell you to call him, and he'll tell you where y'all can meet up," speaking in a high country twang. "If you want, you can use the store phone," Jimmy offered. Michael took Jimmy up on the offer and called the number Tim had left for him. On the tenth ring, just as Michael was getting ready to hang up, Tim picked up and piped in, "Joe's pool hall, eight ball speaking." "Hey eight ball, it's me," Michael said. "Where are you?" Tim asked. "Do you have wheels?" "Yeah, but it's time to change it out. I don't want to leave it anywhere close so the wrong people find it. Do you know a place we can dump it for a while…you know, somewhere no one will find it?" Michael asked. "Yeah, I know a place. You sit still and I'll be there in about thirty minutes," Tim told Michael. "I'll be close to Jimmy's work place keeping my eyes open for you," Michael responded. "Thanks for the phone man," Michael told Jimmy as he laid the phone on the counter and walked out the door. "Yeah, sure anytime," Jimmy replied. "What a creep," Jimmy mumbled under his breath as the door closed.

"I look too much like I did when I was at the beach," Michael thought as he caught a glimpse of himself in the store window. Let's see what some dark sunglasses and a Kyle Barnhardt hat from this NASCAR store do for me," Michael said as he made his purchase. As he ambled through the mall waiting on Tim, the irresistible smell of a hot dog stand filled his nostrils. Michael stepped up to the stand and ordered four hotdogs all the way and a tall cold draft beer. Settling down on a bench about a hundred yards from the shoe store, Michael sat back to enjoy his lunch. He enjoyed the cool mountain air as he sipped his beer and ate the dogs. Maybe I can relax a little now...just maybe me and Tim can sit back and chill without the dread of looking over our shoulders the whole time we're up here. Finishing the last of the dogs, Michael tossed the trash into a nearby can, leaned back on the bench, folded his arms over his chest, kicked his legs straight out in front of him and relaxed the best he knew how. Michael kept a sharp eye on the shoe store waiting for Tim, when suddenly, Michael spotted him sporting new blue jeans, a bright red designer parka and Ostrich skin cowboy boots! "Well, so much for staying low key," Michael thought. Michael let out a loud whistle grabbing Tim's attention. Tim whipped his head in Michael's direction and saw him sitting on the bench waving at him. "Long time, no see, where you been? What a tan! You been on some island with those hula dancers or something? Sure am glad to see you, man!" Tim said as he gave Michael a slap on the back. "Won't nothing keeping me in North Carolina one second more the way I saw it, so I took off," Michael replied. Man, I've been living like a big shot on what I call my floating party barge. The heat was getting too close, so I ditched the car, picked up a yacht and headed south down the ICW… ended up in Florida. Figured it was time we met up, so here I am," Michael said. The boys sat on the bench and talked for more than an hour before Tim asked," What you want to do with that car?" "We need to hide it or dump it in a place where it won't be found too easily," Michael responded. "If the cops tie those stolen cars to one another, they'll know where we are. Then it won't be long before they start looking for two guys from the Kranston Corner area flashing a bunch of money around." Michael said. "I know the perfect place… nobody will ever find it where I've got in mind. Get the car and follow me," Tim said. The boys got up and walked to the parking lot. Michael was shocked to see that Tim was still driving the truck he had stolen from Cape Shore. "You know we're gonna have to get rid of that vehicle also, don't you Tim?" Michael asked. "Man I ain't getting rid of my ride! I've become attached to it." Tim snapped. "Okay, you do whatever you think you have to do; but, if you keep it, remember you're one step closer to getting caught," Michael replied. "Ain't nobody up here looking for that truck; besides, I've changed the license plates three times since I left the beach. I ain't getting rid of my truck, man!" Tim again asserted. "We'll talk about it later," Michael said as he unlocked the door on the Chevy. As Michael backed out of the parking lot, he signaled to Tim to go ahead and he would follow him.

Michael followed Tim for what seemed to be over an hour before Tim made a left turn and drove slowly down a muddy dirt road. The road lead deep into the woods, past an old falling down barn, past several piles of trash, a burned down house, behind another barn; and, then turned onto another road that went another mile and a half leading to a gravel road, that seemed to disappear right into the side of a mountain. Tim pulled over and stopped and waved out the window for Michael to pull up next to him. Michael pulled up and asked, "What now?" "You drive in front of me now," Tim said. "Once we get to the end of this road, you'll come up on a big chain that crosses the road. Stop there and I'll drop the chain so you can pass. Michael eased his car around Tim's and followed the path of the road, driving cautiously and slowly. Rounding a small curve, Michael abruptly stopped just before hitting the chain. Tim walked up to the car and said, "We'll pull the car in that mine shaft, and believe me, nobody will ever find it in there." "Sit right there for a minute and let me move that chain," Tim said as he walked over to the post holding up the chain.

The chain looked like it had been hanging there sense the Civil War, orange with rust the chain looked like it had been placed there to lock all the secrets of the mine deep inside. Taking hold of the post, Tim wiggled it a few times and easily lifted it out of the hole and laid it down so Michael could drive across it. "Pull inside as deep as you can and stop," Tim shouted as Michael started down the road leading into the mine shaft. He then eased the Chevy down the mine shaft a couple of hundred feet. "That's good right there," the echo of Tim's voice shouted down the mine. Michael shut off the engine and got out of the car and walked toward the burning head lights of Tim's waiting truck. "Come help me with my gear," Michael said. "No man, I'll wait right here and keep a lookout while you do it." Tim rebutted. "Okay," Michael said a little disgusted as he headed back down the tunnel. A few minutes later, Michael emerged from the tunnel weighed down with guns, camping gear and a knapsack that contained his part of the money. "Man, that would of been a lot easier if you'd helped me," Michael said as he threw his gear into the back of the truck. "Yeah, I'm sure it would of been," Tim said as he turned up the volume on a tape playing…stressing the speakers blasting out "Sweet Home

Alabama." Michael's butt had barely hit the seat when Tim gunned the engine and sped off down the road like he was in a cross country race.

TWENTY ONE

"Michael I'm gonna take you to meet some good ole boys that I grew up with," Tim said eagerly. "These boys got everything you'll ever need, they got women, booze, cards and smoke." "That sounds real good, but I'd like to get a motel room, a hot shower, and a few days sleep first," Michael replied. "No man! You can do all that stuff later. It's your first night in the hills, and you've got to have a drink of shine, and kiss a mountain girl, or you'll have bad luck the rest of your life. That's the law up here, you know," Tim kidded. Michael could see he wasn't getting anywhere talking to Tim, so he decided to offer him a compromise. "I'll tell you what," Michael said, "I'll go with you and I'll have a couple of drinks and after that, you take me to the motel, okay, is that a plan?" Tim glanced in the rearview mirror looking into Michael's eyes, "Yeah man, that's a plan; and, if it ain't, we'll come up with another plan," Tim howled, at the same time leaving a trail of rubber as he sped out on the road.

Tim pulled up to what he referred to as a cabin. Michael expected banjo music to start playing. It was far from what he thought a cabin to be. It was more like a rough honky-tonk dive. "What the devil kind of place is this?" Michael asked with profound uneasiness. "This here is a good ole boy kind of place," Tim came back with. "You could go anywhere on earth and not meet the kind of people you're going to meet in here tonight! Come on in, they're expecting us," Tim said as he slammed the door of the truck and headed towards the door. Rustic didn't come close to describe what the place looked like. Michael paused for a minute after going through the first set of doors and looked inside. The tables and chairs were made up from broken furniture that was probably taken from the local dump. The bar sorta looked like the one Miss Kitty had at the Long Branch, yet nowhere near as nice; and, from the smell of the place…WHEW!... it hadn't been cleaned since the day it first opened, if then. Tim grabbed the inner door handle and slung the door wide open. We could see more than two dozen tough guys sitting around the place. It looked as though they were competing on who could get more ink. Michael followed Tim through a thick cloud of cigarette smoke hanging like a smelly fog throughout the room. By the look of these folks, they had been there all day…maybe all week. Cigarettes were hanging from their lips, ash trays were heaped over, forming small piles of smoldering cigarettes burning over on the tables. With Mason jars half-filled with clear liquor in one hand…a burning cigarette in the other, at best, this was truly a motley crew. Inmates had halos compared to this crowd. As we walked through the maze of on-lookers, we felt their eyes following us, watching every move. The looks were far from friendly.

"Where's Jimmy," Tim asked the big man tending bar. "Jimmy's in the back room…what you want with 'em?" the mountain of a man asked. "We're friends, he told us to meet him here," Tim snapped, as he walked past the bar toward the back room. Throwing back a ratty old blanket hanging on nails across the top of the door, Tim spotted Jimmy through the thick smoke. "Jimmy, how's it going man? I told you we'd be here, didn't I?" Tim said loudly. "Everything is everything!" Jimmy responded. “Come on in and have a drink. It’s good homemade shine. Some folks call it apple pie, but we call it the real mountain dew, and the price is just right.” Jimmy said. Apprehensively, Michael followed Tim, even though his gut was telling him he was in the wrong place.

Tim took a seat at Jimmy’s table. “Come over here, Michael, here’s a chair for you. When Michael sat on the chair, it fell apart. Not so sure how this crowd would react, Michael said, “I guess this one had a lot of use,” He then moved the chair to the corner and took another one from the table next to theirs. Tim and Jimmy, along with all the other dudes let out big belly laughs as if the joke was on Michael. “I meant to warn you about that chair before you sat down!” Jimmy laughed. “It’s okay, everything’s fine,” Michael said a little embarrassed. “Let’s have that drink, then you can take me to the motel,” Michael said. “Man, we just got here…relax…have a few drinks and loosen up…these are my friends,” Tim said. “If we don’t except their hospitality, they’ll be offended and believe me you don‘t want to offend this crowd,” Tim said. Ain’t that right fellas? You don’t want to offend this crowd, do you?” Tim asked with a hint of worry in his voice. “No, I don’t want to offend anybody; I’m just a little tired. Okay, yeah, give me a drink, I’ll relax and have a few drinks with you,” Michael said. “All right, at a boy! You just relax and let’s have some fun. It’s been a long time since I heard you laugh.” Tim said. “Hey, good buddy, don’t worry about a thing. You’re in my town now…I won’t let anything bad happen to you. You took care of me at the beach, now it’s my turn to take care of you,” Tim said as he handed Michael a half-full Mason jar. “Down the hatch, Michael,” Tim shouted over the loud beat of the music. “This will put hair on your chest.” Tim said with a big laugh as he up-ended his Mason jar filled with Waterfall County’s finest mountain dew. Following suit, Michael lifted his jar and turned it bottoms up, empting the jar and slamming it down on the table. "Well, if we're gonna do this thing...let's do it right," Michael said as he reached out and picked up another Mason jar and lifted it to his lips. Michael was determined to match Tim drink for drink. It didn't take long before the boys were both feeling the effects of the strong liquor.

Laughing, joking, loud music blasting, and a hot poker game...YEAH...we got it going on, "Yeah, that's it," Tim bellowed, "What do you say, Michael, let's me and you get in that poker game, I'm feeling lucky. Matter of fact, I ain't feeling much of nothing right now!" "You all got any money?" Jimmy asked. "Yeah, we got money," Tim said, as he pulled out a one inch thick roll of hundred dollar bills and slammed it down on the table." "Yeah, boy, I guess you do," Jimmy said as he stared at the wad Tim had laid out on the table in front of him. "If you want to play for that kind of money, I've got a couple of the boys that are always looking for a money game. I'll call them in, if you want me to?" Jimmy asked. "Yeah, go get 'em, their money is just as good as anybody's else's, ain't it?" Tim smirked. Jimmy got up and disappeared into the main room of the bar. He returned a few minutes later with two grizzly old guys in tow that looked like it had been a long time, since either of them had smiled or bathed. Michael looked up through somewhat glazed eyes and thought, "I ain't drunk enough to know that a shot house, liquor, and high stakes poker, ain't painting a pretty picture."

All of a sudden, the cabin went from a noisy honky-tonk to a quiet seriously tense game room. A few minutes later, Michael was sitting at a table with Tim and three mountain men types, playing in a high stakes poker game. Every fiber of Michael's being told him to fold his cards, get up and walk out of the game but knew he couldn't. I just can't leave Tim here alone among these sharks; they'll eat him alive. Tim you are such a fool, Michael thought as he watched him thumb through the stack of hundred dollar bills looking for a five to call a petty bet. Michael sat with his back to the solid timbers of the oak-walled cabin, being well aware of, and cautiously prepared for whatever might happen next.

As the game progressed, Michael proved that he was quite a poker player. Michael found that the observation and listening skills that he had learned from Snake Woman were also useful at the poker table. Ole Wild Bill, who was sitting across from Michael, had the habit of scratching his right ear, when he was holding a good hand. Next to him, Festus's tell was that he took a short sip from his liquor before laying down a bluff, and Tim…mmmh…thought, no matter how bad a hand he was holding, if he threw down a big enough raise, he could buy the hand. Of the first seven hands dealt, Michael won five of them. Consequently, that would be the trend the remainder of the evening. The more games Michael won, the more shine Tim drank. Over time, Tim's demeanor changed from the loveable, joke telling Tim that Michael had known for the past five years to someone Michael had ever seen before. "Go ahead big man, my boy, you win again, pick up your winnings and deal another hand," Tim yelled as he demanded the waitress bring another round of drinks. "What do you know; my old friend Michael wins another one!" Tim shouted sarcastically. "One heck of a card player you've turned out to be, old friend," Tim exclaimed over and over again, becoming boisterously annoying.

Michael ignored the taunting until he was unable to ignore it any more. "Yeah, I'm the big winner! If you weren't so drunk, you could see the cards in your hand ain't winners and you'd stop trying to buy every pot!" Michael shouted back.

Michael was totally unprepared for what happened next. Tim screamed out, "You sorry bum, you're cheating!" Michael raised his eyes from the hand he was holding, and stared directly into Tim's eyes. "You heard me! You're cheating! As long as I've known you, I would never have thought you'd cheat me. I've known you for a long time, Michael, and I know you ain't that good a card player!" Tim shouted. "You're drunk, Tim. You don't know what you're saying!" Michael responded. "Let's get out of here and we'll talk about it tomorrow," Michael said diplomatically. "I ain't going anywhere, but you are!" Tim shouted. "You can get up and leave but the money stays here." Tim said, as he rose and stood on unsure feet! "Man, I ain't cheating. I've just been lucky, that's all," Michael explained pleading with Tim. "You're cheating, I shoulda known I couldn't trust you, you're just a punk cheat! Now, get up out of that chair and get the devil out of here, right now!" Tim said as he lifted his tee shirt, revealing the butt of his 9mm Beretta.

Michael slowly rose from his chair and reached for the stack of bills in front of him. "Nope, ain't happening bro! You're gonna leave that here!" Tim said irately. "Tim, you don't have to do this…we can both walk away from this… don't push this play. It's the liquor talking Tim," Michael said as he stood steadying his footing. "You made the decision on how this would play out when you decided to cheat me!" Tim shouted with intense anger. Michael stood looking directly into Tim's eyes, when in a blink of an eye; Michael threw back his jacket and drew the Colt .45 from his waist band, and "BAM" firing one deafening shot that struck Tim squarely in the middle of his chest. Tim stood stunned staring at Michael in disbelief for a brief second before slumping forward; face down onto the card table, dead. Michael wheeled the pistol in the direction of the players, who were glued in their seats in shock. "Don't get any ideas," Michael said as he reached over and took the Beretta from Tim's hand laying prostrate on the table. "What the heck have you done?" Jimmy screamed. "You've killed him... you crazy? You killed Tim!" Within an instant, Michael heard the sound of a pump shotgun having a round racked into the chamber. Michael froze perfectly still waiting for a blast. Looking over his shoulder toward the sound, Michael found himself looking straight down the barrel of a 12 gauge shotgun pointed straight at his head by the bartender.

"I didn't want any of this to happen," Michael uttered as he slowly turned toward the bartender, sticking the .45 back into his waistband. "It was a fair fight," said one of the players. "I don't care about no fair fight." the bartender bellowed. "Take that dead guy and git him the devil out of here, all of you! Git out, git out now!" Without further instruction, several of the players picked Tim up and toted him toward the front door, while the other bar patrons watched. "What you driving?" Jimmy asked, as he and others tried to balance Tim's body on their shoulders. "That blue Ford right there, that's Tim's truck." "I guess I have to take that," Michael answered. The men tossed Tim in the back of the truck like a sack of potatoes. Reaching over the side rail, Michael rolled Tim up on his side and reached into his pocket and took his truck keys. "Now get your butt the heck out of here and don't ever come back! I don't need no law coming 'round here asking no questions. You ain't been here, I don't know you. I ain't never seen you before! Now, you git as far away from here as you can!" Jimmy shouted as Michael started up the truck and drove away.

Michael's head was buzzing, not only from what had just happened, but from the moonshine. His ears were ringing form the explosion of the .45 and the confusion that was racing through his mind. Michael shook his head violently trying to clear the cob webs that had taken over his normally clear thought patterns. "What am I gonna do now?" Michael said over and over, as he drove full speed down a dirt road not sure where it would take him.

Waterfall County Sheriff's Deputies, Bill Moore and Elton Michaels pulled up to the Country Cobbler Restaurant for their supper break. The clock on the dash read seven-twenty-five p.m. They got out and walked up to the take out window. Bill leaned around Elton and ordered his usual: two BBQ sandwiches, crispy french fries and a diet coke. Elton leaned around Bill's wide shoulders and said, "Give me the same thing that he's having, he'll pay for it. I'm gonna wait in the car and listen to the radio, bring mine when it's ready," Elton told Bill. Sitting in the car, Elton could smell the thick wood smoke mixed with the aroma of fresh pork cooking on an open fire behind the drive in. He was thinking about how good the sandwich was going to be before it even got to the car. Bill climbed in the car and tossed the oil spotted brown paper bag of food between them on the patrol car seat. "Hey, what you think about us going over to the Baptist Church on Stone Mason Road and listen to choir practice while we eat?" Bill asked as he pulled out a hot french fry from the top of the bag. "Sounds good to me," Elton responded, as he fired up the patrol car. The Baptist church is only about five minutes from the Country Cobbler Restaurant. Bill and Elton picked at the french fries during the short drive before preparing for the wonderful goodness waiting for them in the greasy brown paper bag.

Elton pulled the patrol unit right up next to the church so they could hear the heavenly music coming from the slightly ajar windows while they enjoyed their supper. With the choir belting out, "Give Me That Old Time Religion," Bill unloaded the bag preparing to enjoy the delicious food, "Man, it don't get much better than this, does it Elton?" Bill asked. Before Elton answered, he said, "Bill, take a look at that truck coming toward us…that guy is all over the road!" Bill watched the truck weaving back and forth as it sped toward their position. "Good thing there ain't nobody else on the road, cause that guy would kill them," Bill said as he re-wrapped his sandwich and pushed it back in the paper bag. "Yeah, I guess we better check him out," Elton said as he started up the car.

Just as Michael passed the church, the patrol car pulled out right on his tail. "Tim, darn it, I told you to dump this car," Michael said in a loud voice as if Tim could hear him! "If they run that tag, I've had it." Suddenly the inside of the truck turned blue with the flashing lights for the patrol car.

Michael hit the gas and began looking for an advantage. "I'll never be able to get away from them out here on the highway. I'm in a four wheel drive truck so I need to find a dirt road," Michael thought talking to himself. "There's one up ahead on the right." Hitting the brakes hard, Michael slid the truck down the dirt road sideways. The dirt road was dark and the only thing he could see was the darkness and trees as he passed them at more than sixty mile an hour.

The patrol car couldn't keep up once the truck turned down the dirt road. "742 Waterfall County, we'll be checking out a possible 10-55 on Stone Mason Road," Elton called as he pulled in behind the blue Ford. "742, county get me a 10-28 on MKL-0899 North Carolina." "10-4, 742 stand by one." "County, 742, MKL-0899 comes back to a 1964 Ford Comet four door registered to Betty Norden, New Craven, NC." "742, be advised there is a stolen report on that tag," County reported. 742 county we'll be 10-61 with that vehicle one mile east of the Stone Mason Baptist Church," Elton called. Bill reached over and flipped the switch on for the blue lights. "742 County we are 10-43 with that vehicle, we are just passing the Stone Barn Country Club on Stone Mason Road, send backup," Elton hollered over the radio with excitement! "County, 742 10-4." "Keep me advised of your 10-20 updates," County advised. "742 County 10-4, we're turning down a dirt road with no name on the right side of the road between Stone Mill Road and Rock Quarry Road!" Elton yelled. The only thing the deputies could see in front of them was the dimming of the tail lights on the truck they were chasing. They soon began to fade as it got farther and farther away from them.

Michael could see there was a fair distance between him and the patrol car. "This is my chance to get out of the truck and get into the woods, he thought. They'll never be able to find me if I can get into those woods." Michael said to himself confidently. "Next time I go around a curve where they lose sight of me, I'll throw them off my trail!" Michael shouted. Suddenly, right ahead of him was a sharp left turn. Michael had to slam on brakes to keep from losing control of the truck as he rounded the curve. All clear, Michael reached over and turned the head lights off and drove into the first break in the woods on the left side of the road. Pulling in and stopping quickly, Michael took his foot off the brake as the truck went totally dark. Michael reached into the floor and picked up the Mini-14 and held it in the ready position as he pointed it back towards the road. Michael could hear the siren blasting down the dirt road as the patrol car neared and quickly passed his position and drove down the road out of sight. Michael jumped out of the truck and quickly walked to the back of the truck where he retrieved his backpack, bedroll, several canteens and the load bearing vest still filled with extra magazines for the Mini-14. Pausing only a second, he looking at Tim's lifeless body, and thought how this could have ended so much better, if Tim had only dropped him at the motel like he had asked. "Well, no time to worry about that now," Michael said, as he slung the back pack onto his shoulders and disappeared quietly into the dark woods. Michael moved as deeply into the woods, as fast as he could, before stopping to take a bearing and looking back to see if he could see the cop car. Stopping to catch his breath, Michael could see the patrol car driving slowly back down the road, headed toward the abandoned truck with Tim's body in the back. On its first pass, the patrol car drove right past the truck that Michael had driven deeply into the woods, partially obscured by trees and heavy bushes. Michael could see the patrol car turning around and then the side lights came on, "If those lights hit a reflector on that truck, that thing will light up like a Christmas tree," Michael whispered as he rolled down his sleeves and prepared to head deeper into the woods. The patrol car moved slowly down the road coming to a stop right alongside the road where Michael abandoned the truck. Michael didn't wait to see what was going to happened next. He knew that when they found the truck they would find Tim's body, and this would be the beginning of a brand new game.

TWENTY TWO

Taking a fix on the stars, Michael headed due north. "I'm making good time but I have no idea where I'm going," Michael said quietly as he put as much distance between him and the truck as humanly possible. As the sun began to rise, Michael found himself in a thicket on the side of a hill about two hundred feet high overlooking a huge pasture. "There ain't nothing like this down at the beach… looks like a dairy farm or something," Michael thought as he surveyed the pasture and the surrounding woods line.

It was easy for Michael to see at least one airplane and two helicopters buzzing around looking for him. "All I have to do is stay in the woods line and they'll never see me," Michael mumbled as he contemplated his next move. Suddenly several miles behind him, Michael could hear the sound of a pack of dogs on the hunt. Michael wasn't sure if the dogs were on his trail, or if they were somebody's hunting dogs asking for breakfast. Michael knew one thing for sure, he didn't want to find out. Deciding this probably wasn't a good place to wait and see, he moved to the edge of the woods to take a better look. Squatting behind some bushes, Michael looked around the pasture that lay before him with his field glasses. "It must be at least two miles wide and two and a half miles long. Man, this would be a terrible place to be in the middle of, if the cops were on the edge shooting at me. I don't want to lose all this valuable time, but I don't want to be caught out there in the open either," Michael said. Scanning the edge of the pasture with the glasses, Michael said, "I'll make my way around the edge staying in the tree line, and when I get right there, I'll move up that gorge to the top of the hill. I'll be able to get a good look at the whole valley from that ridge...might not be a bad place to take a quick break," Michael whispered to himself. "No time like the present," Michael said as he picked up his pack and slung it onto his back. It took Michael the better part of two hours to go all the way around the pasture and up the hill to the location he had spied from down below. Leaning with his back against a sweet gum tree, Michael said, "Man what a view," as he sat catching his breath. From Michael's perch, the valley laid out in front of him was like a huge bowl. Michael could see every approach to the pasture, except the ones behind him. Closing his eyes, Michael said, "I'll catch a quick nap and figure out my next move. Michael dropped quickly off to sleep, but didn't get much rest, as he harrowingly dreamed of Tim's demise.

Awaking to the sounds of a body of men moving through the woods, Michael quickly readied the Mini 14 for action. Not seeing anyone, he reached into his knapsack and took out his field glasses to see who was making the noise. Across the pasture, Michael could see a small group of lawmen standing just inside the woods line looking out over the pasture.

Tom Hassel was a Captain with the Waterfall County Sheriff's Department, and had been with the department for more than twenty five years. Tom was a law-enforcement officer who didn't take much of anything too seriously. Tom had lived nearly his whole law-enforcement career with an attitude that bad things happen to other people, it can't happen to me. Many of his co-workers thought this was just the kind of attitude that was going to get him killed one day, and prayed they wouldn't be next to him the day it happened.

"Listen to me, I ain't gonna walk all the way around the edge of that field, when we can put a man right here with a high powered rifle, and cover us while we walk straight across to the other side." Capt. Tom said. "Elton, you been bragging about how good you are with that deer rifle the past five years, now's your chance to prove all that talk. Go get that deer rifle with the scope on it and you and Bill are going to stay here and cover us while we cross that field. When we get to the other side, ya'll come across and we'll cover you." "Yes sir, Captain Tom!" Elton snapped. "Get your gear and get ready to move," Capt. Tom yelled, as Bill and Elton moved behind a large rock to cover the field with Elton's old faithful deer rifle. "Sure hope Capt. Tom knows what he's got here, this ain't a typical situation," Elton said.

Taking the lead, Capt. Tom started out into the field with the other officers following single file. "I sure am glad I'm the one who's got the rifle," Elton said to Bill, as the other men started across the field. "Me too, I wouldn't want to be anywhere near that open field if anything goes wrong," Bill, shaking his head, answered.

Michael sat calmly watching the men as they entered the field. "That may be the last mistake some of them will ever make," Michael thought, as he gingerly laid the Mini-14 across his lap, and methodically began to disassemble and clean it. Carefully taking the rifle apart, Michael cleaned each part before laying it on his leg. The disassembling and cleaning took Michael only about four minutes. Michael then quickly, but carefully reassembled the weapon and snapped a fresh magazine into the feed well and racked a .223 round into the chamber. Without getting up or giving away his position, Michael slithered like a snake behind the sweet gum tree he had been leaning against, and raised the rifle taking aim on the deputies, who were now nearly three hundred yards from the edge of the woods. "Five hundred yards from me, and four hundred yards before they can reach cover… this ought to be like shooting fish in a barrel," Michael whispered. "I'll give them another hundred yards, and then I'll nail the door shut on 'em!" Michael uttered coldly.

Following the deputies in the rifle's sights, Michael watched as they entered no-man's land. Targeting the lead officer, Michael eased his finger into the trigger guard and flipped the safety off on the Ruger. BAM! …a single shot rang out from the rifle as the group leader fell face-first dead in the bright green grass of the pasture. Immediately, the other officers began to scatter like chaff in the wind. Carefully and coolly, Michael took aim at another officer and BAM!...a second officer fell. Michael targeted another and then another, and with the sharp report of the rifle, two more officers went down. Taking aim at the only remaining man on his feet, Michael said, "Okay, that's enough, that'll keep them busy for a while. That'll give 'em something to think about, and give time to put distance between them and me," Michael said, as he picked up his pack and headed up the hill, out of sight.

When the shooting began, Bill and Elton anxiously watched the hillside looking for any sign of trouble. "Tom is down…I repeat…officer down… call it in to county!" Elton screamed. "Where are the shots coming from?" Elton screamed, as report of the rifle echoed throughout the valley! "Bill, get some help quick, he's killing all of them, get some help, right now…need help now!" Elton raised his rifle and fired off a shot, hoping to distract the shooter. "Maybe he'll duck his head and the guys will be able to get out of that field of fire. Scanning through his rifle scope intensely, Elton hollered, "I don't see anything …I can't see where he's firing from." Bill continued to scream for help over the radio! Deputy Tom Hassel dead, two deputies critically wounded, and two police officers seriously wounded was the toll of the cow pasture incident. It took more than two hours to clear the hillside before anyone could go back into the pasture to extricate the dead and wounded officers.

"We've got to have a lot more help to get this guy. Call for all available backup including surrounding counties. It's going to take an army of officers to catch this one. Bill interjects, "Call EVERYBODY! I don't know who that guy is, but he sure knows what he's doing," Elton said to Bill, as the last wounded officer was being loaded into an ambulance. "You don't learn ambush tactics like that accidentally!" Bill reacted. "I think we're looking for somebody with military experience here, you just don't set a trap like that without some professional training," said Elton. He's crazy like a fox!" "What was Captain Tom thinking… going out in the open like that, I can't believe he's dead. He never did believe it could happen to him. I just can't believe it. I don't want to believe it!" Elton continued.

"Let's go back to the truck and see if we missed anything. Something tells me that we ain't getting the whole picture here. The truck is at Charlie's garage in Highland, let's go take another look at that truck," Bill suggested.

Arriving at Charlie's garage a little more than an hour later, Elton said, "Hey Bill, look at this," as he took three license plates from under the front seat of the truck. The license plate on the truck was stolen from New Craven…that's down close to the coast, right?" "The truck was stolen from Kranston Corner and whoever stole the truck was smart enough to take the license plates off and switch them with other plates to make it harder for us to trace them," Bill surmised. "Let's go to the sheriff's department and look at the APB's for this month and see how many other cars were stolen from the Kranston Corner area this month."

Arriving at the sheriff's department a short time later, Bill and Elton pulled all the APB's for the month and started looking for a pattern on stolen cars in the Kranston Corner area, as well as any other crimes that may be linked to theirs. "Bill, take a look at this bulletin… there was an armed robbery at Cape First Bank in Cape Shore." Elton continued, "This one says the only suspect identification they have is two males, average body types, using handguns, shotguns and high power rifles." Bill weighed in, "It might be a far stretch, but it's the only lead we have right now. Let's call the Cape Shore Police Department and see if they've been able to develop any suspects in their robbery." Bill continued. "I'm already on it," Elton said as he picked up the phone and dialed 411. "Chief Swain, this is Deputy Elton Michaels with the Waterfall County Sheriff's department. We've had an incident that we believe may be related to a bank robbery that occurred in your jurisdiction a few weeks ago and I'd like to ask for your help." Elton went on to tell Chief Swain about their incident involving the shooting death of one of their officers and the injuries to four other officers. Chief Swain was more than cooperative in sharing the information he possessed with the deputies. Chief Swain advised Deputy Michaels that his department had been able to develop Michael Schomeck, a local trouble maker, and an unknown male as viable suspects for their armed robbery. "Up until now we have had no clues on where the suspects may be," Chief Swain told Elton. "Because of the size of my department, I will be unable to send any officers to join in on the manhunt." "I will contact the Seaside County Sheriff's Department and have the Chief Deputy call you."

"I'm sure the deputy who had his truck shot all to pieces, by those two, would like to come up and lend a hand," Chief Swain said. "I'll get this working on my end, and get back in touch ASAP. One other thing, have you been able to identify the other suspect yet?" Chief Swain asked. "Yeah, Chief we identified him by fingerprints; his name is Timothy Blackhardt, a local trouble maker from Taylorsville, a little town about thirty miles South of Highland. So far, we haven't been able to tie Blackhardt to our suspect, but we're working on it. "I can't say I ever heard that name before," Chief Swain said, changing the subject, "I'll be back in touch as soon as I make contact with the Sheriff.

The next afternoon Deputy Sheriff's Aaron Hill, Francis Gaza and Special Deputy Fred McDaniels departed Valley Field Airstrip, en route to Highland Airport. Two hours later they landed at Highland Airport, where Bill and Elton anxiously waited for them. After making introductions, Deputy Gaza briefed Bill & Elton with the information they brought regarding Michael Schomeck. Deputy Gaza read from Michael's arrest file; "Michael Schomeck, white/male, twenty years old, raised by his father Master/Sgt. Joseph J. Schomeck." "Michael served four years as a juvenile offender for residential arson. He is currently wanted on an open warrant in Seaside County for carrying a concealed weapon and felony escape. Michael is an expert woodsman; he is expert with edged weapons, knives, hatchets, axes, rifles, shotguns and handguns. He is highly skilled in escape and evasion. I guess he learned that stuff from his daddy," Francis continued. "Other than that, we don't have a whole lot on him. He knows how to handle a rifle," Aaron added, "He darn near sent me to the hereafter a few weeks ago, and I'm ready for some payback." Bill joined in, "He waited on the side of that hill for our men to get to the middle of that pasture and shot them all to pieces. I'll tell you the truth, I don't know how any of them got out alive." "Only because he wanted them too," Fred said. "This boy really knows what he's doing," Elton said. "He's just an animal doing everything he knows how to do to survive. Fred McDaniels piped in, "Listen to me fella's; this boy learned everything he knows from a witch in Seaside County and he learned real good. He's probably the best you've ever seen, he may be the best there ever was," Fred continued. "But if you can show me where he was last seen, I'll lead you to him... after that, he's all yours." "I don't want to be in on the kill," Fred said. "I ain't gonna say I'm superstitious, but whoever makes the kill on this hunt, better have his juju right, 'cause if not, he'll be short-timing in this world. That boy's protected by the witch! Fred informed the crew. As Fred talked about Snake Woman, he reached inside his collar and pulled out a leather cord necklace with a small leather pouch hanging from it. He nervously rubbed the leather pouch with his thumb and forefinger, as if he was warding off a potential spell cast on him just for talking about her in that way. "I wouldn't be surprised if she didn't have a bunch of them voodoo dolls made up in our image, sticking pins in them right now," Fred said as if he really believed it." Stop all that bull, Fred," Snapped Aaron. "Michael Schomeck ain't nothing but a wild animal, and believe you me, if I get the change to bust a cap in him he's mine, juju or no juju." "Like I told ya, I'll track him, I'll put you on him; and, if I get pushed up in a corner, and it's him or me, I'll put him down. I just want to go home to mama, but I ain't gonna go out there looking for this kill," Fred stated. "I don't have any intentions of getting on the wrong side of Snake Woman. This woman is mean when she needs to be. Don't nobody go 'round her, if they're smart. Too many folks been hoodwinked into thinking she's a friend. For one thing, I ain't too sure how anybody wants to be ‘round her, I don’t think she’s ever had a bath. She’s treacherous, boys. Anybody who takes to her has one thing in mind…survival! Steal, cheat, lie, swindle, even kill…whatever you have to do to survive, you do it! She’s been fending for herself for a long time. If you do something to somebody she cares about, she’ll hurt you! I’ve seen it. One thing I’ve come to know is that she loves this kid. Just telling you what I know to be true about this witch, and witch she is, boys!

TWENTY THREE

Michael reached the top of the hill and could see no one was following him, so he eased off a bit. "Conserve your energy, you'll need it later when they're on you heels," Michael gave thought. Coming to a clearing, Michael could see a small wood framed house. "Somebody's home, I see smoke rising from the chimney," Michael ventured. "Let me get a little closer and see what I can see," talking to himself. As he slipped up next to the house, he could see a lady standing at the cook stove fixing breakfast. She looked like somebody's grandma. Michael never knew his grandmother. He had moved so much, the only people he was close to was his immediate family, if you want to call it that. As Michael stood there watching the woman move about in her kitchen, he had reflections of how his mother would hug him and remind him that his father did love him, he just didn't know how to show it. His thoughts then went to Snake Woman. "Whether it was real or not, I felt Snake Woman loved me, by simply helping me survive, and that's all that mattered. I loved her too, despite how others saw her," Michael reminisced.

Walking around the house, quietly taking a look inside, it appeared as if no one else was there. Michael stepped up to the back door and knocked gently. The lady cracked the door open and asked, "Who's there?" "Ma'am my name is Michael, I'm a stranger in these parts and I need something to eat," he said kindly. "I have money and I'll be happy to pay for whatever you can spare." The door swung open, "Come on in young man, you don't need no money, I'll give you something to eat," the lady said with a big smile on her face as she looked at Michael with her trusting soft blue eyes. My name is Betty. "Thank you Miss Betty," Michael said as he laid his pack down and leaned his rifle against the back door frame.

"Sit yourself down right here, and I'll fix you something," the lady said as she motioned for Michael to take a seat at the kitchen table. Placing a cup of hot coffee down in front of Michael, she said in a soft country twang "Sip on this, while I fry you a couple of eggs. I'm sorry I don't have more to offer you son, but I haven't had any extra money to go to the store and buy groceries in a while," she said as she cooked. Michael was taken back when he looked down at a plate of fried eggs, homemade biscuits and strips of bacon. "Oh, that smell of bacon," he recalled. Michael hesitated for only a moment before bowing his head and silently praying. "It's good to see a young man pray before he eats these days," said the lady. "Thank you ma'am, my grandmother (thinking of Snake Woman) taught me not to eat without thanking the Maker for it." Michael responded as he picked up his fork and began to eat. Finishing quickly, Michael stood up and thanked the lady for the food. "Ma'am, you wouldn't by chance have a map laying around that I could take a look at, do you?" asked Michael. "Are you the one they're looking for, Michael, you know the police?" asked the lady. Hesitantly, Michael said, "Yes ma'am, I am." "I don't know why they're after you, but I'm sure you had good reasons, you know, for whatever you done," said the lady as she opened a kitchen drawer and pulled out an old map. "Ma'am, I only did what I had to do to stay alive and survive. "Everything went terribly wrong. It seems like my whole life has been upside down. I didn't mean nobody any harm," Michael tried to explain. "Michael, I can tell you want to have a good spirit about you. I don't want to hurt your feelings or make you mad at me, but I feel there is an evil presence about you that sometimes takes over. I have a way of knowing these things. I don't know what happened to cause you to be in so much trouble, but I don't reckon that makes much difference now. I'm thinking whatever you done you had to do," the lady stated as she handed Michael the map. "Thank you for the hospitality ma'am," Michael said politely as he pulled open the kitchen door. "Ma'am, I'm gonna leave something for you right here on the door step… you use it for whatever you need," Michael said as he laid a large stack of crumpled money on the door step. "Son, you don't have to do that!" the lady said. "Ma'am, I want you to have it, 'cause I won't have any need for money after today. You were kind to me for no reason, accept because you wanted to be," Michael said obligingly. "Well, I hate to hear that for you, Boy, but I am a little short on money. I do thank you for it, Michael," the lady reacted.

Pausing briefly outside the back door, Michael looked into the old lady's eyes and said, "Would you do me a favor if I asked you to?" "Yes, Michael," the lady answered. "If you hear that I got killed today, would you say a prayer for me?" Michael asked. "Yes Michael, I'll pray for your soul," answered the lady. "You kind of remind me of someone I'm close to back home, and I know she'd pray for me, that's why I asked," Michael said. "No matter about that, son. I'll pray for you because we all need someone praying for us once in a while, don't we?" "Yes ma'am, we sure do," Michael said as he picked up his gear and started back into the woods. "Michael," called the lady. "Yes ma'am," he answered. "God bless you." "Thank you ma'am," Michael responded as he walked out of sight, back into the woods. The old lady stood at the back door, watching Michael as he faded into the deep green and golden brown color hues of the woods. As the lady watched, she quietly began to pray for Michael.

Officers from more than twenty police departments, five sheriff's departments and the highway patrol around Waterfall County were assembled at the county court house for a briefing on the suspect Michael Schomeck. Deputy Sheriff Francis Gaza and Aaron Hill conducted the first part of the briefing, before turning over the meeting to Sheriff Morris.

Pointing to a large county map with a pointer, Sheriff Morris spoke, "We believe our suspect is located in this general area. We will deploy twenty squads of twelve men, each around the base of this hill, and systematically work our way up to the top. If everything goes as I planned, by us making this show of force, we will drive our suspect to an area where we can contain him. Once he is contained in this area, pointing at an area high-lighted with a yellow circle, "He'll have to decide whether he wants to make a stand or surrender. Boys, just between you and me, after what he did to those officers in the pasture, I hope he does resist!" asserted Sheriff Morris. "One of my deputies will lead each group. Once everyone gets into position, I'll advise you over the radio to advance at your own pace. When we get about halfway up the hill, we'll stop for a rest; this time will allow our suspect to move into our target area. I'll check on each squad's status, and when everyone is ready to continue, we'll move on up the hill to the second check point. I want all of y'all to remember one thing. This hill is more than a mile high and right much of the terrain is straight up and down, this won't be a cake walk for any of us." Morris continued. "There are a couple of hundred people that live up there, so if you make contact with the suspect, don't go shooting wildly and kill some innocent bystander. Don't forget this boy, Schomeck has killed two people so far, and I don't want to visit anymore families delivering that news!" Morris said. "It's ten thirty right now. When we leave here, proceed to your assignment location, check in, and stand by for further instructions."

Michael wiped the rain from the crystal on his watch to see the time, it was quarter past ten. "There's an old barn down at the bottom of this valley. I'll slip in there and take another look at the map and see what my next move needs to be," Michael whispered as he looked over the depression in the valley. Michael slowly descended down the slippery grass covered slope and thought out loud. "Not as much air traffic today as I thought there would be, they must be grounded because of the weather," Michael whispered quietly. "If I was the cops, I'd try to surround this hill and try to catch me when I come down. Well, maybe, but I ain't gonna come down from here in the daylight," Michael whispered again as he skidded down a six foot drop on the seat of his pants. "I'll sit here for a minute and make sure the coast is clear before I head to the barn," Michael said as he squatted in the thick brush twenty five yards inside the woods line. Michael watched the area for a little more than a half hour when he decided to move over to the barn. Covering the hundred fifty yards from the woods to the front door of the barn only took Michael a little more than a minute. Hesitating for a stop, look and listen, before pushing open the door, Michael entered the barn with the mini-14 in the ready position.

Suitably surprised to find the barn empty, except for an old hoot owl and some bats that had taken residence there, Michael moved to a horse stall in the middle of the barn and settled down for a quick look and strategy session with the map.

Michael sat down with his back to the stall boards. When he noticed the floor was covered with hay, Michael decided, "This might be a good time and place for a quick nap." Having survived for the last three days on little more than two or three cat naps of ten minutes each, was influencing Michael's ability to reason. Shucking his pack, Michael settled down on the hay and closed his eyes. As Michael listened to the rain softly falling on the tin roof, he drifted off into a well-deserved deep sleep.

Sheriff Morris was on the radio, "All squads begin your search. You are authorized to begin your ascent of the hill at this time. Most of the squads made good time as they climbed the rocky crags, out-cropping and loose stones that the hill was formed by. Fred McDaniels was the lead man and tracker for the fourth squad. Fred was responsible for blazing a trail up the hill and look for any sign of the suspect along the way. "That old man climbs hills like a Billy goat!" Elton said to Bill as they struggled with the steep grade. Seeing some of the men falling behind, Fred stopped and waited for them to catch up to him.

The fourth squad had been climbing for more than two hours when the call came out from Sheriff Morris for all squads to hold their position. "Just when I was getting the hang of this, he wants us to stop," said Fred. "If he's just getting the hang of this, I don't want to see him when he knows what he's doing," Elton said to Bill. "Save your breath," Bill said panting. "Look at him Elton, that old scudder ain't even breathing hard and I'm about to pass out." "Look at him Bill, he ain't even resting... he's looking for sign!" Elton replied. Fred came down the hill quickly to Elton's position. "I picked up some sign," Fred said quietly. "Elton, I've picked up some sign up there close to the edge of that out-cropping. The rest of y'all just sit still; Elton, you come with me," Fred said. Fred and Elton got up and started up the hill. "Hold on, I'm coming too," Bill said. "That's my partner and wherever he goes, I go." "Well, get a move on then," Fred expressed.

"Look right there," Fred said. "You'll have to use your imagination a little, 'cause I know the rain's washed out a lot of the sign, but if you look real close, you can see that someone was going down this hill right here, and slipped. See how there is a rut right here that looks like someone slid down the hill on their butt," Fred added. Elton and Bill looked at the place where Fred pointed, but neither of them could see the sign. "Yeah, I see it Fred!" they both answered in unison. "Boys, let me tell you something; if that mark right there, wasn't made by a man, I'll eat my hat," Fred said vehemently. "I'm gonna follow this sign and see where it leads me. You two sit right here while I check it out. I'll come back and let you know what I find out." Fred said eagerly. "Okay, Fred we'll wait fifteen minutes; but, if you're not back by then, we're coming after you," Elton said with Bill agreeing. Fred walked away saying, "I'll be back, boys." As Fred moved like a ghost across the rain-covered forest floor following the sign, he said to himself, "Mmmh…in fifteen minutes, you'll come after me? You two couldn't find your own butts with both hands, and you're gonna come after me!"

Fred followed a clear trail for a little more than a mile, when he came to the place where Michael had squatted, possibly watching over the valley, looking for movement. "That's it," Fred said silently, "He's in that old barn. Let me get back to the guys and call the troops in, before we move in any closer," Fred anticipated, as he back tracked to Bill's and Elton's location.

"We were just getting ready to come after you," Elton said as Fred emerged from the woods. "I think I found him boys," Fred said as he pulled a plug of tobacco from his pocket and cut off a plug and shoved it into the corner of his jaw. "I believe our boy is holed up in a barn about a mile that way. I think it's time to let your Sheriff know what's going on here," Fred said. "Did you see him?" asked Elton. "Nope," Fred responded. "Then how do you know it's our man in there?" How do we know there's anybody in there at all, if you didn't see anybody?" Elton asked. "I think we need to take a couple of men and go down to that barn and see what we actually have before we call all the men from their search locations," Elton said using his official tone. You go ahead and do whatever you want to, after all, you are in charge," Fred told Elton. "But first, let me tell you about this boy. I've trailed many a man in my days, and the man that left that sign, ain't no ordinary man, who's just taking a stroll in the woods. This man, who left that sign is somebody that knows how to cover his tracks. Another thing… I'll be willing to bet if you crowd go rolling down that hill, on top of him…some of y'all are gonna get dead! Now I've had my say. You do what you think's best," Fred said as he leaned over and spit at Elton's feet.

Elton sat back thinking for a moment. When he got his thoughts together, he transmitted to Sheriff Morris where Michael was hiding out. The radio crackled, "Have Deputy McDaniels get into a position where he can keep a close eye on the barn," said the Sheriff. "You and your men wait out of sight, until I get there. I'll assess the situation when I arrive," Sheriff Morris continued. "Elton, do you copy?" "10-4 Sheriff," Elton answered. "Elton, do you understand?" asked the Sheriff again. "10-4 Sheriff, loud and clear," Elton again responded. Bill piped in, "You know what he's telling you, don't you?" "Yeah Bill, he's telling me that if I don't follow his orders, after this it's all over and I'll be out of a job," Elton said answering Bill. "Yep, that's exactly what he's telling you, so you know what you've gotta do, right?" Bill asked. "Yep, sure do! It means we gotta get down there now, and catch this guy before he gets away again!" Elton said as a matter of fact.

"Fred, the Sheriff wants us to get down there and see if this feller is holed up in the barn or what," Elton said. "Bill, you gather the men around and I'll brief them on our plan," Elton said. Bill called the men in for a quick meeting. Elton conducted the meeting saying, "Fred found some sign he says, just over that hill, and we believe Schomeck is down in that valley holed up in that old barn. The Sheriff wants us to deploy down to the valley and surround the barn. Be as quiet as possible on your approach to the barn; because, we don't want him to know we've surrounded him, until everyone is in position. I want us to set up a one hundred yard perimeter all the way around that barn, and keep it covered while me, Bill and Fred approach the barn to see if Schomeck's in there," Elton said.

"I ain't going down there to that barn!" Fred said in protest. "I'm telling you right now, Schomeck is down there in that barn. He's heavily armed. He's already killed his partner in crime, one deputy and crippled two others, that we know of, and Fred McDaniels ain't gonna be his next victim! Elton, you may not want to hear this, but if Sheriff Morris told you to move down there on that barn, with just the twelve of us, without waiting for the rest of the troops to get here...well, he's a bigger fool than you are! This ain't like playing cowboy and Indians when we was young'uns, Elton. It's a bad plan, and I ain't gonna have any part of it." Fred said as he sat down on a log nodding defiantly. "I'll get in position where I can keep an eye on the barn, and let you know if there's any movement; but, I ain't going down there to get killed," Fred said as he cut a new chaw from the plug of Black Mariah chewing tobacco. "Morris to Elton, come in Elton," squawked over the radio. "Go ahead

Sheriff," Elton answered. "Give me that radio," Fred said, "I'll tell him what I think about that plan of yours!" Sheriff Morris speaking, "Elton, have you deployed Deputy McDaniels yet, like I told you too?" "Negative Sheriff," answered Elton. "Well, what the heck you waiting on boy?" asked the Sheriff. "I'm ten minutes away and I want the latest on that suspect's location as soon as I get there. Is Deputy McDaniels right there?" asked the Sheriff. "10-4 Sheriff, he's listening." "Deputy McDaniels, can you get into a position so you can keep an eye on the barn until I arrive on your scene?" Sheriff Morris asked. "Yes sir, Sheriff," answered Fred. "Deputy McDaniels, take whatever resources you need and take up a position where you can observe the barn from a safe distance. I do not...repeat...I do not want anyone to approach that barn until we deploy all of the officers to their field positions." Fred turned and stared at Elton. "Yes sir, Sheriff, I copy," responded Fred. "Sheriff, I'm gonna turn you over to Elton now. I'm gonna get myself into a position where I can observe the barn. Come find me when you get here and I'll brief you," Fred said, as he handed the radio back over to Elton, then turned and headed up the hill. "Elton, I don't know what's going on up there, but if you like you job, you'd better not screw this up!" Sheriff Morris said over the radio. "No sir Sheriff, I ain't screwed nothing up, we're sitting right here waiting for you before we do anything, just like you told us to," Elton said. "10-4, I'll be at your location in less than five minutes, meanwhile, stay still till I get there."

Fred followed his trail back to the spot where he had picked up the first sign. As he approached, he stopped and scouted out a position where he could observe the barn from good cover. "There's a good spot right there," Fred said to himself as he made his way down the hill to a large rock over-looking the whole valley. Fred pulled out a small pair of binoculars and traced the foot prints from the edge of the woods line, through the heavy grass, and up to the front door of the barn. Continuing his sweep, Fred looked all the way around the barn to reassure himself that whoever had gone in the barn was still there. "The boy must be getting tired, that was the second mistake he's made today," Fred said quietly. "Yep, he's still in there," Fred whispered as he leaned over and spit.

Sheriff Morris arrived at Elton's squad location at four-thirty-five p.m. "Okay Elton, where's Mr. McDaniels?" asked Sheriff Morris. "Follow me Sheriff, I'll take you to him," Elton said respectfully. Forty-five minutes later, which took Fred only 15 minutes, Elton and the Sheriff reached Fred's position. Fred heard the officers approaching and went out to lead them in. Moving to the rock from a back door type position, Fred pulled out the tobacco plug from his pocket and offered it to the Sheriff. "No, no thank you Mr. McDaniels," Sheriff Morris responded. "Sheriff, don't think I'm being too disrespectful with what I'm about to say, but calling me Mr. McDaniels is like putting a hat on a pig, it just don't fit. You'd be doing me a personal favor if you'd just call me Fred." "Okay Fred, I'll do that," the Sheriff replied.

"Okay Fred, run me through what we know here." Morris said. Fred began, "Look straight down that draw to the tall dark shaded bush at the edge of the field on this side. See how there's a darker area that runs toward the barn leading from that bush?" Fred asked. "Yeah, I see it," Morris answered. "I believe those are Schomeck's foot prints that are running toward the barn. I say he was running because you can see how long his strides are, and they're way too far apart for him to have been walking. Besides, he probably didn't want to be out in the open that long in case airplanes and choppers start back flying." "Here, take these glasses, Sheriff," Fred said as he handed the

Sheriff his binoculars. “Start right at the front door and look all the way around the barn. Maybe your eyes are better than my old worn out eyes are, but I don’t see any footprints leaving the barn,” Fred said respectfully. “Fred, I doubt my eyes are near as good as your old worn out eyes are, but I’m just like you, I don’t see anything that would indicate to me that anybody left the barn either,” the Sheriff replied. “Well then Sheriff, in my opinion, whoever went into that barn is still in there,” Fred said confidently! “Fred, how much more day light do we have before the advantage we are enjoying turns into his advantage after it gets dark?“ asked the Sheriff. “Sheriff, the way I figure it, we’ve got just over an hour…maybe an hour and a half, before it’s gets dark and then another hour when it’s dark enough for him to slip out of that barn and back in the wood,” Fred answered. “Sheriff, if that boy gets back into the woods, there ain’t no telling how long before he makes another mistake like this one,” Fred said. “If it was me, I’d take what men we have and deploy them all the way around the barn. This part might sound stupid… but, then I’d have them make enough noise so that Schomeck knows we’re out here. Maybe we can keep him in there until its morning. Once that sun comes up, we’ll have the advantage. Sheriff, let me tell you something right now, that boy don’t know it, but we got him right where we want him...just like when you’re hunting a wild animal, we’ve run ‘em to ground.

Sheriff instructed Elton, “Get the men into position so they can watch the barn from every side. Once they get into position, have them sit still, until I give them the signal.” “What kind of signal, Sheriff?” Elton interrupted. Sheriff responded, “You know to stand by the radio Elton and wait for my signal like we usually communicate, got it?” Sheriff continued, “Once everyone is in a safe position, I want the men to intentionally make enough noise to let Schomeck know we’ve got him surrounded. Elton, let me make it perfectly clear to you, so you can make it clear to the men; they are NOT to engage the barn unless they are fired upon first, is that clear?" asked Sheriff Morris. "Yes sir, perfectly clear," answered Elton. "Bill, you go with Elton and don't let him screw up any of this," Morris said, "I'm holding you responsible to not let Elton screw up." "Thanks a lot Sheriff, but please...please don't hold me responsible for what Elton does," Bill responded. Elton and Bill relayed the Sheriff's message verbatim, before breaking the twelve men into two man teams and sending them to their assigned positions.

TWENTY FOUR

Michael woke from dead sleep in panic not knowing how long he had been asleep or where he was. Shaking his head trying to clear his confusion, he glanced at his watch and his eyes nearly popped out of their sockets in disbelief. "It's five-ten p.m…what was I thinking…I know I can't let my guard down like this, not if I expect to make it out of here alive," Michael said disgusted at himself. Grabbing the Mini-14, Michael ran to the back of the barn and peeked out through a crack between two boards. As he scanned the edge of the woods, Michael couldn't see anything, but had an uneasy feeling in his gut. Suddenly, like a hammer strike, Michael's greatest fears were realized.

Deep in the woods, a few hundred yards behind the barn, Michael spotted a uniformed deputy moving from behind a tree to a big rock, where he dropped down and concealed himself. Michael furiously ran to the other end of the barn and looked through the crack between the doors. Scanning the ridge above the barn, Michael spotted two more officers a hundred and fifty yards out and seventy five feet above him. "I'm in a heck of a fix here. They've got me in a cross fire…if anything gets started, they'll cut me to pieces," Michael said out loud. Running back to the center of the barn, Michael flopped down in the stall, pausing just long enough to gather his thoughts. "It'll be dark in another hour, I'll make my break then," Michael said to himself, with more composure this time.

Five-thirty p.m. Sheriff Morris sent out a radio message for the officers to make their presence known. Officers all around Michael began to make subtle sounds to let Michael know he was surrounded. Michael was already a step ahead of the officers as he moved from one side of the barn to the other. Michael checked the front and rear of the barn making mental notes to where each officer was located in the woods. Michael took out his knife and cleared away a place on the floor of the barn to make a drawing in the dirt showing each officer's position...how many officers there were...their locations... whether or not they had long guns, shotguns or hand guns.

Looking up after studying the drawing, Michael dropped his head, knowing that he was badly outnumbered. "If I try to make it out of here, I won't stand a chance," Michael whispered feverishly. Michael felt like a rat caught in a trap. "I ain't going out there, so they'll have to come in here and get me," Michael said as he looked around the barn to see what he could use to help defend his position. "Sure ain't much help here," Michael said as he leaned his back to a ten by ten inch post that supported the roof. Michael spent the rest of the evening in the darkness listening to the movement of additional officers moving into their positions to cover him. "I wonder how many there are out there." Michael asked himself. "Too darn many," he quickly answered.

Michael leaned his head back against the post, closed his eyes and thought, "This must be how the men at the Alamo felt while Santa Anna surrounded them. If they try to come in here, they'll have to pay for this property just like Santa Anna did," Michael said out loud. As Michael sat thinking about the battle to come, he used the heels of his boots to dig an indention into the dirt floor of the barn. Retrieving a broken board from the stall next to him, Michael began to scratch and scrape out a hole in the dirt thinking, "I'll dig a fox hole for protection, or am I digging my own grave?" nervously laughing to himself.

All was quiet in the woods as the officers took turns trying to get a nod or two in before daybreak. The wet cold mountain air made it a long night for the officers as they took turns watching and sleeping. The last thing they wanted to happen was for Schomeck to slip out of the barn into the darkness.

"Zero-five-hundred hours," Sheriff Morris said as he reached over and shook Elton awake. "It's gonna start getting light in about an hour Elton, get up, clear your head. I'm gonna need you wide awake for this." "Yes sir Sheriff, I'm up," Elton said as he sat up, stretched, and tried to shake the sleepiness from his mind. "Where's Bill?" asked Elton. "I sent him out to check the troops and make sure everyone is in position. I told him to report back to this location when he finished," Sheriff Morris said, "he's been gone a long time…the better part of two hours. He ought to be getting back any time now. I hope that little son of a gun is still in there, and didn't get out before we got the men deployed around him," Fred said as he listened carefully for Bill's return. "Sheriff, Bill will be back anytime now. I just heard him…he's about a hundred yards out," Fred said softly. "Fred, how is it you know Bill is a hundred yards away?" asked Sheriff Morris. "I can tell it's Bill 'cause I know his gait. He'll take two or three steps, stop, shuffle his feet, and then walk three or four more steps a little faster, then slow up. You point your ear over toward that sweet gum tree and listen up. Don't you hear that rustling of the leaves coming this way? Fred continued. "Wait a minute; I do see Bill dragging himself up the hill!" Sheriff Morris said astonished.

Ten minutes later, Bill came up the hill huffing and puffing out of breath. Wiping the sweat from his brow he addressed the Sheriff, "I...I went to every post and...I... told them not to move ...and...not to fire unless...unless they were fired at first. Let me sit down a minute... and catch my breath," Bill said as he flopped down hard, behind the rock at the Sheriff's feet. It was about five minutes before Bill could re-tell the results of the assignment to Sheriff Morris. "Sheriff I went to every post, and told ever man, to sit still, not to make any move on the barn, and not to fire, unless they were fired at first. I told them that you were going to go down to the valley and make contact with Schomeck at first light. You would then try talking him into giving himself up. I told them that whatever happened after that was up to Schomeck," Bill reported. "Okay I guess we're ready then," said Sheriff Morris as he reached into a turnout bag and pulled out a bullhorn. Morris flipped open the battery door cover and tilted the bullhorn to the side dumping out the old batteries. Quickly reloading the battery compartment with fresh batteries, the Sheriff turned on the power switch and observed the power LED turns on.

"Fred, can you lead me down the hill to that large rock at the bottom of the valley?" Morris asked. "Yes sir Sheriff, I sure enough can. I'm ready when you are," Fred responded as he rose from a crouched position. He gathered his gear and walked toward the ridge line. "Elton, get your squad ready, we're gonna move down to the valley floor. Tell everyone to take their time and be as quiet as possible. If we do this right, maybe we can get into position without alerting whoever's in that barn," Morris said. "Elton, make sure to tell the guys not to bunch up as we go down that hill," Morris continued. "Make sure to keep at least twenty feet between each of those officers as we go down this hill," Fred snapped. "We've come this far, and ain't got nobody shot yet, so let's don't give Schomeck a bunched up group of men to shoot at now," Fred added. "Right on, Fred! Right on! If the Sheriff would put me in charge of this whole operation, we'd have this over and done with, and be eating BBQ before noon." Elton answered. Fred turned his head, looked at Sheriff Morris, shook his head as he asked, "Where'd you get that guy, Sheriff? You know if he was a dog...where I come from, we'd a drowned him when he was a pup." "Yeah, I know Fred, but his mama is my wife's sister, so I'm obligated to do the best I can for him," responded Morris. "Well, that clears a lot of things up for me," Fred said with a chuckle, as he headed out just before daybreak.

Trudging through the heavily overgrown weeds, staying between the trees and working at a better than forty degree decline, it took Fred and the men more than forty minutes to descend the hundred and fifty feet to the valley floor. Once everyone was on an even plain with the barn, Sheriff Morris deployed the squad to positions with natural cover so they could watch the front and both sides of the barn.

Zero-six-forty-five-hours the sun had just begun to break over the horizon, scanning from side to side, Sheriff Morris checked his officers' positions one last time before engaging the suspect, Michael Schomeck. Flipping the power switch to the on position and raising the Bullhorn to his mouth, Sheriff Morris took a deep breath, squeezed the trigger and announced, "Michael Schomeck, this is Sheriff Morris with the Waterfall County Sheriff's Department. We have you surrounded, throw out your weapons and come out with your hands up. Releasing the trigger, Sheriff Morris could feel his pulse pounding in his forehead as his adrenalin pumped wildly through his veins. Turning to Fred, "I hope the next thing that happens is that door swings open, and I see guns being thrown out!" said Morris. "Don't count on it." Fred replied calmly.

Michael eyes popped wide open at the first squawk of the bull-horn. "I guess it's time," Michael said as he cautiously rose to his feet and grabbed the Mini-14 that had been leaning against the wall of the horse stall he was resting in. Michael quickly, but carefully, moved to the end of the barn where he had heard the Sheriff's announcement coming from. Peeking out the crack in the door, Michael began to count and memorize the positions of the officers who had surrounded the barn. "Holy cow, there must be at least three hundred cops out there and they're everywhere!" Michael said, as he dropped his glance to the ground and blew out a long labored breath. Turning to the door, Michael yelled, "I ain't coming out…y'all have to come in and get me!" Hearing Michael's challenge, Sheriff Morris called out, "We've got your position surrounded, son. There's no way out. Throw out your guns and come out with your hands up. You don't have to die here today. Come out with your hands up." "Don't call me son, I ain't your son!" Michael yelled, as he eased the barrel of the Mini-14 up to a crack in the door and pointed it in the direction where the bullhorn was coming from. Depressing the trigger of the Mini-14, Michael emptied a full magazine in the direction of the Sheriff. As soon as the last round left the barrel, Michael sprinted to the center of the barn and dove into the hole he had dug, covering his head with several heavy boards he had pulled from the stall walls.

Without notice, rounds began striking the rocks where Morris and several of his men were secluded. Having time to do nothing but duck their heads, the men huddled as low as possible until the last report of the rifle sounded. "Fire…Fire…Fire," Sheriff Morris screamed as he raised his head from behind the rock and began shooting in the direction of the barn. Almost simultaneously, the officer's stationed all around the barn began to fire into the barn as well. Bullets were whizzing everywhere. Rounds went in one side of the barn, passed straight through and headed in the direction of officers on the other side of the barn. Officers who heard the rounds whizzing by, thought Schomeck was firing at them from inside, so they fired back with even more fervor.

The officers were actually shooting at each other without knowing it. With Michael hearing the hundreds of gun shots, he did everything he could to make himself as small as possible, digging himself into the ground even deeper. After more than five full minutes of continuous gun fire, Sheriff Morris got on the bull horn and ordered everyone, *"Hold your fire…Hold your fire!"* "Sheriff you know they're shooting at each other, don't you?" Fred asked, as he raised his head from behind a rock. "What do you mean?" asked the Sheriff. "I tried to tell that numb nuts," nodding towards Elton, "Not to set these men up in a cross fire position, but he don't listen too good, do he?" Fred asked. "No, apparently not," Morris answered. "See how you've got your men surrounding that barn? If the men continue to shoot at each other, all Schomeck needs to do is keep his head down waiting for the men to use up their ammo so he can escape. "How do you think we need to be set up then?" asked Morris. "We need to cover the front and the right side with most of the men, and then you set two squads of ten or twelve men each, and have them cover right flank and the rear. That way, if we have to return anymore fire, we won't hit one of our own guys," Fred determined. "Elton, did you hear what Mr. McDaniels…Fred, just said?" Morris asked. "Yes Sheriff, I heard him," Elton replied. "I want you and Bill to get on the radio and coordinate the movement of the men into those positions ASAP. Is that clear?" asked Morris. "Yes sir Sheriff, perfectly clear!" answered

Elton. "One more thing Elton, said the Sheriff, "If you screw this up, family or no family, your fired, is that clear?" "Yes sir, perfectly clear," Elton answered again. "Well then, get to it!" barked Sheriff Morris.

As soon as the gunfire stopped, Michael lifted his head out of the hole, and looked around to determine which directions the officers were advancing before an assault on the barn. At the same time, he dropped the empty magazine from the Mini-14 and slapped a full one in its place. Racking a round into the chamber, Michael ran to the door fully prepared to engage the advancing officers. Michael was completely surprised when he looked out and didn't see anyone advancing on his position. Michael stood behind the door contemplating what their next move would be.

"Michael, this is Sheriff Morris, throw out your weapons and come out of the barn," announced Sheriff Morris again. Michael's answer was loud and clear as he took careful aim and fired two; three-shot bursts from his rifle striking the rock directly the front of Sheriff Morris sending chips of rock into his face. "Darn, that was too close for comfort!" Morris yelled as he ducked back behind the rock, wiping blood from his face. "You all right Sheriff," asked Fred. "Yeah, it's rock fragments that cut me, I'm okay. I'm not hit," Morris replied.

With thoughtful hesitancy, knowing he had to send his men in harm's way, Morris replied, "Are the men in place yet, Fred?" Fred replied without any hesitation, "Yes sir, Sheriff. I believe we're ready this time." "Give the order for the officers to fire at will." Sheriff Morris said. "Picking up the radio, Elton relayed the Sheriff's orders verbatim, "All units…fire at will… I repeat fire at will!" For the next thirty minutes, the only sounds that could be heard were the steady echo of the blasts of gunfire echoing through the crisp mountain air. Simi-automatic rifles, pistols, revolvers, shotguns and high power hunting rifles were releasing a constant stream of hot lead into the barn from every possible angle. As soon as Michael heard the first shot fired from the officers' weapons, he turned and sprinted toward the protection of his foxhole. Before he could reach the safety of the hole, Michael was struck by a bullet in the right shoulder, spinning him around violently and knocking him to the ground. Seriously wounded, Michael crawled the rest of the way to the hole, and slid inside while applying pressure to the wound with his hand; at the same time, keeping his head as low as possible trying to avoid being hit by another round. As Michael lay in the hole, trying to get the bleeding from his wound under control, he wondered how long the shooting would go on before the officers took their next cease fire.

TWENTY FIVE

Although help consisting of hundreds of officers, Sheriff Morris realized they did not have the training, nor had they faced such an intense manhunt. He gave careful thought to protecting his men from this suspect who was determined to kill anyone who threatened him. The situation had escalated into far more than his team could handle. It was necessary to summon the SWAT experts to stop this cop killer.

The Sheriff met with Captain A.O Lea of the SBI SWAT Team. "Capt. Lea's team had been requested to report to the location of the siege by Sheriff Morris when he saw that he wasn't going to be able to talk Schomeck out of the barn at the beginning of the siege.

"It appears that while your men are firing on the barn, the suspect takes cover, and when the firing stops, he comes out of his hole, and returns fire on your positions," Lea said. "We'll need to keep his head down while my team approaches the barn. If your men can supply suppressive fire on the barn, I'll get my men into position to make an entry into the barn and confront the suspect as soon as your men stop firing," Capt. Lea advised Sheriff Morris. "We'll do whatever we have to do to end this incident, without any more of our officers getting hurt Capt. Lea," Morris responded. Capt. Lea explained, "Sheriff here's the plan… I'll have my men assembled right here, ready to cross the field to the barn. I'll have a sniper positioned on that ridge," pointing to a position above the rally point. "If our suspect comes close to the door, my guy will go ahead and take him out. If not, he'll be in position to provide us with close support, as we make our way across the field to the outside of the barn." Lea continued. "Once my men are into position, it's important that all officers on the outer perimeter, know not to shoot into the barn! As soon as the officers stop firing, my team will force entry into the barn and confront the suspect. Depending on how the suspect responds to my orders to drop his weapon and comply with our arrest order, will determine our response to the suspect," Lea added.

"Sheriff, just to make the facts of this situation perfectly clear; I understand that this suspect has killed at least two people, one of them a law enforcement officer. He has wounded several other officers and he has been ordered to comply with your lawful order to come out of the barn and surrender himself to law enforcement, and he has failed to comply on each and every occasion to your lawful orders. Are all of those facts true and accurate to the best of your knowledge, Sheriff?" asked Capt. Lea. "Yes, those are the facts," Sheriff Morris confirmed.

"Sheriff, are you at this time, requesting the assistance of the SBI to assist your department in the apprehension of this suspect, Mr. Michael Schomeck?" Capt. Lea continued. "Yes, Capt. Lea," Sheriff Morris answered. "Thank you Sheriff. I had to ask you those questions for the record. Now that you have officially requested our assistance, we'll be glad to help you anyway we can," Capt. Lea said respectfully.

Following the established pattern of firing for a long barrage and then ceasing fire, Michael waited in his hole nursing his wound, waiting for the cease fire. Then, as suddenly as the firing began, it stopped. Michael raised his head out of the hole and reached for his backpack. Dumping out its contents,

Michael reached into the pile and grabbed a tee-shirt. Lifting his blood-soaked jacket, Michael shoved the tee-shirt inside and pressed it down hard on the wound. Slowly rising to his feet, Michael moved over to the door and again peered out waiting for the Sheriff's next demand for him to surrender. Michael was offset a little when the demand didn't come, "What's changed?" Michael thought. "Why has he changed his pattern?" Michael's alert level immediately was elevated by the change in the Sheriff's pattern...he's preparing for an assault. I'll be ready for him!" Michael assumed.

"Okay Sheriff, my team is assembled and we're set to assault the barn at exactly zero-eight-forty-hours," Capt. Lea advised. "The officers on the perimeter have been advised about the plan, and at exactly zero-eight-thirty-hours they will start firing on the barn," Sheriff Morris explained. "All officers will concentrate their fire to the left side of the barn, leaving your team a clear lane to move up to the barn. Once your team is in place at the front door, all officers will cease fire and wait further orders from your team," Morris concluded. "Okay Sheriff, I'm going down and join my men now. We'll begin our move to the barn at exactly zero-eight-thirty-five-hours. Wish us luck," Capt. Lea said. "Don't take any chances with this guy Captain. If your guys get a clear shot, take it," Sheriff Morris said calmly, yet coldly. Pausing a moment, Capt. Lea nodded at the Sheriff, turned and moved slowly to the staging area where his team was gathered at the bottom of the hill behind a large rock. Capt. Lea watched the hands of his wrist watch as the minutes clicked by. At exactly zero-eight-thirty-hours, the first shots began, intensifying rapidly increasing until the sound of gun fire was nothing but a steady roar. The minutes clicked by steadily until the hands read zero-eight-thirty-five-hours. Capt. Lea held two fingers in the air at shoulder level and made a small circle signaling the team to perform their last equipment check and prepare to move out. Upon seeing this signal, the team members locked and loaded their weapons, and rose to a crouching position anticipating the short move across the field to the barn that was only a hundred and fifty yards and a few seconds away. Rising to a standing position Capt. Lea held up his hand and motioned forward as he left his position of safety, and led his men across the open field that ended at the front doors of the barn. At that very moment, Sheriff Morris gave the order to cease fire. Within seconds, all officers on the perimeter stopped firing.

Braced for the next round of fire Michael slowly walked back over to the foxhole, easing himself down, he laid the Mini-14 across his chest preparing his mind for the next onslaught of wild firing by the officers. Lifting his jacket, Michael looked at the gaping wound in his shoulder and thought about everything that had happened to bring him to here and now. Michael put down his head and dreamed of swimming in Bogue sound one more time.

Looking down at his watch, Capt. Lea held up one finger, signaling ten seconds until entry. Each officer was at their sharpest, mentally and physically, waiting for the signal to breach the door.

Lea, with his MP5 nestled into his right shoulder, holding the weapon in a position with his right hand, held up his left hand, and began to count down using hand signals to the assault team; Five...Four...Three...Two...one...Breach... Breach...Breach! Upon the breach order, each team member, two by two began to pour into the barn, scanning for hostiles, and seeking protective cover. First team member to the right, second one to left, alternating right and left until all team members were inside barn.

Suddenly, the end barn door slammed against the inside barn wall. Michael jumped to his feet and raised his rifle. Go... Go...Go... echoed through the barn as several black uniform clad SWAT team members rushed in through the barn door. Michael pointed his rifle in the direction of the deluge of officers and started firing from the hip. Immediately, several team members returned fire. The deafening sound of gunfire rang throughout the barn. Expending the last bullet from his magazine, Michael calmly reached for another mag and reloaded his weapon quickly. Snapping back the bolt, he was ready to resume the heated gun battle that had begun only a few seconds ago.

SWAT team members moved through the barn in unison like a well-oiled machine. Seeking cover, acquiring a clear sight picture of the suspect, reloading their weapons; and, at the same time, avoiding bullets whizzing by their heads, then pressed forward just as expected, of these highly skilled warriors.

Capt. Lea moved toward the suspect's position, he was struck in the chest by a round from Schomeck's weapon, and fell prostrate to the floor of the barn. Luckily, divine intervention was with Capt. Lea. The round struck a magazine he carried in his vest pouch, causing the round to ricochet without penetrating into his body armor. Rolling to cover, Capt. Lea reached under his vest, checking to see how badly he was wounded. He was relieved to find that the bullet had not penetrated his vest and he was only slightly injured.

The gun fight continued to intensify, as SWAT members moved in closer to Michael's position. Before being overwhelmed, Michael decided to fall back to the rear corner of the barn, where he took a position behind a heavy supporting beam, before he continued to return fire on the advancing officers. Suddenly, silence fell over the barn, as all gunfire stopped.

"Michael, give it up, you don't have a chance," Capt. Lea yelled out! Michael responded, "I can't...I can't go back to jail." "It's better than dying," Lea replied. "Listen son, I ain't gonna lie to you, things don't look very good for you right now, I know. It's time to show everyone you can make a good decision when you're forced to...give yourself up!" Capt. Lea restated.

Michael quietly reached down and extracted the nearly empty magazine from the Mini-14, and replaced it with a full one. He knew he would never be taken alive. He was adamant about never going back to prison. Within seconds, Michael recalled his short life of crime as his emotions and adrenalin took over. "If only I had listened to my gut when I was just nine years old," Michael thought. "Maybe being alone and having no friends wasn't so bad. I've killed the only one I knew had my back when we were in prison. I don't know if I killed that cop at the bank or not. I probably did. He should have never come over there. I had to do it. I had to kill that cop coming over that open field for me. There was no way I was going to let him think I couldn't get him first. Snake Woman may have been a witch, but she loved me and I knew it. She spent time teaching me things. Might not have been the right things, but I had to survive somehow. Fairlane, why'd he rag me every chance he got? I'd like to put one of these bullets in him. Why did my father turn me away? Why was I so stupid to get hooked back up with Tim? I had it good with Snake Woman, if she had only asked me to stay. Maybe I would have, maybe I wouldn't. That sorry Buddy Thompson. That's who caused all this mess I'm in. I wish I'd killed him too. I suppose there's hate inside me and I ain't wanted to believe it. I figured it was survival just like the wild animals in the woods. Snake Woman always told me if I wanted to survive, that's what I'd have to be like. I did what I had to do. That's what I gotta do now," Michael said, as he sprang to his feet. Leaning forward to see where the SWAT team members were located, Michael ran from the stall toward the center of the barn firing wildly.

Sgt. Murdock, armed with a shotgun, was moving from outside the barn door to the interior of the barn when he heard the commotion of the automatic gunfire and spotted Michael running toward his position. Having seen Capt. Lea take a round and go down, Sgt. Murdoch raised his shotgun and pointed it in direction of Michael's advance and squeezed the trigger.

Cautiously, the members of the team moved to the center of the barn, covering Michael with their weapons as Capt. Lea approached Michael to check for vital signs…there were none. Reaching for the walkie-talkie on his side, Lea called Sheriff Morris and advised, "Sheriff, the suspect is in custody and be advised he is 10-7." The shotgun slug had found it's mark striking Michael in the right temple. Michael was dead before his body hit the floor.

Snake Woman's day began just like all the rest. Before dawn, out of bed to begin her chores, fix breakfast, feed the chickens, slop the hogs and stoke the fire under the well-seasoned black cauldron. Blowing on the embers, Snake Woman made them breathe life once again. As the embers began to glow, Snake Woman added a couple of pieces of oak, bringing the embers to a roar. "The rays of the morning sun appeared especially bright today as they burned off the heavy mist in the pines," Snake Woman noticed.

Headed back to the cabin, she was surprised by a strange howl from deep in the woods. Turning quickly, she lowered her gaze and peered deep into the woods. "What in the world was that?" she whispered faintly.

Nearly two hundred yards away, she spotted a swirl of smoky colored mist twirling at the base of an old Pine tree.

Pausing only a second, she leaned back into her rocking chair, took out her pipe, struck a match and held it to the pipe while she deeply puffed. Blowing out a long ribbon of smoke, Snake Woman's eyes filled with tears…she knew her prediction had been realized. Slowly raising her head, Snake Woman wiped the tears from her face, and smiled. "I will always thinks of you, Michael, when 'er I sees the mist in the pines. Peaceably, Snake Woman said, "Welcome home my Son. Welcome home!"

The End.

About the Author

As many young men of Carteret County, Mel too, grew up fishing the waters of the Atlantic Ocean, Bogue and Core Sounds. At age 13 after school, Mel would fish his 100 crab pots, sell his haul of crabs to his uncle's crab house, do homework, get a little sleep, attend school, only for a full repeat the next day. When the seafood seasons changed, so did his work and workload. Summers meant trawling all night for shrimp. Cold weather meant harvesting scallops and oysters. And then there were the clams that had to be raked. He then worked preparing the seafood in his family's seafood restaurant, Mom and Pops on Atlantic Beach. Self-discipline and strength training was key to his ability, so much so he lettered in wrestling; however, his deep desire of becoming a cop was still 'wrestling' within him as his family was steeped in law.

In 1975, Mel started what would become a 30 year career in law enforcement moving upward from dispatcher to chief. He received numerous commendations and awards over the years including an Honorary Doctorate from Emanuel Baptist University for his work in Humanities. After his retirement, Mel decided to put his experiences to ink by beginning a series of crime novels. Although the names have been changed to protect the innocent, many of you will remember some of his stories.

Mel proves truth in 'once a cowboy, always a cowboy' by continuing his sport of cowboy action shooting and leather-crafting gun belts, holsters and roping cuffs, among other hand-carved and hand-sewn leather products. This is just a sampling of his many hobbies. As a Sea Captain, he will always have the salt water of the Atlantic Ocean running through his veins.

Mel and his wife, Frances, actively serve The Lord at Bogue Banks Baptist Church on Atlantic Beach, NC.